Also by Ellis Sharp

Novels

I0460333

The Dump
Unbelievable Things
Walthamstow Central
Intolerable Tongues
To Wetumpka
Lamees Najim

Short Fiction

The Aleppo Button
(with Mac Daly) *Engels on Video*
To Wanstonia
Driving My Baby Back Home
Aria Fritta
Quin Again and other stories
Dead Iraqis: Selected Short Stories

Non-Fiction

Sharply Critical

For Anna and Daniel

ELLIS SHARP

LENIN'S TROUSERS

Zoilus Press

First published in Great Britain by Malice Aforethought Press, 1992

Reissued by Zoilus Press, 2019

ISBN 9781999735968

Contents

"Proletarians and free-thinkers of the world, unite against the fascist tyrants!"
Winston Churchill, 20th August, 1938

Martina

A blob, a far distant dark and blurry blob barely a quarter-inch tall, several metres above the ground and swelling slowly, is how she first entered my vision and my life, in Death Valley, all those years ago.

Death Valley! I remember it well, Horatio. Mallet in hand I trudged back of Badwater and Zabriskie Point. I was twenty-seven years old and dying of thirst. All that day I had felt like someone stranded forever amid the desolation and wreckage of Yves Tanguy's *The Furniture of Time*. In the early morning, scraping the flanks of a mesa (something I used to adore), I had discovered a curious lump of stone. It was half a metre across and had the same shape as Phobos. I realised at once it was almost certainly a dinosaur egg. Ten minutes later my car refused to budge. My ecstasy began rapidly to evaporate in the heat.

I was about ten miles from Dante's View, well off the road, out of sight of the tourists. I sat motionless in the shade, my heart pumping sluggishly and my mouth dry. Bathed in conventional electromagnetic radiation I gazed blankly at the place where sky and land rubbed at each other, a far, shining place where, amid a heat-haze horizon jitter curtained by a spectral net of red dust, she first appeared and began to approach, the filaments of her shape and form rushing towards me at a spritely, irrepressible 186,283 miles per second and growing all the while in size, igniting a faint momentary memory-flash of Omar Sharif's initial slow, shimmering approach in *Lawrence of Arabia,* getting closer, taking on a human appearance as the electric churning melted behind her and she came slowly down to earth, my eyes focussing at last on a woman, a woman wearing dark glasses and driving a space-ship-style crimson dune buggy of a type unknown and bearing the letter "M", moving at speed and trailing immense bright Wordsworthian clouds, clouds which still boil darkly

7

behind her ghost gliding towards me as I recollect all this, binoculars always at the ready, in a green English garden marred only by Maddock's grinding machinery, the self-same well-watered green of the lawn at the back of dark Dove Cottage which we explored together and where I closed my eyes against the August sunlight and the cottage gloom and saw only an ominous row of red bars and a remote, shrinking scarlet dot, a time that came later, camped out in a bleak, sloping Lakeland field, a faded Polaroid snap revealing a section of the tent interior, her shy smile emerging from the opening of a double sleeping bag, next to my massively swollen big toe and its four gross companions, each amputated tentacle sprouting tufts of eerie black hair and preposterously distorted by the lens, a juxtaposition reminiscent (to me, if not to you, Horatio) of Stanley Spencer's *Leg of Mutton Nude* (1937), a ghost, a crimson-bright insistent ghost doomed to walk along a quaint Scottish castle battlement which we haven't yet reached – be patient – and along the tops of romantic mountains with extensive and well-worth-photographing views where I kissed her against the vista and on into a demolished apartment, there to remove ghostly clothes, a phantom at any moment liable to be hurled back in time by the soft devastating drag and suction of Proustian recall (dust whirled by the wind on a dry summer's day, a blood orange, the winked HALT! of a traffic light), to that first spectral encounter in Death Valley, sloughing the great sandy wastes wearing scarlet ski pants and pressing on the brake with an ox-blood coloured shoe as she draws alongside with a flashing smile and enquires in a cracked foreign voice if I need anything, a question which transforms me from a statuesque chump on his rump huddled in the shade of a motionless Corvette on an old Olympia Portable into quivering flesh again, a chump who reaches inside and turns down the car radio on which Smoky Robinson is singing "The Tracks of My Tears"', a chump at first lost for words, with dust in his mouth tasting like gravel, a ridiculous figure dressed in khaki shorts and a white cotton shirt with a handkerchief knotted at the corners draped over his head, the sort of person you would half expect to be called "Griswold" or "Hans Pfaall" or even "Ned Lip", an entity perhaps liable to unnerve anyone not acquainted with Monty Python's Flying Circus or with an extensive knowledge of science fiction, the mop of limp Mohican hair bifurcating his brow like the bent conical cap of a Fool, an English Fool with a too-tight shirt, a clown with enormous shoes and a turned-down mouth fit only to be hooted at, who, feeling himself reddening, begins, penguin-like, to flap his arms and to nod vigorously, until at last he is in a position to say, in a thick English accent, Yes. *Yes, as a matter of fact I do, actually. I'm right out of petrol – that's to say, gas. Silly of me, I know, but –*

And on I gabbled, as one does, when face to face with a radiant creature from another world. From the green lustre of her large liquid eyes and the tan of her skin I judged she was from California. I felt her scan my Englishness. She looked to be about thirty. Her hair was streaky and wild. She gave a broad smile and commanded me to climb aboard. In the grip of strange forces, my heart suddenly lively as a washing-machine on its final spin, I reached stiffly for my Olympia Portable and obeyed.

Ghosts, like plesiosaurs in Scottish lochs, are best seen out of the corner of the eye; turn your head and they are gone. Ghosts dislike people who tiptoe after them at midnight, burdened by cameras and flashlights and tape-recorders. They are creatures of shadow and reflection; they come when least expected. I am old and growing older, but I am prepared to wait.

Twenty years ago, Horatio! How far, how near. I am grown weary and sullen and restless as Heathcliff. The moon never beams without bringing me dreams, and my head has increasingly come to resemble an egg. I am going bald like Shakespeare, with that same inordinate expansion above the regions of the temple.

The hot days of summer are the worst. I cannot help myself. Abandoning the small cool room where, upon the altar of my vast black leather desk, stands the Trinity of keyboard, computer and Epson dot-matrix printer, I step out of my modest English terraced house on to a sun-drenched lawn. The clump of forsythia by the back fence billows and arcs like a melancholy willow; here and there a yellow ranunculus winks from the grass; on the borders, where upturned bricks yield gleaming amber slugs, thistles sprout like baby triffids. At the back, casting an oppressive Dickensian shadow even at noon, is the high brick wall and grimy impenetrable windows of Maddock's Factory, in the roaring interior of which, under strips of artificial light, underpaid Asians toil a ten-hour day amid a stench of oil and chemicals, manufacturing Formica breakfast trays bearing representations of jolly hunting scenes, contented cows by sunlit windmills and Constable's immortal "Hay Wain".

I always go into the garden with the best of intentions – to sit down in a deck-chair and re-read *Ludwig Feuerbach and the End of Classical German Philosophy*, say, or perhaps something by Victor Serge – and before I've read more than two or three pages I find my gaze slipping away from the printed page and rising towards the sky. Could there be anything more ridiculous than a revolutionary socialist keeping half an eye out for a flying saucer?

The silvery glint of an airliner high in the stacks can cause havoc in my heart. My shaking hands grab for the binoculars. I know I will be disappointed, and I know that I have always been disappointed, and yet, and yet...

I could never tell any of my comrades this. I have heard their whispers. They are beginning to have doubts about me. They are not sure what to make of my liking for canal holidays. Comrade Derek rose grim-faced at a branch meeting, glared in my direction and sternly pointed out that there was no record of Marx, Lenin and Trotsky ever having been on a canal holiday. In order to avert Comrade Derek's implicit accusation of petty-bourgeois deviationism I have had to stock my narrow boat with a massive ENGLISCH-DEUTSCH Brockhaus Illustrated Dictionary and the forty-one volume *Marx-Engels Werke*. I sail through the Norfolk Broads playing *The Internationale* on my ghetto blaster, attracting the scowls of fishermen. Once out of sight I quickly change to a David Bowie tape or the Bournemouth Symphony Orchestra playing the first movement of Holst's *The Planets.*

Then there are the binoculars. I have had to pretend that I am a keen bird-watcher. Though utterly bored and indifferent to the behaviour and whistlings of the Lesser Redpoll, I feign enthusiasm at the sound of its monotonous moronic twittering. A glimpse of its red forehead and rose-pink breast does, admittedly, ignite a tiny spark. I purport to peruse with ornithological passion the tinge of pink on its rump but my passion is merely colour-coded. It might just as well be a fallen pink petal from a dying rose. My focus is elsewhere, set – the stars never rise but I feel her bright eyes! – to infinity, roaming far beyond the Redpoll's brown blur of piffling tail-feathers, scanning the wide blank sky, that zone of endless possibility which, once in a blue moon, coins silvery vessels, parodies of kitchen pans, burlesques of tubs and tubes, cigars, fifty-seven unbending varieties of ithyphallic phenomena, cymbals and dishes and triangles and balls and saucers, the complete contents of a cutlery drawer, the emptyings of a giant's lumber room and kitchen, the clutter of advanced civilisations still faithful to stainless steel, gravity-defying saucepan lids with ping-pong balls clinging tenaciously to their undersides, evidence of a celestial poltergeist's anarchic fun with agricultural implements, policemen's helmets, ice-cream cones and a tipped, titillating cornucopia of other strange, cavorting, spinning, undulating, leap-frogging impish shapes.

All this is a long way from Ludwig Feuerbach. How could I ever explain? But Comrade Derek (who more and more reminds me of the young Iosif Visarionovich Djugashvili) suspected something was up. He rose grim-faced at a branch meeting with statistics about the wages of women who manufactured binoculars. He cried that the only aids to perception anyone needs were *these* (waving his three volumes of the Penguin *Capital,* the second and third volumes with suspiciously unbent spines). I stoutly referred to both Marx's and Engels's keen interest in the natural sciences. Did not

Marx himself refer to Fraas's *Climate and the Vegetable World Throughout the Ages* as "very interesting"? Did not Engels denounce his own "arrogant narrow-mindedness" and beg the duck-billed-platypus's pardon for his former scepticism about its ability to lay eggs?

Comrade Derek muttered something inaudible, and the branch moved on to a discussion of the troubles at Maddock's.

Twenty years ago ...

It was the start of the hottest summer of the century. She drove me back to my apartment and, as in *Finnegans Wake,* the outlines of words began to blur, walls collapsed, time accelerated, there was a fuzzy luminous edge to the events taking place, and one thing led to another. We made small talk, banana fritters, two gin slings, jokes, popcorn and love. Nowadays I am a Consultant in Chaos Theory, but in those days I was a Blepharospasm specialist. My apartment was in L.A. and overlooked the ocean. There was a waterbed, a jacuzzi, an orange-keyed chamber pot. The apartment was rented and I was due to leave the week after. She explained mournfully that she had a husband. He was working in China. He fixed walls. He was not due back until the fall, on the thirtieth anniversary of the day Bill Monroe and the Blue Grass Boys, with Earl Scruggs on banjo, recorded "Will You Be Lovin' Another Man?". In bed I held her tightly and described my passion for plesiosaurs, and where one might still be alive, mischievously defying Darwinist orthodoxy. I told her it was my intention to find it. She laughed. She asked if she could join me. We could spend the summer together. I was over the moon. She seemed to find me an interesting specimen. But why, she enquired, the unusual name?

I felt myself blushing. Wearily, I explained. My drunken father, about to set out for the Registry Office on the afternoon of my birth, yelled up the stairs, "What shall we call it, then?", at which my partially-deaf mother, believing she was being asked what she wanted for tea, cried back, "Omelette!" – and so Hamlet it was.

This, to say the least, was unfortunate, in view of my surname – "Gimlet". Gimlet was the bright idea of my dim grandfather, Graham Gibbet, a whiskery optician, who, despite his curious facial resemblance to Karl Marx, failed utterly to grasp the realities of economic recession in a capitalist society and blamed the decline of his business on his name – a misfortune he sought to ameliorate, without any success whatsoever (he cut his throat two years later, in 1929) by deed-poll, ridding himself of those double-noose "b"s and substituting an enticing "m" and what seemed at first to be a lush, mellifluous "l" but which in time came more and more to resemble a good sharp knife.

And my creature from another world? Her name was Martina. Martina Nameless. She was not from California at all. "Nameless" was an Americanisation of Gnaemmelesski. She explained she'd been born in Illyriar, a backwater of the Ukraine, a region of lush foaming rivers, poppies and golden corn. She spoke of quaint onion-domed churches and country priests and stout, loveable old women who sat on porches dressed entirely in black, chuckling as they peeled their way through forty pound sacks of potatoes, while not far away ruddy-cheeked merry harvesters passed along the lane singing homely folk songs at dusk, the red bloated sun hanging in the sky like an aerostat, casting a ruby glow over the village pond where mother duckling led her fluffy brood through the emerald slime, and reddening the gnarled nose of the wise old village commissar who fingered his Stalin moustache in a thoughtful manner as he gazed upon the cottages, the overflowing barns, the abnormally white sheep and other quaint, mostly rose-tinted picture-postcard props and scene-boards plucked from magazines or improvised from her imagination, wonderfully convincing to someone who had never in his life been further east than Lowestoft, and all, in retrospect, beautifully redolent of the idiocy of rural life.

In London it was hot and getting hotter. I left my lump of rock with the Natural History Museum, and showed Martina around the capital. The flowers in the parks had turned into withered stalks; the fountains, switched off to conserve water, were grey and dirty. I trudged along Oxford Street with the weary gait of a deep-sea diver, mopping the shine from my cheeks with a sodden handkerchief, feeling fat and scant of breath. Martina glided beside me, lithe and gay, her tiny feet barely touching the ground. Drifts of old crackly sweet-wrappings lay underfoot like sand; by Hyde Park Corner, chuckling, she held one against my eye. The raspberry cellophane counterfeited a Martian vista of pink dying trees under a frumious sky.

If I had to sum her up in a single word it would be *insouciance*. She was out of this world. Whereas I was earthbound and clumsy and had stains under my armpits, she was fresh and crisp and clean. It was as if she'd spent her whole life in the desert; the heat didn't seem to bother her at all. Her skin had a strange leather-metallic smell, which I found unique and exciting and which I have sought to renew ever since, unsuccessfully, with flaring nostrils and frantic doggy sniffs in innumerable furniture departments and DIY stores of the better sort.

She seemed to like London. We toiled up and down paralysed escalators, lay motionless on the yellow dying grass in Hyde Park. Like the couple in *Brief Encounter*, we rowed along one of the little moats in Regent's Park, the water level low, the banks cracked and dry and smelling of weeds and death. She said it reminded her of home.

The sunlight had a reddish dusty tinge; the traffic on Red Place sounded blurred and slowed down, like a disc losing its momentum. Gubble-gubble-gubble, choired the birds perched on high ledges. Honk-honk, replied the big red buses. Every patch of baked earth seemed occupied by ecstatic sparrows taking vigorous dust baths. The Thames stank, airliners crawled mutely across the burning sky, a band in Embankment Gardens played a Janacek melody. Sweating like a pig, dripping like a stalactite, slippery as an eel, I pulled her into the tomb-cool darkness of Southwark Cathedral then towed her across the river, into the white-as-a-refrigerator interior of

St Magnus Martyr. Then on, on, and up the spiral stone steps inside St Paul's, where we spoke soft words to each other, inaudible, meaningless as Martian gobbledygook, like stranded astronauts from different worlds, straining to communicate across the vast cosmic space of the whispering gallery, thereafter descending to the crypt to gaze at Wellington's black, preposterous funeral wagon.

We quenched our thirst in bars, we plunged into empty afternoon cinemas and saw *One Flew Over the Cuckoo's Nest* and ("When will I see you?" "Quite soon") *The Day the Earth Caught Fire* and *The Man Who Fell to Earth* and ("... a cove in Cornwall where the rocks turn red at sunset") *Quest for Love.* Love! We made it drowsily first thing in the morning; we made it on a sunlit mattress in the bright afternoons; we made love at night, the window wide open, our gleaming bellies so wet with sweat that they fused and clamped together, joining us as if glued, so that we rocked and swayed as one in the writhing toils of passion, tight as a bivalve mollusc, until an age later when the cold, clammy hands of duty and time prised us apart with explosive slurps.

At the end of that week we returned to the museum where a smug palaeontologist with a sickly smile explained that my lump of rock was indeed the fossilized remains of something deposited by a dinosaur – only it wasn't an egg. We ran from that place, rented a car and headed north for Loch Ness. Loch Ness! Where, as anyone who has read the books knows, a breeding herd of not less than two dozen multi-coloured plesiosaurs still lurk and sport, mysteriously attuned to the vexing presence of photographers, merrily defying that preposterous washed-out band of small-minded, blinkered poltroons commonly known as scientists.

I had a hunch that if anyone was going to get film of the fabled monster it was me. Were not conditions for plesiosaurs perfect? The weather was hot, the loch's surface had dropped several metres, salmon (and everybody knows that plesiosaurs like nothing better than to crunch half-a-dozen fresh salmon between their fearsome jaws) leapt and jigged about at the surface, making ripples and sudden splashes liable to induce a massive surge of emotion and perhaps even a red-hot thrombosis in an older and plumper monster-hunter, but in your humble ratiocinator, in those days fit as a fiddle, provoking at most a mere mild tremble of the fingers and faint flicker of the pulse.

With Martina at my side, I waited. How I waited! Tourists came and gawped. I said nothing; my face wore that quiet, beatific, slightly smug expression (you can't possibly understand, and I understand you can't understand, but believe me, *I know*) of Christ dying on his cross. I waited patiently, calmly, like Lenin in Zurich, or Estragon.

And?

Nothing.

Nothing at all.

Shadows spread across the loch at dusk; shadows crawled up the sides of the glowing mountains and extinguished their amber crests. Day after day this happened. We explored the loch's many tangled bays and beaches. We wandered the ruins of Urquhart Castle; filed along the broken battlements; ascended the disfigured tower. The word "return" rang like a chill reverberating gong through our final days together. It was time for her husband to return from China, time for us to return to London, time for Martina to return ("You know what I think is going to happen to us now? We're going to drift away from each other, you and I") ("No! Don't say that!") to California.

On the way back we stopped off at the Lakes and pursued the ghost of Wordsworth. Words-words! Whose percentage of diamond is embedded in vast sheets of shale, buried under scree, caked in dross, lost amid numbing granite. In the desolate valleys, under a restless sky, specks of plutonium blew gaily in from Windscale; at a stall selling walking sticks and Kodak film and Hay Wain trays I purchased a Selected Poems, which needless to say did not contain the sonnet to Toussaint L'Ouverture; in Keswick I left my menthol cigarettes behind in a pub and had to run back for them; in Cockermouth Martina

16

yelped with rapture as she cocked her head, applied pressure to the knob and greedily imbibed the silvery spurts ejaculated by the red drinking fountain erected in 1896 to the memory of William and sister Dorothy. In London ("You're so less – alive – now than you were just a day or so ago... do you know that?") we kissed goodbye.

At the Terminal she lost all solidity; the tears in my eyes converted her to a shimmering blob, a colourful jumpy crimson amoeba that slipped through passport control and withdrew to the departures lounge in a single swift alien movement. A mutant limb seemed to wave in the direction of my misery, then shrank to a scarlet dot. The dot sprang away and vanished and she was gone, gone, gone.

For a long time afterwards I felt like Candace Hilligoss in *Carnival of Souls*. Life had a strange dislocated feel to it. Later, jobless, with a broken heart, I bore a superficial resemblance to Ludwig Feuerbach. Cobweb-spinning eclectic fleacrackers (to use Engels's masterly invective) had taken possession of the chairs of philosophy, while Feuerbach "had to rusticate and grow sour in a little village".

Ludwig *who*?

Ludwig Feuerbach (1804-1872). The man who blew away the fog of Hegelianism that stifled intellectual life in Germany in the nineteenth century. The man whose writings had an electrifying impact upon Marx and Engels. The man whose work inspired the young Dr Marx, in the spring of 1845, in a small terraced house in the rue de l'Alliance, Brussels, to scribble down some reflections on where he disagreed with Feuerbach – eleven short paragraphs climaxing with the perception that even today causes intellectuals and academics to scowl, and fidget, and flush (Goethe knew men of education who found intolerable the sight of a person dressed in scarlet) and shake their heads in a weary superior manner, and want to get back to their leather armchairs and their fine port and their very important research and their peaceful senior common rooms, away from the vexing influence of the doctor's voluminous writings and quarrelsome students calling themselves socialists and the grey, dreary, peripheral news of disputes, strikes, and pickets in places (factories, mines, workshops, ambulance depots, fire stations, bus stations, railway stations, building sites, shipyards) where they would never, ever wish to go. *Die Philosophen haben die Welt nur verschieden interpretiert, es kommt daraufan, sie zu verändern.*

In later years I was enlightened and inspired not simply by Marx but also by Fort, not just by the Paris Commune or the Bolshevik Revolution but by a number of other remarkable events. Barney Hill, for example, went to his doctor about a pain in his groin, and found his life transformed. On 15 December 1957 a Brazilian farmer had an unusual encounter with a woman of Slavonic appearance. At Valensole, France, very early on the morning of 1st July 1965, while working in a lavender field, a farmer, M. Masse, saw a strange machine approximately the size of a Dauphine car. "It was standing on four metallic legs and a central support. It looked like a monstrous spider." M. Masse was reluctant to discuss what happened next.

In North America an Algonquin legend tells of a hunter who encountered a great circle where the grass had been crushed down. A more recent report from Queensland speaks of mysterious circular depressions in the ground. New Jersey sign-writer Howard Menger met an exquisite woman sitting on a rock by a brook, and his life thereafter "became one of exciting activity", including a tour of ladies' underwear shops. Truck driver Truman Bethurum never regretted that day he met the captain of a space ship in the Nevada desert. As experts have observed, these things are portents of great changes. Is it my imagination, or does my little plaster bust of Lenin seem to half-nod in solemn agreement?

The television announcer was wearing the grave, blank-eyed, gosh-isn't-this-awful expression that television announcers adopt when about to convey tidings of death or mishaps involving royalty, politicians, cormorants, aircraft, whales or retired newscasters.

It had happened four hours out of Heathrow, over the ocean. Ships were diverted; aircraft searched. A man in a blue suit with a baton pointed enthusiastically at a map of the Atlantic and described how the plane had simply vanished from the radar screens. A small oil-slick had been discovered where it was presumed to have gone down. No wreckage had yet been found. Relatives at the airport in Los Angeles were shown throwing themselves at the ground and weeping hysterically. Sickened, I switched off and reached for the whisky. Amid my grief I found myself wondering which of those grim-faced men in plaid jackets seen being hurried away from the cameras had recently flown in from Peking.

My darling died slowly, her cheeks puffed out, her pale face distraught. She had always been evanescent and now she was effervescent. A stream of bubbles poured from between those lips which had given me such pleasure. The mute, contorted, adorable O of her mouth, oddly reminiscent of my namesake's last gasp, emitted a stream of Disneyish bubbles, each of which contained letters that made up my name. Her head tilted contemplatively to one side and a crown of pale sea-urchins formed upon her hair, which billowed out, Botticelli-fashion. Two dainty star-fish descended to hang upon each of her tennis-ball breasts, then an octopus punched its way through the paper walls of her ribs and reached in greedily to clutch at her congested, bursting heart as it sent out its fading flickering line of pulses like a message from a far, parched planet.

There was no detail I could not imagine of my drowned love in her metallic tomb beneath the sounding sea. The aircraft lay on the bed of the ocean, an enormous murk-filled tube with two hundred seat-belted skeletons where rare deep-sea fishes with monstrous sci-fi bodies, bored with exploring the Titanic, approached excitedly, gliding by with bulbous dispassionate eyes.

All the night-tide I longed to lie down by her side whispering something mournful and full of *Angst*, something along the lines of: *The starry floor, the watery shore, is given thee till the break of day.* But as I discovered many years ago on a zany middle-of-the-night trip to Scratby, sand is, after sundown, even when you are clutching a throbbing, exciting, nineteen-year-old female bundle of warm breasts and melting limbs, surprisingly cold and uncomfortable to sprawl on, so I gave the lying-down-by-the-tide notion a miss. Besides, I never really believed what they'd said on the TV news. The oil-slick was a trick of the gods, a greasy coincidence, the evacuation of a shifty Greek tanker-captain with an Errol Flynn moustache, furtively cleansing his tanks in the unpatrolled ocean vastness, a flag of convenience drooping from his rear, the crew a crowd of cowed non-unionised Asiatics working for less than the minimum rate.

It was a strange, unearthly time. A shower of blood was reported to have fallen in a remote region of India; an unimpeachable case of spontaneous combustion was recorded from a South Carolina dance-hall; in Britain the Labour Government's commitment to a major redistribution of wealth from the rich to the poor vanished one sunny afternoon in conditions of clear visibility. What was more, the tabloids reported that a UFO had been seen over the Atlantic at about the time of the disappearance of Martina's plane. It had been observed by the crew of a French herring trawler, the *Attrape*. They described seeing a gigantic fish-shaped craft almost one-mile in length. It was of a reddish hue, except for its nose, which was purple.

Charles Berlitz, winner of the Dag Hammarskjöld International Prize for Non-fiction and an expert on these matters, was interviewed. He said it seemed to him there was more in this than met the eye. He mentioned the disappearance of Flight 19 back in December 1945, when five Avenger torpedo bombers vanished without trace, as did a Martin Mariner PMB flying boat sent out to look for them. Twenty-seven airmen and six planes gone, in the words of one naval officer, "as if they'd flown to Mars". He spoke of the mysterious last words – "Something is happening to the sky... the sky is opening up – " – of the pilot of the Kawanishi HK-8 flying boat which vanished in Mano Umi, the Devil's Sea south of Japan. He suggested, tentatively, excitingly, that some air travellers find themselves passing through a strange portal to another world ...

Yes! Yes! She is not in the ocean deep but up there somewhere, rising above our cold grey streets like a moth straining for an amber planet perched atop a lamp-post, like Candace Hilligoss eluding at last her pasty-faced pursuers, like a remote glittering disc soaring across the vast blue firmament, not where the sportive swifts glide and drop but higher, higher, through that pesky gap in the ozone layer, to the realms of silence and velvet blackness where astronauts resembling the Michelin-man perform slow-motion important tasks against a wall of shining stars. I remembered Charles Fort's great work, begun in 1915 and simply entitled *X,* which demonstrated (with the aid of tens of thousands of notes recording anomalous phenomena) that life on earth had long been controlled by events or beings from Mars, a work even today scarcely less momentous and refreshingly relevant than Lenin's *Collapse of the Second International,* but which Fort, alas, in a fit of despondency, burned the following year.

Bunkum!

Illusion, delusion. The wishful thinking of a mind not facing up to things. A mind buffeted by gales in a season of bleakest misery. A mind that mused, fruitlessly, about her whereabouts, for long and weary hours, its attention riveted by the motion of the branch of a rose, or absorbed in quaint shadows falling aslant the floor. And then I put away the whisky and the past, pulled myself together and became a socialist.

When I say I became a socialist I should explain that I joined the Labour Party. I did not then realise the glaring incompatibility of these two things. The Labour Party! Nowadays that phrase conjures up a party of portly men gathered around a committee table upon which sprawls a bloated motionless figure in the final pangs of a phantom pregnancy, straining to bring forth a torrent of very moderate wind.

Lukewarm tea in the committee rooms, ward meetings devoted to two solid hours of correspondence and reports, and a complete absence of political discussion except for the ever popular subject of faraway South Africa, which always provoked animated exchanges and the passing of passionate motions to be forwarded to Walworth Road, in the knowledge that since this was a subject about which the membership was not obliged to make practical choices or actually do anything, it was a safe one and something everyone could feel very good about. (And if at some future point in history a Labour government should actually be elected, there would no doubt be very good reasons why it would be unable to do anything about South Africa.)

Of course in those days I suffered from historical amnesia, which is an essential condition of Labour Party membership. Historical amnesia is characterised by feelings of apathy and a strange fever. Hallucinations sometimes occur. Visions of a future, tough-minded Labour Government squeezing the rich and building gleaming new schools and hospitals are commonplace. Sufferers sometimes gabble "1945!" or "Don't rock the boat!". Some feel compelled to scrawl Xs on scraps of paper, others compose fierce conference resolutions.

One day I was accidentally struck on the head by a stout book, which left me dazed and quivering. Soon afterwards I left the Labour Party and became a revolutionary socialist.

Now as anyone who reads the newspapers knows, people become revolutionary socialists for one of a number of reasons:

(i) a bad fall in childhood;

(ii) unnatural craving for excitement;

(iii) gross ingratitude to one's parents, who scrimped and saved for that school uniform with the Latin motto, and the matching tie and grey socks;

(iv) pathological dislike of policemen with moustaches, who are simply trying to do a job impartially and to the best of their abilities in very difficult circumstances;

(v) rigidity;

(vi) spots, madness;

(vii) abnormal liking for long books with small typefaces and difficult words written by hairy foreigners;

(viii) unwillingness to snap out of it, grow up and face realities.

There are other reasons.

The memory of the 26 Commissars of Baku, say, or the belief that we live in a world of stupefying barbarism and exploitation deriving from the relentless motion of the capitalist system in which the means of production is concentrated in the hands of a minority ruling-class who extract the surplus value of the working-class, and that political struggle cannot be separated from the economic struggle of workers, and that the system cannot be reformed from within by working through a capitalist workers' party within a bourgeois parliamentary democracy in which the Queen has powers of Stalinist proportions, where the state (in the last instance: bodies of armed men) serves the interests of the ruling-class, where the real power lies elsewhere and in which the five-year pseudo-democratic system hinges on a combination of poor education and the mass manipulation of information through TV and radio networks which are under ruling-class control, manipulating in myriad subtle ways, ranging from the constructions of television news to drama, sit-coms, and even ("a general knowledge is an idiot's knowledge" – William Blake) quiz shows, the thought processes/"common sense" of those who remain the only medium for overthrowing the present system by a revolution resulting in workers' control of production and an authentic democratic system of workers' councils, i.e. the working class.

In my case I have often wondered if I was not simply (complexly!) drawn to revolutionary socialism by a liking for the colour red born out of a strange intuition – even, perhaps, a premonition. Although I didn't know it in those days, my favourite colour was also the favourite of Marx and of Zola.

I do not wish to hear of the achromatopsia of hysterics; rather, let me assert that red is especially dynamogeneous!

As a child I always preferred to be a Red Indian than a cowboy. In adolescence I collected magazine photographs of red cedars. At twenty I admired Napoleon, and was thrilled to learn that he was accompanied by a familiar which guided and protected him, sometimes taking on the form of a shining sphere but more often than not the figure of a dwarf clothed in red. My favourite novel is *A Study in Scarlet*.

Even my faithful companion Horatio, now on his last legs, seems to testify to the trend of my destiny. A red setter, with lugubrious bloodshot eyes, he is now hideously old and decrepit, his rust-coloured hair dropping away in handfuls. He spends most of his days asleep, tormented by old memories, wild doggy dreams, scenes articulated by low growls, mutterings, grunts and coughs. His rear legs were turned to a bloody pulp, crushed by a car; I had the bright idea of fitting him up with a pair of cheerful scarlet pushchair wheels, which he seemed to appreciate.

What, in the end, led me to perceive the truth about Martina? Why have I become that strange, contradictory thing, a red with an interest in UFOs?

There were two causes.

First, my clumsiness. I am forever banging into things, muddling my words, dropping glasses, growing older and wearier, as if my body was gradually disengaging from this world, as if the machinery was wearing out and there were no spare parts.

Secondly, my abandonment of a manual typewriter (farewell old Olympia Portable, you served me well) in favour of a computer with a word-processing package.

I have now spent years of my life boxed-in, inhabiting a grey prison light, staring at a small screen, watching letters lengthen into words, the words into sentences, sentences reflecting the full weight of my crime in losing her, sentences with no time off for good behaviour, sentences without syntax, blurring together, not plural but singular, in short a long, agonising, almost unending life sentence.

One day, on a whim, at the end of September, not long after the equinox, the leaves reddening everywhere as they died, I took a break from Chaos and decided to set down the story of Martina and myself. What a red-letter day it turned out to be! With a lamentable lack of imagination I decided to call the story "Martina". I booted up (as we PC buffs say), changed the directory to WORD, created a new document entitled "Martina", faced manfully the blank brutal screen, pressed the capital lock, and began. I began by tapping out the title of my story. And that is where I went wrong.

It was the merest slip, a trifle, a trifle that drove a rod of red-hot iron into my heart, that made me crimson and flush with a sudden fever, that made me roar out, tears of delight and wonder coursing down my blazing cheeks, and sent me running out into the starlit back yard, delirious as Gerard Manley Hopkins, staring up at the sky, cursing my ignorance of all those remote cartwheeling floodlit globes and rocks and white pulsing pricks of fire up there, of the constellations of the northern hemisphere and of the whereabouts of the planets, let alone the location of Elysium, Cerberus and Zephyria, the observations of Giovanni Schiaparelli or Hubble's crucial discovery that the light speeding towards us from the galaxies lengthens in wavelength. Yes, a slip that made me throb with ecstasy and boil with rage, affording me a strange vision of my old love sledging down a sunlit rust-coloured slope in Araxes, steering a straight course from Memnonia to Mare Sirenum and hobnobbing (or worse) with muscular blonde Venusian males. My jealousy was only finally quelled by the placid, pleasing image of a tranquil underground apartment lit by luminous panels of amber light. Here, by now divorced, she lived alone, frequently watched *ET* and thought wistfully of the child we'd never had.

Comrades, remember what happened to Lenin (and what so nearly happened) near Juvisy-sur-Orge! Let us not deny the role of accidents in history. Sometimes I wonder if a strange invisible force was responsible, guiding my forefinger, twisting it off course like an anti-missile device. Was it – it surely was!

– a signal from another world. A semiotic trick or tease? The little game of a punning, orange-complexioned entity with stalks on its turnip-shaped scalp observing me sympathetically through its long-distance telescope from its home in Eridania? As it was for the band of revolutionaries rushing into the Winter Palace that October night in Petrograd, though the consequences of my enlightenment were complex, the event itself was simple. It was merely a matter of hitting the wrong keys. The wrong keys? Yes, the wrong keys, the keys that gave me the key and the clue to everything. Ah, Martina, Martina! How the past slips suddenly into focus, how everything becomes symmetrical as a canal network and clear as the outline of a shining planet.

Comrades, I do not believe that the existence of extra-terrestrials in any way negates the fundamental tenets of Marxism! In defence of this thesis let me point out to you that science fiction seems to hold a particular attraction for revolutionary socialists, and why not, since there is no one who sees more clearly into the future than a Leninist! Those of you who have seen Sean Connery in *Outland* will know that capitalist exploitation can continue into deep space! Nowadays everyone laughs at Percival Lowell and at his books and maps, yet those of you who have seen *Capricorn One* will surely share my scepticism about the pictures sent back by the Viking space probes of 1976! Who can doubt that they were faked at Zzyzx! We are property! Truth lies on the margins, with Lenin and with Fort! Was Marx (I have often wondered) secretly sent here by an advanced civilisation of workers' councils impatient to bring our miserable botch to an end? Is Marx an anagram for Xram, oldest and wisest of the inhabitants of Deimos?

No. I could never say such things. My comrades would think I was mad. If I hadn't met Martina I'd feel the same way. Flying saucers? Rubbish! How can anyone with a clear perception of our planet's barbarous and bloody realities possibly waste their time on all that outer-space nonsense? Life on earth, deformed, twisted and stunted by capitalism, is quite enough to be going on with, without worrying about how things are on

Mars.

What is to be done?

I long ago gave up my plan to become an astronaut and wangle my way into a NASA crew. For that you need to be young, fit, blue-eyed and One-Hundred-Per-Cent American, cheerfully unconcerned by the pits and mounds of the dead in Chile, Honduras, Indonesia, El Salvador, Guatemala, the almost innumerable places, not to mention good with a screw-driver and advanced electronic circuitry, whereas I am middle-aged, English, overweight, with bloodshot eyes, a troublesome leftist with Leninist leanings, my past (remember that dinosaur egg) a murk of ineptitude and folly.

Do not think that I underestimate the gravity of my position as I sit here stiffly in my deckchair in an English garden, beside a clump of dying irises, whirled around on a preposterous oxygenated speck of cosmic dirt circling a third-rate star and crawling with parasitic organisms in the grip of capitalism. From Brazil come reports of UFOs, from South Korea: riots. Did you know that today in South Korea alone there are more workers than in the entire world in the lifetime of Karl Marx? A Red Admiral flutters past, stirring a hurricane in my heart and squalls over Acnahannet. How carelessly it sails over the stalks of dying poppies! The clouds darken and the baby triffids restlessly move in the breeze. The shadows from Maddock's Factory fade; the noise of the machinery has ceased. The workers have walked out, demanding a pay rise and union recognition. Tomorrow the management have promised to bus in scabs; tomorrow at five-thirty my comrades and I will be on the picket-line with the strikers.

Every strike conceals the hydra of the social revolution; any movement of the proletariat, however small, however modest it may be at the start, however slight its occasion, inevitably threatens to outgrow its aims and to develop into a force irreconcilable to the entire old order and destructive of it! The movement of the proletariat, by reason of the essential peculiarities of the position of this class under capitalism, has a marked tendency to develop into a desperate all-out struggle, a struggle for complete victory over all the dark forces of exploitation and oppression!

It said just now on the news that an oceanography team has discovered the remains of an airliner lying on the bed of the Atlantic. Sheer coincidence, eh, Horatio? And then I remember: Horatio died a week ago, deep in a dream of a romp on a sunlit beach with a bright bone for supper. I decided that what was good enough for Effi Briest was good enough for dear old H, and so I buried him in the back garden, under a white marble stone. Farewell, old friend. I had hoped to be able to introduce you to Martina, but evidently she is still away on an important mission. Though clouds of obscuring matter and interstellar gas and dust and luminous and opaque bodies whose motions are in different directions still come between us, I am confident that she will return one day. My hair may whiten and fall away, my face may crack and blotch like an old painting, but she – she will never grow old. She crackles in my heart like that old translucent sweet-wrapping held up fatefully by Hyde Park Corner.

Horatio departed; he left me where I have always been, watchful and alert, ever since that trifling, incandescent, keyboard error. Comrades, I mean the simple transposition – unearthly, illuminating, marvellous, stupendous – of the last two letters of her name.

Shooting Americans, With Emily

We used to lie in the undergrowth, shooting Americans. Emily seemed to like that more than anything. More even than music or sex. She was a surprisingly good shot.

Those were grand days when I used to go out shooting Americans with Emily. Just grand. I first met Emily in the bar of a hotel in Realejo. It was dark in there. In a corner, on a raised platform, a pianist with greasy hair was playing "I Wish I Was in New Orleans" real slow. Behind the bar, illuminated by a candle in a bottle, was a print of Crunlop's famous aerostat engraving and a shelf on which the proprietor had lined up his collection of bone china plesiosaurs and toby jug bigots. Emily was dressed in black and almost invisible. Getting closer I could smell the whisky. She was picking her nose with the index finger of her left hand. The index finger of her right hand was slowly moving across a grid of figures on a timetable. She was staring at the timetable and frowning. "Can I be of assistance, ma'am?" She recognised my accent at once. Me hers. I wondered what a girl from the West Riding was doing so far from home.

Her family, she explained, pulling something from her sack under the table and chomping on it. Yes, she would have another whisky. A dribble of mango ran down her chin. Her family. They drove her to it. Sister Charlie a real bitch, sister Anne a pious worm. Her brother (who could blame him?) a drunk. Her father nowt but a whinging hypochondriac, obsessed about bad air and the menace of infection. Christ, what a bunch! Luckily three of them were short-sighted. As for the fourth, Branny, he was in a perpetual stupor. Branny would not have blinked had an elephant borne down upon him in a white lace dress, bellowing that its name was Queen Victoria.

In the winter of 1846 Emily bribed a girl from the village to impersonate her. They tried it for a week while Emily sheltered in a cave, reading a revolvers catalogue. The village girl was thin and pasty. She dressed in drab black clothes and was of a moody disposition. Nobody noticed the difference. Emily drew up a contract stipulating that the girl should impersonate her for a period of not less than two years. In the summer of 1847, having made the final revisions to her manuscript, Emily headed for Liverpool. There she disguised herself as a cabin boy and obtained employment on one of the vessels being used to transport British troops across the Atlantic.

That was the version I liked best. There were many others. Panning for gold, harvest moons, a torrid romance with a short story writer in Newport News. A fling with a Bronx banjo manufacturer. Great cities, perfumed bedrooms, mornings with icicles dripping from gutters. Stallions, rivers, paddle steamers, grizzled sea captains, an ivory toothbrush. A device for removing hairs from the ear. A surgeon specialising in tumours of the gut. Emily was a great fibber. She blamed it on her Yorkshire upbringing and the heat.

British troops across the Atlantic? At the beginning of 1848, British troops occupied Nicaragua's only Atlantic port, San Juan del Norte. The port was to be the terminus for a proposed canal. The British troops expelled the Nicaraguan authorities. England now controlled the Atlantic terminus of the proposed canal.

At the end of March 1848 Elijah Hise was appointed U.S. charge d'affaires for Central America. His instructions from Secretary Buchanan spoke of the importance of cultivating friendly relations with the states of Central America. The political turmoil of the region was deplored. Hise was advised to enlighten the indigenous population of the shining example represented by the U.S.A., where all political controversies are decided at the ballot box. Hise was enthusiastic about his mission. He had a dream. His dream was to see slavery introduced into Central America.

I'm only trying to explain. When I say we used to enjoy shooting Americans I should explain. We didn't just shoot any Americans, only the ones that *deserved* shooting. Of course what I didn't know then was just how many Americans deserve shooting. You meet them, you think, what amiable open-hearted folk. The men genial, the women bubbly and bright. Sweetly perfumed, even. With healthy, shining skin. Moreover genial, good with a flow of words. A little pig-ignorant of their nation's foreign policy, perhaps, maybe a smidgeon dumb concerning the sources of the pillaged wealth that makes America great, a trifle paranoid, a little arrogant and self-centred but nevertheless a warm friendly people. Then next thing they go do something which shows what they deserve, and with a weary sigh (because although shooting Americans can be good fun it also tiring and tremendously time-consuming) you make for the carved oak chest where the rifles are stored.

Emily was no fanatic. She was capable of looking ahead to the time when shooting Americans would no longer be necessary. "One day," she whispered, bleeding copiously from a wound in her breast, "we will be free of these Americans. We will put away our rifles and settle down together in a ten-room villa with many books, two cats and a grand view of a tranquil brown river..."

The thing that really bugged Emily was what the Americans on the river did. 1848 was the year Gordon's Passenger Line of New York opened their fast route to San Francisco. First there was a boat trip down the east coast of the United States to the port of San Juan del Norte. There the passengers transferred to large canoes for the long trip up the San Juan River to Lake Nicaragua. They then sailed to Granada, 120 miles across the lake. From there they went by horse (of if you were a second-class passenger, by mule) to the Pacific port of Realejo. From Realejo it was a short trip by boat to San Francisco.

What the Americans on the river did was this. As the canoes glided up the San Juan River, the Americans opened their stout valises and their leather cases and their carpetbags and took out their revolvers, their pistols and their rifles. Then they opened fire on the Indians who lived along the lush, fertile shore of the great river. For 122 miles the American passengers had tremendous sport, blazing away at large breasted half-naked women washing clothes, blasting down angry muscular young men waving spears, plugging white haired village elders holding up magical wooden carvings, blowing away dark skinned gesticulating boys, pumping lead into plump perplexed babies, licking their wet American lips at the hilarious, glorious sight of jets of blood spurting from Indian backs and Indian bottoms and Indian breasts, of hands blown clean away, of legs smashed and broken, of bodies writhing, falling, dancing, of heads exploding like rotten turnips, and roaring with loud, hearty American laughter at the sound of shrieks, screams, agonized cries, wailings, death rattles, gasps, chokings and weeping, sailing on into the distance eating ham sandwiches and drinking beer and saying "Boy oh boy!" and "Hey man!" and "How about that!" and "Did you see the one I blasted up the ass?" and all the other things that Americans say when they are having one hell of a good time.

After her fourth whisky Emily confided that she thought it would be a good idea if we broke into the Realejo gun shop and headed east to do something about it. And so we did. Long after all this happened I paid a mainstream painter to execute a handsome oil entitled "Shooting Americans, with Emily". This was in London, of course. I kneeled on a sofa and aimed a broom handle at The Monument through the window of my apartment. I was trying to remember the colour of the river at noon. Emily the painter did from a faded snap. I asked him to come up with a *sometimes a woman knows what she must do* expression, which he managed superbly. The painter's name was George Arnold Wilkinson and mostly he specialised in Scottish glens at sunset. I had to pay him extra for a midday painting. He wanted to include a stag and some jovial hunters, but I wouldn't let him. We compromised by letting him portray the Americans not in a humdrum canoe but in a paddle steamer. The paddle steamer he copied from a book about paddle steamers. If memory serves it was entitled *The Glory of the Paddle Steamer*.

I was so pleased with the painting that I decided to commission Wilkinson to paint another one, entitled "Hunted". I knew he would find the title enticing and that when he learned that it did not include a stag or a line of jovial huntsmen he would grow querulous and expensive but that was a risk I would have to take. I had in mind a vast canvas, a good thirty feet long and fifteen high, with myself and Emily Brontë in the far left upper corner, ascending a Nicaraguan hillside pursued by U.S. marines, a dribble of blue ants the far side of a far-distant sunset-drenched canyon located at the far right.

Unfortunately my letter came back marked "Addressee Dead". Wilkinson had contracted typhus from his close friend Potato Jones. He left an unfinished oil of "The Hunt by Urquhart Castle" and debts amounting to eleven thousand guineas.

The U.S. marines hunted us for four months before they finally caught up with us.

I can still see Emily sitting down on that moss-covered tree trunk in the nameless valley where they surrounded us. She puts the rifle down. Leaning forward a little, she vigorously scratches her rump.

In those weeks, towards the end, she suffered greatly, heroically, from constipation and wind. The U.S. marines had laxatives, and we had none. For days on end her only expression was a grimace. She pressed her few remaining teeth together tightly, sending shivers through her gums. She dug deep until she bled, for the comfort of a different pain. How she suffered! A single turbulent rush was enough to send an entire flock of hummingbirds rushing in a blind thrashing panic to Honduras. Her matutinal eruptions panicked even the most hardened of vultures. I waited, rarely disappointed, for her gloriously sustained expulsions to rip and bubble through the soporific noonday jungle like the scrape and squeal of a thousand saws. I watched, entranced, sniffing the air keenly as, swathed in sulphur, she descended the mountain slopes like an early morning mist.

Emily, Emily.

Since I was a muck-smeared lad of three I have always been

fond of grubby girls who reek, and no one stank more pungently than little Emily. Her breath smelled excitingly of putrefying grass. Her body was washed by a tide of foul, lifeless crabs. Rotting lilies drooped from her dank, thrilling scalp. Aphids had dripped upon her back, impudent birds had voided their wastes across her shoulders. The jungle brought us together. Its steaming dankness and hot earth fertilised the firm dry ground of comradeship with billowing desire. I have never forgotten that first morning when I seized Emily Brontë, crushed her against my chest, smothered her in kisses and stripped away her rags. It was like passing through a rainbow of deep, shimmering odours. Beneath her daiquiri-splattered chemise lay soiled, complicated undergarments stained lemon-yellow at the crotch. When at last I laid her gently on the grass and licked her naked body I was astonished at her saltiness. She was crusted with the deposits of all the tears of all the men who had kneeled there before me, weeping helplessly. My tongue grew frenzied and numb as it wormed and burrowed and ploughed its way through the tidemarks and the dirt. Beneath the salt surface of her unwashed contours lay the rich, damp, fertile, dark chocolate dirt of Nicaragua, which after a good hour of licking gave way to the sharp, peppery, dusty dirt of Mexico. More impetuous licks brought me to a hot strange unidentifiable dirt which whispered of cotton fields and banjos and wild moonlit nights. Then there was a dry, stale unpleasant dirt, as if my naughty, dirty waif had lain in doorways in Chicago or amid dark alleys in the Bronx. There were traces of other brief, filthy adventures, mere specks and smears, until at last I reached the moment when, aged twenty-five, my darling had first renounced hygiene. It was marked by a delicious, final, admirable layer of no-nonsense Yorkshire dirt, its creamy stench redolent of insanitary drainage systems and dead sheep.

Up until this moment if I had had to sum up Emily Brontë in a single word it would have been *grimy*. But now that word would no longer do. She lay there naked and pale as cream cheese. Her breasts had been sketched in a hurry and left incomplete; the skin of her belly sagged between the stark frame of her rib cage. Calculation shone through the slits of my alligator's eyes; goatishly I lifted up her papery, insubstantial body and flipped her over on to her red, bony knees.

She glared at me but said nothing. I sensed in her a steely commitment to the propriety of the missionary position, the consequence perhaps of a narrow, backward religious upbringing. I tore off my clothes and crouched behind her, the chill breeze at my rear fanning my lust. My hippopotamus bulk, my elephantine limbs, my hairy body fell upon her waif's thin form. I was earth and water, gross, heavy, sweating; she was fire and air, elusive, temporary, ungraspable. We came together with a sudden soft squelch. My stony lust met her moist acceptance; my throbbing desire sparked and jetted against her motionlessness; my gasps and grunts and bellowed ardour soared above her open-eyed silence. At the height of my passion she glanced back disapprovingly. She remained mute throughout.

Sex with Emily Brontë was always like that. While I was inquisitive, athletic, feverish, she remained cool and detached, often occupying the time by picking shreds of pineapple from between her teeth. Now I began to understand about the thick crust of salt which had formerly coated her skin.

Ping! went the bullets. The repercussions multiplied along the valley walls. Emily sniped eight marines before they finally got her. She held them off until dusk, enabling me to slip away under cover of darkness. I hid out in the mountains for a year, living off roots and berries. Then I returned to England, disguised as a philosopher.

In London I became friends with a delightful German émigré named Karl Marx. "Stay off drugs," he cautioned. "Get a grip on yourself. Do something useful. Join the International Working Men's Association." We drank a few beers and discussed that bastard Vogt.

I offered Marx a spoonful of opium but he waved me away. "Can't you see I'm busy?"

I asked whether it was his opinion that the 26 Commissars of

Baku were beheaded or shot, observing that while there seemed to be no doubt as to the fact of their execution and to the fact that the atrocity was carried out by British troops there did seem to be some doubt about the manner of their murder. Marx irritably pointed out to me the irrelevance of the question. "What matters is to study in depth the policy of British imperialism in the Caspian region at the beginning of the civil war."

I promised that I would.

I played him some Victor Jara tapes. I introduced him to *Various Positions*. Marx nodded approvingly. "That's good," he said. I remarked that whereas a writer's best book is always the first, a singer's best album is always the second. Marx immediately disproved this with references to Malcolm Lowry and Joni Mitchell. Marx confided that he preferred jazz. He seemed a little down in the dumps but hauled out his borrowed copy of Barton's *Observations on the Circumstances which Influence the Condition of the Labouring Classes of Society* and read a few pages. It was not long before anger had driven off the blue devils.

Oh! Just, subtle and mighty opium! Eloquent opium that summonest to the chancery of dreams. My addiction, I regret to say, put an end to our friendship.

Now it is almost the end of the century and I am slowly, gloriously, sluggishly-squalidly, going out of my crumbling serpentine mind. The trumpeters play bright in the street, a guitarist plucks at the overhead wires. A crumpled cherub thumbs his grubby lute and I – I have a greater compass both of mirth and melancholy than another. A circus clown bangs a broken drum in the yard, an actor in black tosses a human skull from palm to palm. Wreathed writhing emerald leaves swarm and copulate along the sill. Mustard and lilac butterflies skip and multiply only inches before my eyes, a glockenspiel vibrates painfully in the derelict villa. The dust tickles the emerald leaves' lush, sweating erogenous zones. Leathery lizards scamper across the stained walls, hide behind dark paintings of sodden England. I am waterlogged and clumsy, at the mercy of the moon. It stares as I roll with the tides. Leathery lizards skip across the bathroom sink and vanish in a flash of light that hardens into foil. Soot in my throat as the sun turns the raging gladioli into fire and the bougainvillea explode.

We live, Emily Brontë and I, in a ramshackle ten-room villa at the edge of a cliff. Tens of thousands of books are lined up on shelves, or lie in heaps, or are piled in towers by the bedside. Our bedroom is large and empty apart from the big double bed. Our bedroom is large and shining. The walls are the colour of custard. In the mornings we watch the steam rising from the jungle and hear the shrieks of the frantic, copulating monkeys. In the morning Emily writes, in the afternoons she potters about the garden wearing a Panama hat and holding a watering can. The monkey-puzzle tree is in good health, the bougainvillea is in blossom. The hedges are rich with white roses and the mountains are higher than the Alps. Our two cats, Flossie and Gradgrind, chase butterflies or paw at rivers of ants or bring us gifts of mutilated mice. Money seeps in through the walls, enabling us to make periodic trips to Buenos Aires for new books and cushions.

Emily had her first orgasm last year and since then things have gone swimmingly. She is no longer papery and motionless but animated and flushed. Explosions of pleasure erupt from her throat and multiply among the canyons. She shrieks and gasps and I am in sudden torment, sudden terror. She strokes the sweat from my brow, she speaks tenderly to me, but her words are no sooner spoken than they become that most dreadful of all things, the past. Her words fall away like the inflamed leaves of autumn. Her words are gold, then a dangerous cardiac purple; a moment later, a forlorn shrivelled yellow. The clarity of her love for me turns murky inside a minute. Her smile is streaked with rigor mortis. Her body no longer tastes of dirt and salt but of ash and marble. She gets up from the bed and leaves the room and the bed becomes a raft, swept at sea. I am alone with my addictions, my appetites. I am spooning opium, I am feeding my habits. I am drifting in gorgeous interspace like a stunned gull. And Emily? She has gone to other occupations – peeling potatoes, cutting the grass, picking her nose, finishing her novel, lying down alone to die. She is gone from the room forever, and I am what I always was, a slippery hairy fellow, a sort of eel which has evolved into a monkey, tormented by time and tapping at a keyboard.

Nonsense! (he cried, with a hearty smile, slapping backs, robust as ever).

Emily has just come into the room. She is wearing a Mona Lisa smile. She says she has news for me. She smiles shyly, tenderly. She is going to have a baby. My baby. Our baby. A baby! A wibbly-wobbly-glubbly-wubbly-dribbly-drubbly baby! A baby that will cry and sob and shriek and whimper and leak and gush and stink and laugh and smile and gurgle and wake us up, night after night after night after night! A radiant prospect! I grin like a clown, I whoop like a lout! I embrace her, press my gross hairy hands across the rumour of her bulge.

HOOOOOT! Sudden, unexpected. Hoot of something in the distance, noise of an engine. The sunlight evaporates, dense dark cloud slides across the sky. Between rapture and rupture is a single slurred vowel, the grunt of someone shot. We step out on to the balcony. An enormous paddle steamer moves round the bend and comes towards our house. It is packed with laughing Americans. They whoop at the sight of the Indian families washing their clothes at the river's edge. Some of them start taking potshots. An Indian woman is thrown back onto the ground, a purple gash in her dark breasts. A child's head explodes. The Indians begin to flee, run to the cover of the trees. The laughter and whoops of the Americans ring across the valley. Two more Indians fall, shot in the back. A baby abandoned at the water's edge begins screaming until its head bursts like a paper bag.

I look at Emily and she looks at me. I know what she's thinking. It's easy not to get involved when you're white and on the side with the best weapons and the most killers. Don't get involved and nothing's going to happen. Think of the baby.

Misery or bliss, contentment or death. Emily doesn't spend more than a moment or so thinking about what her response should be. She looks at me and nods. Death; misery. *Hurry.* I unlock the old oak chest and take out the rifles.

From rapture to rupture is a single slurred vowel, a bullet's sludgy impact. Emily Brontë lines up a plump American in her sights, a triple-chinned man with baggy twills and a yellow plaid waistcoat, a gross overweight bigot soundly in need of a good puncturing. She is smiling a grim smile, her eyes hard with the knowledge of the injustice of things. Her face is thin and pinched; her body feels like marble. She looks so old, she's coughing. She tightens her brawny Yorkshire finger on the trigger. Stretched out on the black sofa, she shiveringly perceives that between rapture and rupture lies that little linkage, a child's streak of ink, black ink, and a child she'll never know. The deck of the paddle steamer is slippery with blood, the Americans are shrieking, indignant. The paddle steamer is turning, leaving a huge wake. Washington will hear of this. Events like this cannot be tolerated. *Send for the marines.*

Emily is very weak, now. She opens her eyes once, smiles, closes them again. Her pulse is the merest flicker. Bullets continue to ping and crash in the deserted rooms of the villa. I put Emily over my shoulder and slip out the back. I head for the mountains. We'll find a cave, a cool cave. It's so hot, so hot. On through the wreathed writhing emerald, the trumpeters playing brightly, the glockenspiel ringing. Leathery lizards skip past and vanish, gladioli burn fiercely, butterflies everywhere. Orchids, eucalyptus, Elijah IIise, vultures.

Exhausted, I lie Emily Brontë gently on the ground. She is limp, unconscious. I feel in my pocket for the cartridges. The sunlight magnifies and clarifies everything. The United States seeks to cultivate friendly relations with the states of Central America (a circus clown bangs a broken drum nearby). The political turmoil of the region is deplored (scarlet and indigo butterflies skip and multiply only inches from my eyes). In the United States all political controversies are decided at the ballot box (we have our rifles, our cartridges; when the Americans come we shall be ready for them).

Lenin's Trousers

Our story begins – But perhaps it is best to begin with the trousers. Trousers, in concealing legs, reveal much about the wearer. The lack of interest in Lenin's trousers on the part of historians and journalists is curious. Examine a man's trousers and you begin to touch his inmost being. Consider the case of the novelist, Thomas Hardy. At the height of his fame Hardy refused absolutely to let go of his trousers. As the nineteenth century moved towards the twentieth royalties poured down upon him as copiously as Dorset rain. His wife fretted and badgered him unceasingly. In vain. Though he could have had a brand new pair every day of the year, Hardy continued wearing the same trousers for twenty years.

Two conclusions follow. Either Hardy was pathologically mean (a common fault in the super-rich) or he despaired of ever again finding a pair as comfortable as the ones he was wearing. Of the two possibilities, and for personal reasons, I favour the latter.

Let me make a confession: I have legs of an unusual shape. Slender at the shin, thickening at the thigh, my legs have never yet found a pair of trousers that fit with the precision and the comfort that sets the soul at rest. Worse, the whole process of purchasing a new pair of trousers is one that almost physically sickens me. I stride towards the brightly lit menswear in a state of acute anxiety. Nauseous and nervous, I paw at the racks and try to remember if I am a 32" waist or a 34" waist. Am I short in the leg or long in the leg? What if I am a 33" waist with short-long legs? The low hum of muzak blanks out my mind, an ingratiating eager-to-please assistant bobs at my shoulder, chattering, making recommendations, urging me towards the changing room. Once inside, the torments continue. I am panting, in the middle of struggling to force on the new pair of trousers, when the curtain tweaks back. It is the smirking assistant, anxious to know if everything is fine – as if everything could possibly be fine in a world ravaged by disease, starvation, grotesque inequalities, homelessness, poverty, torture and repression. "Fine," I whisper, my face scarlet, my armpits dripping, my arms straining to drag on those accursed trousers in that cramped floodlit cubicle which multiplies my humiliation in the floor-to-ceiling mirrors.

I know one thing: if ever I find the ideal pair of trousers you can be sure that I shall hang on to them, through thick and thin, through war and revolution, through fame or obscurity or whatever else the future may hold in store. This, I am convinced, was also Hardy's position.

If Hardy had heard about what happened to John Reed his tenacious grip on those trousers would surely have doubled in intensity. After publishing his classic account of the Bolshevik revolution, *Ten Days That Shook the World* (1919), freelance journalist Reed returned to Russia. In the summer of 1920 the thirty-two year old Reed went on a five-day train trip to a conference in Baku. Everywhere the railway stations had been destroyed by the Whites; everywhere the sidings were full of the half-burnt wrecks of coaches. After Petrovsk the track ran alongside the shore of the Caspian Sea, and whenever the train made an extended stop Reed rushed off for a swim. Once, in his haste to get dressed again, Reed tore his trousers. A fellow comrade described this as "a tragic event, since of course he didn't have any others with him".

Ten days after his return from Baku, Reed fell ill. His clothes were in rags, his trousers still torn. His temperature shot up; he felt dizzy. Headaches pushed and blundered behind his temple. Because of the imperialist blockade of Russia no medical supplies were available. There followed a stroke, paralysis, death. Typhus, the doctors had said. Typhus? Most probably typhus. Almost certainly typhus. But it is a curious coincidence, is it not, that from the moment Reed tore his trousers his life went into a spectacular decline? Not only did Reed suffer the anguish of a torn pair of trousers: back in Moscow he was unable to obtain a new pair. Is it an exaggeration to say that when a man tears his trousers he tears something irreplaceable, deep inside himself?

To be sure, yes.

No.

That is –

As far as Lenin's trousers are concerned... The documentation concerning Lenin is mountainous; the data relating to his trousers of vexingly microscopic dimensions. I have always believed that to understand any man or woman of historical significance, whether they are novelists, metaphysicians, politicians, critics, philosophers, sociologists, military strategists or revolutionary socialists, it is necessary to read not only *everything* they ever wrote – books, articles, letters, memoranda – but also all the books in their library. It maddens me when I encounter lecturers on Sterne who know nothing of the letter to Dodsley sent (most probably) in October 1759, let alone prattling economists grossly ignorant of the tables attached by Marx to his letter of July 6, 1863. Even among those who call themselves Marxists it is common to come up against those who look blank when you mention Boxhorn, say, or John Forbes Watson, let alone Tuckett, Vanderlint and Urquhart.

In the case of Lenin these difficulties are exacerbated by the sheer volume of his writings as well as by the size of his library. Lenin's energy was prodigious, both as a writer and a reader. His *Collected Works* amounts to some 47 volumes. He may have owned only a handful of pairs of trousers in his lifetime, his shirts may have been grey and unfashionable, his wardrobe generally risible: not so his bookshelves. Lenin owned 10,000 books in 20 languages. His addiction to books (often the dreariest books imaginable, books stuffed full of statistics, books by Hegel, books crammed with trade figures, Herbert's *System of Synthetic Philosophy,* books bursting with obscure data on wages, profits and interest, books about supply and its relation to demand, not to mention *Nerves,* a book discussing the nervous system, its intricate mechanism, and the strange phenomena of energy and fatigue, together with some practical reflections) was not unique. Trotsky was similarly addicted, a journalist who visited him at his home sardonically observing, "In all corridors and passages there were piles of books, and once again books – the nourishment of revolutionaries, as ox blood used to be the nourishment of the Spartans."

The awesome total of books owned and written by Lenin is, however, dwarfed by the fantastic quantity of books which have been published *about* Lenin. Tap in that solitary pseudonym to a library mainframe and watch it trigger a flashing, massive avalanche of titles. *Vladimir Ilyich Lenin, Biografiia; Lenin: Building the Party; Lenin: All Power to the Soviets; Lenin: The Revolution Besieged; Lenin's Government; Lenin: The Man, the Theorist, the Leader; Lenin and the Bolsheviks; Lenin Lives!; Lenin and Philosophy; Lenin's Last Struggle; Leninism Under Lenin; Lenin's Moscow; The Life and Death of Lenin; From Lenin to Stalin; A Film Trilogy About Lenin* ... not to mention *Lenin* by Conquest and *Lenin* by Gorky and *Lenin* by Lukács and *Lenin* by Pospelov and *Lenin* by Shub and ...

One or two of these authors had the advantage of knowing Lenin; one or two have taken the trouble to learn Russian and read all the way through the *Collected Works*. I am certain not a single one of them has read those 10,000 books which Lenin drew on to formulate his thoughts. Sifting through the books about Lenin it quickly becomes apparent that there is not one Lenin but three Lenins that people write about.

Firstly, there is Saint Lenin, born into a progressive family; an instinctive Marxist and revolutionary who at the age of thirteen understood profoundly the need to build a revolutionary party; who grew up, never breaking wind or picking his nose like other boys; who redeemed mankind, aided by his faithful comrade-in-arms Joseph Stalin, a comrade who (as is proved by many inspiring oil paintings) always stood deferentially yet commandingly beside Lenin at moments of danger or when great decisions needed to be made, often indicating with his pipe the correct course of action, which Lenin, not having perceived it himself, agreed to at once with a smile and a profound wise nod; who, on the rare occasions that he frowned, frowned at the activities of Lev Davidovich Trotsky, a rabid and bitter enemy of Leninism who was admitted to membership of the Bolshevik Party in 1917 but who did not accept Bolshevism and who continued his lifelong activities as a splitter, waging a hidden and open struggle against Leninism and the Party's policy and constantly opposing the Party's general line and its programme of building socialism in the USSR; Saint Lenin, whose body, smoothed and plumped by beeswax and mortician's fluid, was laid beneath a glass sarcophagus in a massive mausoleum of porphyry and granite; Saint Lenin, whose mummified body, over the years, has, as one might expect of a saint, turned from that of a wrinkled, old, grey, tired man with discoloured hands into a much younger, healthier, sprightlier figure, with rosy hands and a splendid complexion, looking for all the world as if he has just popped into his coffin for a nap on a drowsy summer afternoon; Saint Lenin of the innumerable paintings and the folk art; Saint Lenin of the busts and monumental reliefs and the painted papier-mâché boxes; Saint Lenin of the hand-embroidered banners and bone china dinner plates; Saint Lenin of the pedestals, reaching out for something, clutching his cap in the wind, gazing intently at something, or cupping his bearded chin just like Shakespeare, deep in the deepest of thought.

Saint Lenin had a twin and his name was Joseph; so, too, has the second Lenin. The second Lenin's twin is also named Joseph; they are, moreover, identical twins. If Joseph was a terror, why, so too was Vladimir. Indeed, responsibility for Joseph's misdemeanours must be firmly pinned on Vladdy, who set a very bad example and should have known better. I cannot think of a pithier summary of this particular Lenin than that coined by Professor Alfred Meyer, for whom Lenin's career expressed a "deep-seated hostility towards everything that exists". This hostility can clearly be seen in the many Soviet statues of Lenin: Lenin grimly leaning forwards to crush a passing butterfly in his fist; Lenin scowling at the fierce wind which obliges him to hold on tight to his cap; Lenin reaching up to yank with brutal, unnecessary force at a just-out-of-reach lavatory chain of the sort nowadays only seen in the homes of the very poor or the very rich. I speak, in short, of Lenin the Monster, Lenin of the fanatical will, Lenin the heartless, ruthless conspirator, Lenin the cynic, beguiling, crafty, collusive, pitiless, insidious; Lenin the schemer, the nullifidian, the tergiversator, Lenin the ascetic, cold and hard as stone, hard as nails, hard boiled, heartless, icily detached, inhuman, whose cold laugh would have sent shivers down your spine, Lenin the splitter and scoffer, obsessive, crushing complexity with his dogma, his precepts and principles, his system, his tenets and articles, his rubric and catechism; Lenin the ideologist, the Marxist, Lenin of the closed mind, doctrinaire, foul inventor of Democratic Centralism, authoritarian, unshakable, totalitarian from the tips of his toes to the brutal blunt bald cranium; Lenin the man whose frightful example demonstrates the folly of socialist ideals, and how preposterous and unrealistic notions of equality, control of the means of production and other chimeras lead with inevitable logic to coils of barbed wire, mass graves, walls, jackboots, guards, watchtowers, empty bakeries, guard dogs, economic chaos, low living standards, bad weather, and the persecution of poets; Lenin, a man at the mercy of dark impulses of destruction, terrible as Lucifer, chilling as Dracula, a man to make you tremble and give you sleepless nights. Lenin, whose face, in death, looked restful and untroubled, until some days had passed, when the skin began to shrink and twist, contorting the features of his face so that, as one scholar sombrely notes, "he looked angry and sullen, tormented by guilt" – as well he might!

Lastly, dwarfed, overshadowed, sandwiched between the first two Lenins is a third Lenin, a homeless Lenin, a short stocky figure with a big head set down on his shoulders, bald and bulging; a Lenin who disappeared in the dead of winter, a Lenin scattered across the continents, a man who, if you had met him, you would never have realised was a leader; Lenin whom Mrs Zelda Coates remembered getting down on to his knees at her sister's house and hooting and shrieking with the children; Lenin the incomparably great revolutionary figure of the twentieth century; Lenin who wrote of the way in which, after their deaths, attempts are made to turn revolutionary leaders "into harmless saints, canonising them, as it were, while at the same time emasculating and vulgarising the real essence of their

revolutionary theories and blunting their revolutionary edge";
Lenin, whose widow urged that there should be no memorials,
no naming of palaces after him, no vast commemorations in his
honour: "to all these things he attached so little importance in
his life"; Lenin with a hole in his shoe; Lenin whose *Collected
Letters* has never been published; Lenin of the shabby cap;
Lenin ("Without you the sun would set forever on my life and
the world would be a cold and empty place...") of Kollontai's
stupefyingly banal novella; Lenin who seemed colourless,
uncompromising and detached; Lenin who was sometimes
wrong, who made mistakes; Lenin without picturesque
idiosyncrasies; Lenin who had the power of explaining profound
ideas in simple terms; Lenin who was irritable, depressed, shy,
good humoured, exasperating, exasperated, human, brilliant;
Lenin who combined with shrewdness the greatest intellectual
audacity; Lenin whose voice may yet be heard in the importance
and noise of tomorrow.

Whichever of these three Lenins you happen to prefer, it is a
fact that none of them showed any interest whatsoever in
trousers. Lenin the Saint was in a dimension far removed from
anything so vulgar and common as trousers. For Lenin the
Monster trousers were, at best, simply something he wiped his
blood-drenched hands upon; he was far too busy designing
concentration camps to worry about fashion. Lenin the
Revolutionary Socialist, if he thought about trousers at all,
would not have thought of how he looked in them but of their
manufacture, of power looms and mills and worsted, of
machinery and factories, of Factory Acts and legislation and
inspectors, of wages and the extraction of surplus value, of rates
of profit, of imports and exports, unpicking those tattered
trousers until they had revealed the oily and bloody nakedness
of capitalism and war.

Did Lenin know of trews and breeks and galligaskins and of
the historical development of trousers; did Lenin, with his
insights into the future of capitalism, envisage future trends? In
a turbulent era of mass graves and imploded empires, in a world
of cords and flannels, did Lenin ever consider the possibility of

47

drainpipes and bell-bottoms and Levi's?

I think not. There is simply no sign that Lenin ever took the slightest interest in clothes at all, let alone in his trousers. He showed none of the keen dress sense of his comrade Stalin, for example. Can you believe that when Lenin died the undertaker was actually tactless enough to dress the corpse in Lenin's dark double-breasted suit? You might well ask, what on earth is the point of being a revolutionary if you don't *look* like a revolutionary? Luckily Stalin was soon on hand to give a flourish of style to the proceedings, insisting that the corpse change its clothes at once. And so it was that Lenin was displayed in his open coffin wearing a nifty semi-military khaki jacket, which, as I'm sure you'll agree, shows that whatever else may be said against Joseph Stalin, he knew a thing or two about PR.

Now about those trousers. There is no evidence that Lenin favoured a particular pair. He was not obsessive; he was not like Thomas Hardy. During the long periods of exile Lenin may well have hung on to his trousers for four or five years, but never for twenty, and only because of poverty. There was no vanity in the man. He would never have dreamed of deliberately wearing shabby clothes as a pose. When things looked up Lenin was perfectly willing to buy a new pair. Given that these matters are not in dispute, why, then, did the British Government, in 1918, spend 1,200,000 roubles on a plot to obtain Lenin's trousers? This was what vexed my Uncle George.

Our story begins (ah, how I have always, always, wanted to tell a story which begins with *Our story begins*) (my second dearest wish is to write one which ends with *But that is another story*) with a sheet of paper. To be more precise, a sun-yellowed foolscap sheet which had originally mellowed on some portly, important person's desk, in London, many years ago. Rubber stamped, signature scrawled, approval given, the sheet had been passed to Accounts, filed away, forgotten. Forgotten until that cold November day in 1957 when Maureen Hopper, owner of three grey hairs, the same age as the dying John Reed, whose trembling hand gave advance warning of the disease which was shortly to incapacitate her, collided in the basement corridor with Uncle George, spilling her three o'clock tea over his brown leather shoe and scalding a small area of his right foot, causing him to gasp with pain, let go of the file in his hand and fall on to his left knee, in the conventional posture of an enraptured lover about to make a proposal of marriage, which for a few incandescent moments Miss Hopper believed to be the case, her heart thudding, loneliness, her taste for cheap paperbound romances and the excess of wax in her ears conspiring to misinterpret my uncle's groans as the sighs of a long hidden passion, a pleasing fantasy terminated only by the rising pitch of my uncle's excruciating sufferings and the strange sight of her suitor peeling off his sock and staring at a red-raw area of skin.

"Grog!" my uncle, sprawled now on the mud brown linoleum, seemed to be repeating, sometimes in German, which encouraged Maureen Hopper to become aware of the mishap which had occurred and sent her rushing off for bandages and a jug of water, leaving my uncle stranded in a solitude during which he at last perceived the trifling slip of paper which had fallen from the fat dusty file he'd been carrying along that long, cold, dark, narrow corridor in the basement of the great grey building on Whitehall – a slip of paper upon which was written *Lenin's trousers* and a sum of roubles which made his eyes swell with amazement.

Plump, pink, bland, rubbery, deferential, lacking strong feelings about anything much, and with a passionate interest in filing systems, my uncle was the perfect civil servant. His employment as a clerk had begun in 1937 at the age of eighteen. In those days, before he purchased Gordon, he was pale, slim, hard-working, quiet, polite and trustworthy. He always wore a poppy for Remembrance Day. He saw no reason to conceal his admiration for the Royal Family, whatever their ups and downs. On major royal birthdays he drank a half pint of stout to celebrate. He did not smoke; he never overindulged. He believed a woman should know her place and ought never to expose her armpits – not even to her husband. His superiors found him to be an admirable little fellow and, now twenty years later, Uncle George was on the verge of promotion from Clerical Officer

Grade Four to Administrative Officer Grade Seventeen, the thought of which made him dizzy with excitement, especially on those occasions when he panted after Gordon through the well trampled undergrowth of Epping Forest. My uncle lived in a bachelor's one-bedroom maisonette in Walthamstow and Gordon was his goose, which he kept behind chicken wire in the eastern half of his west-facing garden. Gordon was a wild, ill-tempered goose and he was always escaping; both he and my uncle were a familiar sight in the quiet suburban streets of Upper Walthamstow in the early nineteen-fifties, Gordon screeching and hissing hideously and darting after terrified cats and dogs, or skipping gaily towards the Forest, with my uncle (clutching a broom handle, a leash and a butterfly net) in anguished pursuit.

The slip of paper lying on the floor beside his scalded foot perplexed and disturbed him. A glance told my uncle that the sheet of paper did not belong with the neatly bound file entitled War Office Lead Pencil Expenditure 1926-28 but somewhere else. Evidently no one had missed it, which was perhaps not surprising, as the sheet was dated 1918. Hearing the slap of heels getting closer, and mesmerised by the incredible words *Lenin's trousers*, my uncle impulsively and furtively slipped the receipt into his pocket, a few seconds before Maureen loomed through the swing doors and handed him a refreshing glass of lime juice. He gulped down the lime juice, experienced agonizing pains in his stomach and was rushed to hospital, where, after an excruciating medical examination and a drugged sleep, a psychiatrist talked amiably to him, asked him to tick some boxes (he was delighted: there was nothing George liked more than putting ticks on important pieces of paper) and went away and wrote a report about my uncle's reduced vigour and suicidal inclinations – a report which obliterated at once my uncle's prospect of promotion, and led him to curse Maureen Hopper's absent-mindedness, which had caused her to confuse her bottle of lime juice cordial with an adjacent green bottle containing a fluid which, when used regularly, prevented chalky limescale deposits forming under the rim of lavatory bowls and other important household surfaces.

Embittered and angry, my uncle said nothing about the intriguing receipt for Lenin's trousers. He was a changed man with a dull ache in his stomach and a burning sensation in his throat. He cursed Maureen Hopper for her clumsiness and her idiotic error. He cursed the fatuous psychiatrist for his ridiculous report. He cursed the Civil Service for requiring psychiatric reports on all staff who needed their stomachs pumping. He cursed his pet goose, Gordon, for escaping into Epping Forest again. He cursed the weather on the day he went back to work.

My uncle's formerly affable superiors now regarded him with sombre suspicion and spoke to him coldly. They did not want to have anything to do with a man who might well cause a future delay on the Northern Line by hurling himself under a train. Consumed by fury at their ingratitude, my uncle devoted the next few months to a private quest to find out more about the mystery he had stumbled upon. He had always understood (upbringing, school, newspapers) that Lenin was a Monster, a Menace and a Madman. My uncle chuckled at the unseemly thought that perhaps in some as yet obscure but sensational way he could be revenged upon his superiors by causing them *embarrassment*. There is nothing the Civil Service fears more than embarrassment and *bad publicity*. My uncle wheezed; he chuckled; he drank two pints of stout in ten minutes and felt light-headed and very happy.

His secret work prospered. He discovered that approval for the attempt to obtain Lenin's trousers had been given at the very highest levels, that the trousers had not been obtained in 1918, and that the matter had evidently been dropped. There was clear evidence – numbers of files which turned out not to exist or which had been missing for fifteen years, brittle crisp-shaped fragments of paper still clinging to filing rods – that most of the material had been removed and destroyed. HMG, having failed to obtain Lenin's trousers, did not want anyone else to know what it had been up to. My uncle could understand that. HMG wouldn't want the French or the Americans to succeed where it had failed.

What was it about Lenin's trousers that made them so valuable? This was what my uncle couldn't understand. Were priceless jewels stolen from the Tsar hidden in the turn-ups? Was a top-secret chemical formula sewn into the inside left pocket? Had the Bolsheviks secreted their plan for world domination somewhere inside the legs? He had borrowed a biography from the local lending library and looked at the photographs. Lenin's trousers looked just like everyone else's at that period in history. Uncle George peered for hours through a magnifying glass but was unable to discern any suspicious bulges, not even when he turned the book upside down. Why had the British Government wanted to obtain such a cheap, common object for such an incredible sum? The only way to find out was to go to Russia, obtain the trousers and subject them to a thorough examination.

After spending some time puzzling over the word "patronymic", my uncle succeeded in filling out his visa application form and, in July 1958, having decided that this time Gordon would have to survive in the forest as best he could, he caught the 8.09am from Victoria. Belgium, the two Germanys and Poland slid by his window. In the second Germany the ticket collector had a sub-machine gun and a snarling Alsatian dog, in Poland the parallel rail line had buckled and a gleaming locomotive lay on its side, as if Lawrence of Arabia had recently passed that way. Warsaw was a dark blur resembling the area around Clapham Junction, Brest was cold and pale and an officious dwarf in a postman's uniform jabbered at him hysterically and threw out his arms when he tried to take a photograph of the sun rising above the shunting yard. The gauge of the track changed at the border; the Soviet train was unexpectedly large and spacious, and an elderly woman dressed in black brought him many glasses of steaming amber tea, shaking her head with a puzzled look when he looked in his pocket dictionary and tried to say the Russian word for milk.

Moscow was dark and dismal, the streets wide and unexpectedly quiet, his hotel vast, cold and glum. The food was appalling. His Intourist guide, a rather grim grey sexless girl called Sasha who occasionally exploded with gobbets of Shelley or lengthy quotations from *Hard Times,* insisted that first he visit the Exhibition of Economic Achievement. This turned out to be in a park, where distortions of Tchaikovsky boomed from poor quality speakers hidden in trees and small boys hailed him as "mistair yank" and badgered him ceaselessly for chewing gum. He trudged through the Great Hall of Tractors, watched a scratchy hour-long documentary on hydro-electric power and wandered gloomily around a House of Folk Art devoted to scenes from the Great October Socialist Revolution. It was, he reflected, even worse than the Festival of Britain. At the end of it Sasha thrust at him a small clay tablet portraying the Winter Palace and angrily told him of the British Government's refusal to allow the USSR a licence to import Cliff Richard's records.

It rained.

Sasha took my uncle to Red Square and showed a card to the guards which permitted them to go to the front of the gargantuan queue of people waiting to enter Lenin's mausoleum. My uncle said their evident devotion and enthusiasm reminded him of those peculiar people who line up in the rain for Wimbledon tickets or who jostle greedily outside Harrods at the beginning of January. Seeing my uncle's officially sanctioned queue-jumping, the people at the front began to shout and shake their fists. Although my uncle did not know more than a few words of Russian he understood very well the suggestions that they were making. Sasha looked grim and hustled him towards the mausoleum entrance.

Inside it was cool and dark except for the blazing lights which shone down on the mortal remains of Vladimir Ilyich Lenin. Jackbooted guards stood at attention, clutching machine guns and scowling. My uncle blinked in the sudden darkness, perceiving a stiff waxwork effigy arranged on a kind of dais, decorated with red velvet trimming of the sort you saw in Indian restaurants. Suddenly, tears swimming in his eyes, oppressed by the viciousness of time, the dead load of the years, the grey lined face that surprised him in the shaving mirror every morning, he remembered a long-ago visit to Santa's grotto at Selfridges when he was six. My Uncle would have liked to linger and step over to take a closer look at the corpse, but Sasha took hold of his arm and pulled him firmly towards the exit. His lasting impression was of a shining yellow forehead resting on a pillow like a priceless jewel, and then he was outside again in the cold Moscow air, and it was starting to rain.

It occurred to my uncle that, though it was commonly acknowledged that Lenin had been laid to rest in trousers, the display in the mausoleum had been so arranged as to keep those trousers out of sight. Was this by accident or design? Had the trousers been removed long ago for safe keeping? It hardly seemed to matter. Whether the trousers were in the mausoleum or buried away in a safe deep inside the Kremlin, they were out of his reach. Fortunately from his researches he knew that there was one other pair of Lenin's trousers in existence...

It rained.

Sasha took him to an exhibition of Soviet Space Achievement and he enlarged his knowledge of boosters.

It rained.

Sasha took him to an enormous department store and bought him an ice cream, which turned out to be excellent.

It took him a week to recover from food poisoning, after which he travelled north to Leningrad, to an equally grisly hotel. It was not until three more days had elapsed that he was at last taken to 52 Lenin Street to visit the V. I. Lenin Memorial Museum. The Museum was situated in the apartment where Lenin had lived for four important months in 1917. Here Uncle George was obliged to leave his shoes with an attendant and put on a pair of felt overshoes. Then he was permitted to enter, Sasha at his side, animatedly pointing out the two iron bedsteads slept in by Lenin and Lenin's wife, Lenin's brother-in-law's desk at which Lenin used to work, Lenin's favourite armchair and Lenin's brother-in-law's dining room table, at which Lenin sometimes ate and around which Lenin sometimes held meetings. Sasha seemed genuinely thrilled by her proximity to these objects, despite having encountered them on eight hundred and thirty-seven previous occasions. My Uncle George was thrilled too. On Lenin's bedstead lay (as if Lenin had just popped out to the bathroom to brush his teeth and would be back at any moment in his red flannel pyjamas) Lenin's jacket and (my uncle's heart went berserk) Lenin's trousers.

Lenin's trousers! As in all the photographs they looked perfectly ordinary. But how to get near the trousers, let alone steal them? A rope shielded the bedsteads, and probably there were hidden alarms and invisible rays. A uniformed attendant stood in the corner, staring suspiciously. Another attendant loitered in the doorway. Sasha herself was a devout Young Communist composed entirely of granite and State purity. It all seemed hopeless. Rain crackled on the windowpane and my uncle's momentary elation began to ebb.

Back at the Aurora Hotel, my uncle sank into a cubicle in the dimly lit bar and ordered a vodka. "Vodka is not made from potatoes," said Ivan with a smile, sliding onto the cushioned bench opposite. "Vodka is a diminutive of our word for water. In Bulgaria they say it drives away boils."

Ivan had engaging blue eyes and a frank, friendly manner. He explained he was an electrician. He loathed the regime. He dreamed of a new life in Bognor Regis, about which he had read in books. "It must be wonderful to live in Bognor. The fishermen's nets flapping in the breeze. The play of sunlight on the sea. The bowling green, the well stocked shops, the greengrocer's where you can buy bananas and pineapples."

"I've never been there myself," said my uncle, adding: "Your English is very good."

Ivan insisted on buying a bottle of vodka, and before the level had sunk to the top of the label my uncle had begun to tell Ivan all about his secret mission. He told him about working in Whitehall and about Maureen Hopper and her stupidity; about the receipt for one million two hundred thousand roubles; about the psychiatrist; about Lenin's bedstead; about his fears for Gordon, all alone in Epping Forest. He did not perhaps quite manage to tell these things to Ivan in a strict chronological order, and he felt that there were perhaps important episodes in his narrative which he had intended to include but had inadvertently omitted, but Ivan, nodding and beaming and stroking a moustache which had surely not been there earlier in the evening, seemed to understand.

My uncle had no memory of leaving the hotel with Ivan but he did dimly recall arriving at a house where someone took his coat and where Ivan ushered him into a large room with mirrored walls and an enormous bed and a delightful young woman who said her name was Olga and who, rather to his surprise, took off her clothes and then began to remove his, beginning an exciting dream which seemed to go faster and faster and faster until he was hurled out of it, and found himself lying in bed at The Aurora once again, the walls of the room, and also the entire contents of the room, spinning slowly around the throbbing axis of his forehead, while in the street below a team of workmen vigorously dug up the road with sixteen pneumatic drills.

Ivan had, thankfully, disappeared; my uncle did not see him again. Nor, equally thankfully, Olga. Indeed, he felt an enormous sense of relief when he left Leningrad and continued his itinerary. The rest of his trip – Moscow again, then Kiev – passed uneventfully. In leaving Leningrad he was of course leaving behind Lenin's trousers, but my uncle convinced himself that his mission had simply been *to reconnoitre* and that he would return at a future date, perhaps with others, and pull off the seemingly impossible. After all, the British government had given up in 1918 and four decades had passed by; it hardly mattered if he left the matter to the following year, or even later still.

At Brest, Sasha gravely shook his hand and presented him with a book about Great Soviet Leaders; my uncle groped among his vests and handed over his one remaining bar of Cadbury's Fruit and Nut. Sasha brightened at the sight of chocolate, then looked glum again. She shook her head and tried to explain with a bogus bright smile that Soviet Fruit and Nut bars of a quality far surpassing those produced in the capitalist west were due in Moscow shortly, delayed merely by snow on the track at Glib. Regretfully she had to decline his gift. Then, clicking her heels, she was gone.

My uncle sat in the vast deserted waiting room at Brest, remembering the events of the previous three weeks. Blurred impossible memories of Olga throbbed in his mind, bringing colour to his cheeks. He thought suddenly of Gordon (poor, forlorn, screeching Gordon) and wondered how he was getting on in Epping Forest. Suddenly a hand tapped him on the shoulder and he started guiltily. He had the crazy notion it was Olga's husband, armed with a pistol, but to his relief and surprise it turned out to be Ivan.

Ivan was no longer dressed in an electrician's smock but in a smart blue suit. He was carrying a small brown case. With a slow, immense wink he opened the case and took out something wrapped in paper. My uncle claimed afterwards that he knew what the present would be, even before Ivan invited him to unwrap it. It was, of course, a pair of dark trousers – Lenin's trousers.

But how – ?

Ivan explained. As a state electrician he worked all over Leningrad. When the rewiring job came up at the Lenin Memorial Museum (they were installing a new lighting system, the better to illuminate the furniture) Ivan remembered his dear friend George. With a gift here and a gift there he had managed to wangle himself a place on the team. It was easy enough to steal Lenin's trousers and substitute another pair: it was simply a question of waiting for the right moment. The right moment had come, the task had been swiftly accomplished and no one had noticed the substitution.

My uncle found himself trembling with joy and terror. How many years would a foreigner caught at the frontier with Lenin's trousers get? Ivan did not share his anxiety. "Easy-peasy-lemon-squeezy," he said. "Simply put Lenin's trousers in your case and pretend they are your spare pair. No one is going to look twice at a pair of trousers."

Sound advice: no one did.

"But how can I ever – ?"

Ivan gave my uncle a hug. "Send me an enlarged colour

57

photograph of Bognor beach. I may never get to Bognor in this life but at least I can dream."

Sobbing manly tears they hugged and parted and waved goodbye, Ivan so consumed with emotion (my uncle recalled) that he actually seemed to be laughing as he walked out of the station and into the large black chauffeur-driven limousine that whisked him away to his next rewiring task. Communist Russia may be evil and grey, my uncle reflected as the train pulled out of the station, but at least their workers do not have to hang around for hours at bus stops.

It took three days to return to England by train. Trembling with excitement and anticipation, like a child on Christmas Eve, my uncle did not dare to examine the trousers until he was back home again in Walthamstow. Before doing so, however, he was obliged to make a fuss of Gordon, who much to his surprise was sitting behind the chicken wire as good as gold, smeared with blood and evidently genuinely delighted to see him again. A glance at the putrefying carcases and bones which littered the garden showed that Gordon had survived by feasting on the neighbourhood cats and dogs. "Good old Gordon!" said my uncle, beaming with approval (he had never liked cats or dogs) and giving Gordon a bowl of brandy as a reward for his loyalty and initiative. Then he went inside to look at Lenin's trousers.

At first he laid them out on his bed and gazed at them as a bridegroom might at his bride. He licked his lips and ran the tips of his fingers along the seams. It may have been his imagination but it was as if he felt a tiny crackle of electricity, making him gasp.

The trousers were in surprisingly good condition. On the other hand, you had to remember that in those days they made things to last. Quite probably they were pre-revolutionary trousers. That would explain their hardly-worn-once look. Dared he?

He dared.

Slipping off his own trousers (which were horribly crumpled after three days spent on trains), my uncle tried them on. No good: they were too long in the leg. The toes of his pink slippers protruded from beneath the floppy turnups like tongues. My uncle sank his hands into the pockets and found that they were empty. He was disappointed. It was exactly what he had expected, nevertheless he was disappointed. He had been counting on Communist carelessness; he had hoped beyond hope that something – something more than just a handkerchief containing brittle samples of Lenin's mucus – would have been overlooked. A notebook, say, containing Bolshevik plans to kidnap a member of the royal family, or to blow up the Eiffel Tower. Something worth one million two hundred thousand roubles.

But there was nothing. There was nothing when he took off the trousers, held them upside down and gave them a good shake; there was nothing when he ran an iron over them to see if there was anything lumpy hidden in the lining; there was nothing when he ferreted around in the turn-ups with a small screwdriver and a toothbrush. When he held the trousers for four hours before a fire no hidden messages materialised on the seat of Lenin's trousers, or on the legs, or even around the flies. The buttons of Lenin's flies were not made of rubies or gold but were ordinary common or garden buttons. He examined every inch of those trousers with his magnifying glass: nothing. He turned them inside out and scrutinised the lining mercilessly: nothing.

My uncle became melancholy. He lost interest in bacon and eggs and pork chops and lamb cutlets and all the other highlights of his old life. Now he ate little more than buttered toast. He began to drink milk and rum and swear at his neighbours. Returning to work, he encountered Clara Hooper in the corridor and set off a fire extinguisher all over her, for which he was sacked. He neglected Gordon, who ran off to Epping Forest and did not come back (crushed by a speeding articulated lorry on the A11). By the time the first blackmail demand arrived, accompanied by a cautionary 5" x 7" print of Olga sprawled open-legged on the bed with my uncle crouched goatishly over her, it was far too late for him to begin a new career as a Soviet spy.

He started wearing a cap like Lenin's and a jacket and

waistcoat like Lenin's. He put on Lenin's trousers and began to make speeches in front of the bathroom mirror. "Comrade Bolsheviks!" he shouted. "Today Russia, tomorrow the world!" Imaginary crowds cheered and applauded; imaginary hands lifted him on to the top of imaginary tanks. He spoke from balconies and stages, he took off his cap and waved it in the direction of the future. He leaned over the sink and was sick.

Cocaine is used in medicine to relieve pain; small doses of cocaine have been given to allay vomiting; it has been said to cure sea sickness. Cocaine may be used to soothe pain in the eye due to the presence of a foreign body. In moderate doses the bodily and mental powers are greatly increased; a feeling of happiness and excitement is obtained; all sense of bodily or mental fatigue is abolished. Vomiting, in pain, with severe eye strain resulting from the presence of a foreign body's trousers, it was only natural that my uncle be prescribed cocaine by his local physician, Dr Ende, a slovenly incompetent whose diet had inflated him like an aerostat.

Bored with Walthamstow, my uncle found a flat in Bayswater, where he spent many happy years in a curtained room listening to Pink Floyd albums and surviving on an inheritance which had arrived out of the Dickensian blue in the conventional nick of time. Lenin's trousers he wrapped up in a supermarket carrier bag and passed on to his mother, a withered little woman named Patience. Patience lived in Tottenham and was very good at canasta, a card game of Uruguayan origin. She must promise, he said, always to look after the package for him. She promised, and there it remained, on top of the wardrobe in her bedroom, next to the box of old postcards, along with a journal in which uncle George set down in code everything that had happened leading up to his possession of Lenin's immensely valuable yet curiously worthless trousers.

Grandma's ninetieth birthday was a splendid affair, with hordes of friends and relatives (just about everyone, in fact, except for uncle George, who maintained a brooding and obscure existence in his Bayswater flat). Grandma had been born on 5th November and her birthdays had always gone with a bang. This one was no exception. My cousin Charles busied himself with the bonfire, the guy and the fireworks; my cousin Eugene volunteered for the drinks and the potatoes. Distracted by the chance discovery of my uncle's journal and the teasing enigma of his code, I avoided volunteering for any tasks. Shutting myself away in the outside lavatory, I began to crack open the long-ago tale of uncle George and Lenin's trousers. For what seemed like hours people kept turning the knob and banging on the door, while I called out "occupied!" or "busy!" in a variety of voices and ingenious accents.

The end of the journal was maddening. Actually to get hold of Lenin's trousers and still not solve the mystery! I felt certain my uncle had overlooked something – something very, very simple. What happened next is, of course, monstrously predictable. Opening that lavatory door I stepped outside into the night. Ignoring the cheers of the crowd as the bonfire was lit, I ran off to seek out Grandma, who was sitting in the parlour playing cards with some ancient white-haired friends. But of course the trousers were not there, and yes, my cousin Charles had taken them for the guy, and yes it was too late, too late, too late.

Or was it?

I ran like a madman down the garden, barging people out of the way. I ignored the intense heat and reached out to seize hold of the guy, whose heart was on fire but whose trousers – Lenin's trousers – were only smouldering. Even as I wrenched them off the guy's straw and paper body the trousers erupted in flame. I let go with a yell of pain. The trousers went WHOOSH! and turned into a black crumbling two-legged ghost. A white, unburnt, angelic fragment soared towards me. I snatched it out of the air, and saw that it was the label. Holding the smouldering fragment gingerly between thumb and forefinger I glanced at the words printed there, words which – I screwed up my eyes, looked again at the label, was forced to let go as flame returned to the charred cloth and gulped it up in a single yellow blaze that burnt the tips of my fingers.

I staggered back from the intense heat. I could have sworn that the label on Lenin's trousers read MADE IN – No! Impossible!

Unbelievable, ridiculous! My heart began to pump with emotion. A thick slew of smoke billowed into my face, choking me. A few dark flecks of fibre rose on a hot current of air, then tumbled back into the heart of the fire. The bonfire blazed with renewed intensity and I retreated up the garden. Tripping over a pile of potatoes, I narrowly avoided being hit by a wailing mis-launched rocket. Spurting cone-shaped fireworks produced a purple and silver daytime through which I wandered, dazed, aware that one or two people were glancing in my direction and grinning.

The bathroom mirror reflected a middle-aged clown with florid, sooty cheeks and a grimy nose. A piece of charred paper had lodged in the clown's receding hair. When I took hold of the paper it crumbled to powder, obliging me to comb and comb until my scalp was sore and tingling. My striped shirt was ruined, my suede shoes smeared and scorched. It was not until the next morning that I became aware of the hole in my anorak caused by a malicious child's sparkler, and the burn mark on the left leg of my expensive green corduroy trousers.

I limped away into the night, sick at heart.

There really was a receipt. My uncle was not deluded in that, only in all the other things. Had he been a little better informed about events in Russia after the Bolshevik revolution he would not have needed to abandon one wild goose chase (Gordon) for another (Lenin's trousers). Had he read *Ten Days That Shook the World* he would not only have begun to understand what really happened in Russia all those years ago but he would also have learned that on the first day of the socialist revolution Lenin appeared at the Smolny "dressed in shabby clothes, his trousers much too long for him".

The Bolshevik revolution came as a considerable shock to everyone. It just goes to show what can happen when a disciplined revolutionary party dedicated to Marxist ideas begins influencing masses of discontented workers and coming up with inflammatory slogans about peace and bread. Once working people start believing they can run their own lives and do without landlords, bosses, newspaper magnates, nobles, princes, kings, emperors or tsars – once working people start understanding dangerous notions like surplus value – once people stop caring about smartness and whether or not their trousers are too long in the leg – once workers start realising that the existing structures of government and the army and the police and the judiciary exist to serve the interests of capitalists – once such things happen a fire is lit which, if not extinguished, can spread.

Enter Sidney Reilly.

In Reilly's opinion Bolshevism was "the greatest danger that has ever threatened civilisation".

Reilly called the Bolsheviks "the Bolos".

Reilly, born 1874, was the only son of a wealthy landowner and contractor. He had two sisters. One, Elena, committed suicide when she was eighteen. His eldest sister, Marie, was terrified of mice and married a doctor. A photograph of Reilly at sixteen shows a scowling youth with psychopath's eyes and thick sensuous lips. A photograph of Reilly taken in 1918 shows a twinkly-eyed lounge lizard with a Mephistophelean moustache and beard. Reilly grew up to become a rich, reactionary charmer. He was a prodigious liar and fantasist. He could never look a camera in the eye. In the handful of photographs which survive Reilly is looking sideways, to his left. The left is where Reilly feels threatened. Women adored him. He possessed eleven passports. He was a talented linguist. He was a bigamist. According to one version of his life Reilly was an expert at "poisoning, stabbing, shooting and throttling". As a slippery, nasty, murderous extreme right-wing thug Reilly was quite naturally regarded as first rate material by M11c (as the British secret service called itself in those days).

Reilly, originally born in Russian Poland, was sent to Moscow by M11c in May 1918. At first Bolshevik Russia was a relatively peaceful place. The Bolsheviks ended Russian participation in the Great War and began to put their socialist programme into practice. In January 1918 someone tried to shoot Lenin, but missed. By May of that year the British diplomatic representative in Moscow, Robert Bruce Lockhart, was conspiring to overthrow the Bolos. He supplied the Foreign Office with a plan whereby on the night of an Allied invasion all the Bolshevik leaders would be murdered, allowing the formation of a new government "which will be in reality a military dictatorship". In fact by that date British troops were already in Russia. On 6 March a division of marines commanded by Major General Frederick Poole landed at the Arctic port of Murmansk. By July there were eighteen anti-Bolshevik governments in what remained of the old Tsarist empire. That same month Lockhart and the French Consul General in Moscow handed over ten million roubles to finance espionage and sabotage by the White anti-Bolshevik National Centre group in Moscow. On 2 August Poole landed at Archangel and seized the town, aided by a detachment of Royal Marines, a French battalion and fifty American sailors. The anti-Bolshevik plots ramified, financed by the governments of Britain, France and the United States. Explosives were stored in the flat of the French government representative. By the summer British, French, American and Japanese troops had landed in Russia in support of the White counter-revolutionary armies. At the end of August, with Moscow and other Russian cities on the verge of starvation, Allied agents blew up food trains at Voronezh station. The British government had previously supplied £1million for the purpose of sabotaging the Russian Baltic fleet: Reilly had a better idea, which was to spend the money on overthrowing the Bolshevik leadership.

Reilly dreamed of the capture of Lenin and the seizure of his trousers. He handed over those 1,200,000 roubles to a man who he believed could bring such an event about. What my uncle never understood was that it was not the trousers that were important but Lenin's legs and underpants. Reilly planned to parade a trouserless Lenin through the streets of Moscow and turn him into a laughing-stock.

The plots thickened. On 30 August a leading Bolshevik, Uritsky, was assassinated in Petrograd, and Lenin was shot and seriously wounded in Moscow. What Reilly didn't know was that the Bolsheviks knew all about his conspiracy to capture Lenin and his trousers. There were mass arrests. Lockhart was imprisoned.

Reilly went into hiding. He spent several nights in a brothel, hiding in the room of a girl in the last stage of syphilis. The girl laughed, said her name began with a "C" and Reilly had to guess. Clarissa? No. Claudia? Niet. Cecilia? Clara? Celeste? No. The girl stank. Her chest was yellow as butter, her cheeks the colour of porridge. Her mouth was foul and oozy.

Syphilis occurs in three stages. A month after contracting the infection a small, hard, painless sore appears. A slight colourless discharge leaks from the sore. The glands in the region of the sore enlarge. The sore goes away, leaving a small blemish on the skin. This happens after two or three months have elapsed.

The girl looked to be about ninety. She had sunken eyes. She shook. She had a squint.

Christine!

No.

After three months the germs have been transported in the blood to all parts of the body. The germs are shaped like a corkscrew. How many spirals? From ten to twenty-five. The germs get down to business: severe headaches, fever, pains in joints and bones, severe anaemia, a dreadful rash all over the body. The germs invade the heart. They drill their way merrily through the walls of the blood vessels. They get into the nervous system.

Cynthia?

No.

If left untreated, the secondary stage appears to clear up and there is a period of freedom from symptoms which may last from two to twenty years. In the third and final stage (Claudine? No) tumour-like masses proliferate disgustingly. Your nose rots. Ulcers and sores as big as oranges erupt across your skin and in your liver and bones and in your mouth and all over your tongue. Cancer of the tongue is common. Your brain and spinal column fill up with pus and putrefaction. You get dizzy. You look awful. You're literally falling apart.

C chuckles, hideously. Wanna fook me, mistair?

Niet.

Guess. You god to guess.

Cecilia.

You had that one.

Hmm.

Her rippled thighs liberally plastered with chancres, excrescent formations reminiscent of fungus, glittery discharges. A tendency to omit words or syllables.

I've got it. Cathy!

Wrong again, Reilly.

The girl shrieked with laughter. She was obviously suffering from general paralysis of the insane. Halted and stumbled over long words. Slurred speech. Said twice parts of words. I give up, Reilly said. He was bored and frightened and disgusted. He hadn't had an erection since he'd entered the room. It was the way he could see the tops of her upper teeth through the hole where her nose used to be. Unforgettable.

"I tell you. My name is – my name is – ". (Hysterical shrieks, general stench, watery oozings, leakages of blood.) "My name is – ". A gobbet of something resembling phlegm smacked against his lapel.

"Cap-eat-all-ism!"

A bad joke! And his lapel smelling like a rotten egg! Reilly screamed and ran from the room. False papers took him to Petrograd. He escaped on a Dutch freighter, feeling itchy. Back in England (the rash was nothing; everybody gets rashes) he was awarded a Military Cross for bravely, if unsuccessfully, attempting to detach Lenin from his trousers.

To cut a long story short (which is the best cut of all), Reilly spent the rest of his life conspiring against the Bolsheviks. To finance the anti-Communist crusade he invented "Humagsolan", a miracle medicine which cured headaches, spots, cancer, constipation and syphilis. Especially syphilis.

"Humagsolan" flopped. Undeterred, Reilly devised a plan whereby (once the wretched Communists had been disposed of) a British banking combine could take over the entire Russian economy. The Central Bank would also run an intelligence network and control the Russian press. The monarchy, naturally, would be restored to the throne. Unfortunately things did not quite turn out that way and, somehow or other, bafflingly and infuriatingly, that tiny handful of Bolshevik madmen succeeded in routing the innumerable armies and the combined efforts of Britain, France, Japan, the USA, and the Whites.

Reilly did not give up so easily. The Bolos might have won the civil war, but that didn't mean their troubles were over. There was encouraging evidence that radishes were thriving under the new regime. Reilly liked the sound of radishes very much. Radishes were Lenin's term. Lenin meant people who were red outside, white within. Under the influence of the radishes the signs were that Bolshevik rule was changing. There was also encouraging evidence that the opposition in Russia might yet act to overthrow the Bolsheviks, a notion which also appealed to Reilly's dear friend Winston Churchill. All that was required was a definite plan of action. If proof of such a plan could be obtained an approach would be made to Henry Ford. "Once his interest is gained, the question of money can be considered solved," Reilly enthusiastically noted. If not, Russian museums could be burgled and their art treasures sold in the West.

On 25 September 1925 Reilly crossed the border into Russia to meet the political council of "The Trust", the organisation which was to overthrow the Bolsheviks. Unfortunately for Reilly "The Trust" was run by the Soviet security service, and was designed to flush out counter-revolutionary conspirators. On this occasion Reilly's false passport did not save him. Removing Reilly's trousers, his captors discovered him to be wearing expensive underpants bearing his initials...

I limped away into the night. Two teenage girls by a bus shelter pointed a finger at me, whispered something and hooted with laughter. I wandered on through empty streets, past illuminated shop windows filled with cheap jewellery, sofas, TVs and videos. Once I slipped on some leaves and some people in a passing car wound down their windows and shrieked something. Soon afterwards I slipped on a piece of discarded fruit, which I observed without smiling was a banana skin. I reflected how I had never found clowns or slapstick amusing. My sides refuse to split with uncontrollable laughter at the sight of people having buckets of blue paint poured over them or having their trousers removed. The very word "gag" makes me gag; I abhor drollery, I loathe waggery, I detest jocosity. Practical jokes make me wince; comic virtuosity is not my cup of tea. You can keep your caprices, your fun, your jests, your clowning. Tomfoolery and buffoonery bores me, funny business makes me scowl. Comic turns make me puke; farce sends me to sleep; custard pie humour makes me yawn until my jaw aches. Life is too short for a laugh a minute; knockabout comedy doesn't knock me out but sends me fleeing. I hope I make my position clear. Give me back my trousers, and a pox on your japes, wisecracks, badinage and leg-pulls.

I remembered the fate of Bim-Bom, the famous Russian clown. When the Cheka arrived in Moscow in 1918 it is said that some of its members were not amused by Bim-Bom's jokes about the Bolshevik government. Some Chekists entered the circus ring to arrest Bim-Bom, much to the laughter of the audience, who thought it was all part of the act. Bim-Bom fled, and the Chekists opened fire. The joke was over: panic and pandemonium.

Historians tell this tale to show what humourless authoritarians the Bolsheviks were. The same historians tell us the story of the plot to remove Lenin's trousers as if it was one of the jolliest japes imaginable. And if it had been successful, and after Lenin had been marched trouserless through the streets of Moscow, what then? Having seen him humiliated in public, the imperialist powers, their prime ministers and their presidents and their generals and their police chiefs and their secret agents all chuckling amiably, would doubtless have made the troublesome fellow go all the way back to Geneva by his original circuitous route and, their troops and moustachio'd policemen guffawing broadly, would have seen the wretch off at the Finland Station to catch the next draughty, cold, uncomfortable third class connection to Geneva.

I think not.

As I walked homeward under a twinkling sky still streaked by rockets and amid a silence punctuated by the distant boom of explosives, I understood that it was not Lenin's trousers they were all after but his life, his voice, his perceptions. It would not have been many minutes after the removal of his trousers before they would have begun the beatings, the torture, the mutilations, the cutting-out of the eyes, the tearing out of his tongue, the crushing and breaking of Lenin's hands, the obliteration of his dangerous brain. There would have been laughter, but it would not have been the pleasant Senior Common Room laughter of the historians.

I must have had a little too much to drink that night, for next thing I found myself standing on top of a red pillar box shouting, "Remember the execution of the 26 Commissars of Baku! Never underestimate the ruthlessness of the British ruling class!" The police were called and I ran off up an alley and crawled into a cardboard box.

"It's a coon," said the first PC, shining his torch on me. This I indignantly denied, assuring him that owing to a sequence of small misadventures I was simply a trifle grimy. Putting on a scouse accent I passed myself off as a homeless northerner seeking to make good in opportunity Britain. I denied having anything to do with the shouting of offensive slogans from a pillar box.

The two young moustachio'd officers held a short conversation during which they decided I was in too filthy a state for them to want to arrest me under the 1824 Vagrancy Act. To relieve the tensions of their stressful and often tedious occupation they therefore relieved themselves upon me, gave me a sound kicking in the ribs and a brisk truncheoning of shoulders and arms and concluded their fun by making a number of colourful threats as to what they would do to me if they ever found me in their manor again. With a squeal of tyres they vanished into the night.

The next day, showered, shaved and changed, and having decided never again to attend a fireworks party or to over-indulge in alcohol, and vowing also always to cross over the road if a pillar box loomed on my side, I strode off to the reference section of the local library to enquire where I might find a revolutionary socialist party in the Leninist tradition.

The rest is history.

I have always wanted to tell a story which begins as this one begins, and now it is done, it is finished with. It is time to draw the curtains and put out the light, time to take off my clothes and put on my pyjamas, time to hang up my trousers (taking special care to see that they are not creased) and to get into bed.

Pyjamas, did I say? Pyjamas remind me of what had completely crossed my mind. I refer to the other pair of trousers in the case. My uncle, wandering off down dark labyrinths of his own devising, never learned about these other trousers, which were worth at least 600,000 roubles. You see, it was not simply Lenin's trousers that the British Government were after but also Trotsky's. Get rid of Lenin and Trotsky and the whole wretched Bolshevik show could be wrapped up once and for all (who knows, perhaps they were right). But as we know, it was not Lenin and Trotsky who lost their trousers, but Sidney Reilly.

It occurs to me that this last sentence is misleading. Some years later Trotsky did lose his trousers, or rather his pyjama bottoms. At the time he was lodging in the House of the Soviets in Granovsky Street, Moscow. On January 17, 1928, early in the morning, the G.P.U. came to take Trotsky away. Trotsky locked himself in his bedroom. The G.P.U. smashed down the door. Dressed in his pyjamas, Trotsky refused to put on his clothes. A G.P.U. man seized Trotsky's pyjama trousers. Another G.P.U. man lifted first one leg, and then the other. His slippers were removed, then his pyjamas. Keeping a tight grip on Trotsky's limbs the G.P.U. men held the great revolutionary out for their colleagues, who were holding Trotsky's clothes.

Soon Trotsky's trousers were forced on to him; his shirt was buttoned; he was dressed.

Some plots involve the forcible removal of trousers; others involve the forcible putting-on of trousers. Some plots fail, others succeed. Sidney Reilly was shot in the Lenin Hills on November 3, 1925. My uncle George died of cocaine poisoning at

25 Powis Square at 9.58 pm on July 12, 1969. As for Trotsky, he was dragged to an empty railway carriage in a lonely Moscow shunting yard. The carriage was taken to a deserted station 50 kilometres from Moscow. There it was linked up to a train travelling all the way to Pishpeck-Frunze. It took a week to get to Alma Ata, across the snowdrifts and the mountains. For three weeks he stayed at an inn on Gogol Street. From there –

But that is another story.

Rubbish

Rubbish. As anyone who knew her would agree. Her? Being horrible to Omar Sharif, who just wanted to work quietly with bandages and sheets, hypodermics and ink, and not get involved in politics?

Ninety-one years old, wrinkled but spritely, walking slowly and carefully towards the post office. She was late and Al would be there selling the papers, anxiously wondering where she'd got to, wearing his old blue raincoat and Lenin cap, wanting to talk about the lock-out and the next day's picket. But Al would understand (as few would) that she'd been so engrossed in re-reading Engels's *Origin of the Family, Private Property and the State* – which reminded her of the time she'd spent in the open prison outside Harrogate – that she'd simply forgotten about the time. When she saw what it said on the kitchen clock she'd reluctantly put down Engels, put on her scarlet headscarf, and left at once.

Empty Tango can rattling along the gutter, spirals of choc-bar wrappings and cellophane whirling beside the kerb.

She came to the zebra-crossing outside Boots and thought, *Nothing lasts really* – not marriages, not governments, not even the design of zebra-crossings. Nobody talked about "Belisha beacons" anymore, probably nobody but her remembered the time when there weren't black and white stripes across the road but just two parallel dashed white lines to walk between. And, checking carefully each way to ensure that no one was coming, she stepped out on to the first dark stripe, hoping Al would not worry too much but would remember all the times he'd called her scatterbrained and forgetful and put her lateness down to the vagaries of age.

Five-forty, it said on the clock on the wall of Boots – or rather 17:40, in funny green lopsided computer numerals she could barely read.

Five-forty!

Nothing lasts really – not even large, busy railway stations.

When she'd read in the local paper that the last line still open was to be closed and the junction with it, what did she feel? Relief? That now the final monument to that far-off, lingering, still-throbbing time was at last to be swept away? No. Not relief. More a queer remote hollowed-out sadness, a rustling emptiness, as if her heart was an old bucket where a quick, elusive spider had left a few strands of silver.

They wanted to turn the site into a multi-storey car park – "They" being the local Conservative Council and the senior planning officers, the usual corrupt bunch of sleazy businessmen, freemasons and freeloaders. And so, that very last day, she had made the effort and gone, before the ticket gate was abandoned and the bar was emptied of its bottles and boxes of crisps and cigarettes and the bulldozers moved in.

The junction was just a shell. She'd hardly recognised it. The water tower was coated in rust. Platform Four was covered in grass and weeds and broken glass, where only ghost trains stopped (the 5.40 for Churley, Lea Green and Langdon, say, its number – L.M.S. 2429 – unforgettable). Only Platform Three was still in use, used not by magnificent, roaring locomotives which wailed past spewing billowing curling coiling alabaster clouds, but by a dingy blue three-carriage diesel which stank of oil and fumes. The underpass up which Alec had run that ghastly Thursday she'd thought he was never going to come was filthy and squalid and covered in spray-painted racist and obscene graffiti. The refreshment room had long ago been boarded-up and replaced by a machine that squirted boiling water on to a polystyrene cup containing three choices of powder – tea, coffee or cola. Hard to imagine a romance blossoming around *that*! Later the waiting room had been turned into a small bar with Gainsborough and Toulouse Lautrec reproductions on the wall to give it style. That was where, on a Thursday in September 1976, she'd first met Al. She'd clumsily spilled her gin and tonic all over his Penguin copy of *Ten Days That Shook the World*. She'd been going through a bad patch then, what with Bobby in the Himalayas sending her postcards of erotic Indian carvings and then his abrupt death, followed soon after by Fred's.

Al was fifty-seven and had been made redundant by British Oxygen. It was Al, twenty years younger than her – "You know what's happened, don't you?" – who had opened her eyes to Marxism-Leninism.

She'd noticed (she could hardly avoid noticing) that the door was still there. Boarded-up, peeling, decrepit, but still there. The door you entered and left by, the door on Platform Three where the sign REFRESHMENT ROOM had once hung on chains, with a disembodied hand pointing a finger, just like the hand on the last page of the first part *of Jude the Obscure* or, for that matter (of course in those days she had never even *heard* of intertextuality, let alone learned to savour the sweetness of its synchronies!), in Chapter XI of *Under the Volcano*, the door through which she'd run, away from Dolly Messiter, away from everything, like Anna Karenin (but not like Anna Karenin!). Behind that door lived many ghosts, reigned over by that strange woman who served tea – what was her name? Mrs Maggot? There were the remains of a poster on the door (put there by Al, or one of the other comrades, probably). THE ENVIRONMENT IN CRISIS, it read. DO THE GREENS HAVE THE ANSWER?

Once upon a time, anxious about depletions of the ozone layer, not to mention the plight of the whales (Walt Disney had a lot to answer for, she felt, remembering *Pinocchio*) and all those cute, grinning dolphins who got caught up and suffered terribly in the nets of the tuna-fish trawlers, she might have thought that perhaps they did, but not now, not since meeting Al.

It was as if she had spent her entire life short-sighted, afflicted by dimness and tunnel vision, and Al was the optician who had corrected her defective perceptions. She had spent most of her adult life burdened by antimacassars, pewter, doilies, cake ingredients, fêtes, and the clatter and thump of the National Symphony Orchestra, her intellectual horizons limited by the *Encyclopaedia Britannica*, the novels of Kate

O'Brien and *The Oxford Book of English Verse*, while other people made a career in electrocardiograms or specialised in antiparticles or worked in laboratories on antiperspirants or discovered a new antipyretic or tended antirrhinums or campaigned on behalf of the anti-sabbatarian movement or wrote experimental fiction which ended in anticlimax (a story, say, that began and ended with the word "Rubbish") while she went on doing the week's shopping and changing her library books and, in the interstices of each stifling day, in the intervals and intermissions and long Sunday afternoons of her busy, desolate, empty petty-bourgeois life, she thought, her heart pumping wildly, of Alec.

She wondered (stepping on to the second white stripe of the crossing) if Alec was still alive. She had often wondered that, all through the 1940s and 1950s, imagining him living under a permanent blue sky in an eight-bedroom villa with immaculate lawns and a tennis court and softly pattering sprinklers and a sweet, whiskery old gardener named Abdul who attentively tended the bougainvillea while his wife Else, a fat jolly woman with an immense bottom, clattered pans in the kitchen and hummed melodious native songs, songs hard to hear because of the droning coming from the lounge, where Else's sister Blanche vacuumed away the grass and leaves that the boys brought in on their plimsolls, while Alec sat upstairs in an air-conditioned study, writing important monographs about pharynxgitis and phimosis and phlebitis and phlegmasia and photophobia and the usefulness of phystigmine, a drug obtained from the calabar bean, while Alec's wife, who had doubled in weight and become an alcoholic, careless about both her personal appearance and hygiene, lay slumped in an easy chair, oblivious to the egg-stains on her unfashionable dress, armpits dripping with sweat, fingering her moustache.

No, not like that. Alec would not have been in Jo'burg long before he'd have fallen for a pretty young white nurse and run off with her to Zambia.

And later there would have been a rather messy involvement with the beautiful young black girl who cleaned the house, who in no time at all would be cradling a coffee-coloured baby with Alec's blue eyes, leaving Alec – who by now was drinking more than was good for him, as doctors are prone to – with little choice but to pack in his African jaunt and go somewhere else, Saigon say, giving up lungs and throats and moving into amputation, a branch of medicine which was then experiencing something of a boom in those parts.

Not that the lives of the Jesson family had exactly kept to the straight and narrow. It had been a terrible shock when their daughter Margaret had announced that she jolly well wasn't going to work at the building society after all. She had decided to become a painter! She had got a book out of the lending library about abstract expressionism. She wanted them to know that she admired Jackson Pollock tremendously.

"*Who?*" had been Laura's first thought, but evidently not Fred's.

Fred had gone through the roof, which was perhaps not surprising, since Fred had always rather resembled a balloon. Of course Fred had rather brought the whole thing on himself, what with his obsession about pensions and the importance of getting a good secure job and his rigid notions of propriety, which committed him never to break wind, not even silently, not even when he was out of the house in the fresh air (for Fred was a stickler for not dropping litter and for keeping things clean and for leaving them exactly as you would hope to find them), which meant that – as Dr Graves explained to her before the operation – the gases in Fred's body had forced their way in among the tubing and bones, forming bubble-clusters and pockets and "bulge-bags", so that Fred's girth had annually increased by one-and-three-quarter inches while his weight had actually gawn down!

"I'm sick of Ketchworth! The people are boring, boring, BORING! I'm sick of living in a mock-Tudor house cluttered up with lamp standards and unopened encyclopaedias! If I hear mother playing her record of Rachmaninoff's second piano concerto one more bloody time I think I'll scream! I'm sick of French windows and rubbers of bridge and that Christ-awful garden with its pixie pool and spotless birdbath, full of idiot gnomes and pensive nymphs and owls and rabbits and crocodiles and shrub tubs and plinths and pots! And another thing: why can't you just let the *grass grow*, for God's sake! Let me tell you I feel physically *sick* living here! As for spending even one hour working for the Blugport and Bumbling Building Society, let alone the rest of my life! Jesus! Don't you understand I want to go places? I want to live! I want to paint like no one has ever painted!"

Margaret's outburst made an instant impression upon her father. His cheeks filled with a dangerous red, abruptly flashed an inflamed orange, and then switched to a queasy green, which instantly re-formed into a nauseous mixture of all three, before briskly impersonating porridge, boarding-house soup and, finally, dirty snow fouled by a flea-bitten mongrel. His arms trembled, his eyes bulged, his chest swelled as if propelling a degenerate capitalist's yacht.

"Painting's not for girls," he said, in an odd strained gasping way, articulating the sentence with painful slowness, leaving a gap of boiling silence between each word. Then, to everyone's astonishment, Fred rose slowly up from the royal-blue deep pile carpet until he was a good six inches off the ground.

"There's no job security in abstract expressionism," he added, shaking his head solemnly, completely unaware of his faintly Biblical ascension.

"I don't bloody care! I'm a creative person – not a bloody cipher!" Margaret clamped her hips with the outstretched thumb and forefinger of each hand. She looked dangerous. Talk about an *ipse dixit*!" she concluded ferociously, the numbness inside her matched by ipsilateral shivers. She thought: if only I could get hold of some ipecacuanha!

Fred went red again. He wobbled from side to side. "Language!" he bellowed. "Go and wash your dirty mouth out, my girl. This minute! If I ever hear you speak like that in front of your mother again, I'll – I'll –".

And then it happened. Fred seemed to expand before their very eyes, and shot upwards, hitting the ceiling with immense force and vanishing from sight amidst a shower of plaster and pink-brown dust, crashing through into the room above (the box room, fortunately), which he passed through at 50m.p.h., crashing through another ceiling before erupting into the black void of the loft, knocking aside packing cases and old surplus rolls of carpet, still rising like a newly launched rocket, before ripping through the roof beams and battering a hole in the tiles in the manner of a mutinous convict involved in a prison protest. Just as Fred seemed about to leave the roof of their house and head out into space there came a tremendous screeching noise as if someone was nipping the throat of a deflating balloon, a noise accompanied by a tremendous rushing stench of putrefaction and faeces and boiled cabbage, the sound and stink of all that stale trapped air rushing out of Fred, whose face was frozen in a scowl of outrage and disapproval, first at his daughter's insolence, secondly at his own out-of-the-blue levitational skills, an expression which remained on his face as, like an elasticated figure of fun out of *Tom and Jerry*, he suddenly shrank to a third of his previous width and plummeted back down through the hole in the roof, down through the attic, down through the hole in the box room ceiling, down through the box room, down through the hole in the lounge ceiling and back onto the royal-blue deep pile carpet once again, landing upright, shaky, his clothes torn off him, bruised and scratched, a hideous parody of his former self, with big flaps of loose, baggy skin hanging from his chest like the withered dugs of a starving African, causing Laura (*I didn't think such violent things could happen to ordinary people*) to scream in shock, surprise and disbelief.

Margaret had by this time taken advantage of the unexpected diversion to run upstairs, pack a case, and tiptoe out by the back door, thereafter making her way to Ketchworth station to catch the 15.12 to Milford, where she caught the 16.04 to Leeds, connecting with the 16.30 to King's Cross, where she took a taxi to Victoria in plenty of time for the 17.45 to Dover, where she had no problem booking a berth on the ferry that left at 23.00 for Calais, where she caught the 4.05 train which went direct to the Gare du Nord, where a speck of grit in her eye led to a chance meeting with Jacques, a surrealist of Algerian descent who lived in an attic in Montmartre, where he introduced her to Max Ernst and later fathered her first child, Jules, a half-caste with brown eyes, who, like Jacques, Margaret's father refused ever to meet, even though his operation had been a complete success, so much so that *A High Wind in Jamaica* was taken out of the locked cabinet in the lounge and reinstated on the bookshelf, and he was even able to attend a showing *of Gone with the Wind* without a flicker of anxiety, and even though that other consequence of Margaret's unseemly outburst – his flaps of drooping flesh – had long since been removed by surgery.

Poor Fred.

"Thank God for Bobby," he'd said to her afterwards. Bobby had a first-rate job at the Midland Bank. If he kept his nose clean and to the grindstone, and didn't loaf, and played his cards right, he might well, in forty-five years' time, rise to assistant chief clerk, at twelve shillings a week!

Poor Fred.

It broke his heart when Bobby was arrested for gross indecency in the urinals at Milford Junction. With Mr Godby, the ticket collector, of all people! What seemed even worse than all the publicity and people giving them funny looks in the street and Bobby losing his job at the bank was that Bobby didn't seem at all ashamed. Fred tried to reason with the poor boy, waving the Bible at him and explaining to him in a quiet voice that he was a filthy fellow, a disgrace and an abomination in the eyes of the Lord. But Bobby just grinned. "It's nothing to be ashamed of, Dad," he'd said, bold as brass. "I just happen to like boys. And men. Big, powerful men like Mr G."

It came as a relief to everyone when Bobby developed an interest in yetis. Things had been pretty tense in the house until Bobby announced that he had to go away for a few weeks. He explained that he had recently become passionately excited by the possibility of a tribe of giant unknown hairy wild men still existing in certain parts of Mongolia and in the foothills of the Himalayas. A monastery near Lhasa apparently had a fragment of fur from an unknown animal, which was kept in a sealed glass case but could be viewed by visitors. There had also been many eye-witness reports from reputable people such as sherpas and even Buddhist monks. He had bought a pair of X8 binoculars and an 8mm home movie camera with a zoom lens. He had booked his flight to Katmandu, and from there he planned to travel on by moped. He was determined to crack the mystery once and for all. Any film taken of a yeti would be priceless, and there might even be a book in it.

Poor Bobby.

He was last seen alive at nineteen-hundred feet, wearing an oxygen mask and a curious black rubber outfit with a Union Jack embroidered on the seat of his trousers. A playful shout of "Watch out, sugars, I'm coming!" – addressed to a desolate mountain landscape where he apparently believed several yetis had mischievously secreted themselves – was enough to trigger the vast white field of thawing snow above. At first, woken by the echoing boom *of coming-coming-coming ing-ing-ing*, it moved an inch or so, groaned once or twice, then surged down the mountainside and gobbled Bobby up as if he was the last pea on a plate. His body was never found.

Poor Laura.

Amid their grief she and Fred had one small consolation – Margaret abandoned her swarthy lover and child and married Jonathan Greech, a wealthy entrepreneur with interests in barbed wire, paper shredders, telephone-tapping machines, listening devices, blowtorches, water-cannon, anti-personnel bombs and miscellaneous torture equipment, which he exported with enormous success to the many governments in the Free World which required them.

Poor Laura.

Hardly had she given away her daughter in holy matrimony than Fred was caught by the police. It turned out he'd been exposing himself to schoolgirls since 1937. Admittedly one paunchy white middle-class, middle-aged male in a pin-striped suit looks much the same as another, and admittedly the police are not very bright, even at the best of times. All the same, it was amazing he'd never been caught earlier. Pervert! Fascist! No wonder (she thought, moving on to the sixth stripe of the crossing) he'd wanted binoculars for his birthday. No wonder he'd pretended to be so keen on bird watching. No wonder it was Fred who'd insisted on separate beds and, after 1944, separate bedrooms. No wonder he had spent much of their married life going off alone into the woods on the pretext that a Godwit had been seen there.

It was typical of Fred that he couldn't even bring himself to look her in the face and tell her of his aberrant sexuality. She used to think he had the sensitivity of a rhinoceros, now she knew he'd just been devious. It was typical of Fred that she didn't even find out until after he was dead. Fred knew the game was up. After being charged by the police, he was freed on bail and went straight to Milford station. One moment he was standing on Platform Three, his *Times* tucked under his arm, the next he had calmly stepped off the edge and into the path of the Boat Train.

At the inquest the witnesses spoke of a sudden, unanticipated shower of rain.

Red rain.

Fred.

One girl – horrid girl! – had spoken at inordinate length about the similarities to her aunt's raspberry jam. She had even brought a pot in to show the inquest jury, who handed it round, dipping their fingers in and whispering. Another girl, who worked in the Heinz factory at Churley, insisted that Fred's remains were identical to ketchup, not simply in colour but also in consistency. A third girl, some sort of beatnik with long straight black hair and a beret, explained that she was very interested in post-impressionism and alluded to the warm fresh reds of Van Gogh's *Poppy Fields*. The fourth witness, a bald Welsh sociologist who sought a safe Labour seat in a deprived part of Glasgow, brushed aside what the others had said and spoke with feeling about the blood-red sunsets he had often seen in late September from the grounds of his villa at

Juan-les-Pins.

Fred's newspaper was solemnly held up and – because of the soaking it had received – was widely mistaken for a copy of the *Financial Times*. The Coroner summed up with a denunciation of coloured immigrants who wantonly abandoned mango peel on station platforms, said it was perfectly obvious Fred had slipped on that sort of peel, and instructed the jury to bring in a verdict of death by misadventure.

Poor Laura.

After Fred had been cremated on the banks of the Ouse she went abroad for a time. First she went to Egypt to see the Sphinx, a rather grubby disappointment, its environs infested with screeching beggars each anxious to show her their sores and stumps, and none of whom had ever heard of a Dr Harvey. Later she flew to Mozambique and sailed up the Zambezi in a canoe, suffering terribly from diarrhoea and not bumping into Alec once.

Poor Alec.

When he had patted her gently on the shoulder and walked out of her life without a backward glance she had been convinced he had gone out to Africa to do good. But now she saw that he simply been running away, that he was a man who would always be running away – from his wife, his duties and responsibilities, his loves, his past. He was a restless creature who, she felt certain, wherever he was, whatever had happened in his life, would never once have devoted (as she had) an entire summer to a reading of all three volumes *of Capital*.

Of course in those days one hardly thought about Africa at all, not even when Alec told her that's where he was going. One had a vague mental image of a continent the shape of a parsnip which was full of sand at the top and jungles in the middle, a place which was very hot and full of crocodiles and elephants and monkeys and giraffes, a land occupied by hordes of beaming black people, who lived in quaint mud huts, people who were anxious to please and who were rather like children, especially when they squabbled, as they did often, because of their blood and the intemperate climate.

If she hadn't met Al she would never have understood why crowds of skinny Africans kept staring at her reproachfully from her television every couple of years, holding up dead babies and ignoring the flies which covered them like a crust. First of all Al explained that the distribution of foreign aid was not in any way related to need and that (for example) in 1989 the top six recipients of U.S. aid were Israel, Egypt, Pakistan, Turkey, the Philippines and El Salvador, who between them got $7,419 million, whereas Ethiopia got just $4 million.

Secondly, he analysed why famine occurred. "Recognise what the roots of poverty are," he told her quietly. "Profit, not human need, determines whether people live or die in the developing world. Starvation is not due to there being too many people. There is famine in Bolivia, with on average just 5 people per acre, and relative plenty in Holland where the comparable population density is 326. Nor has famine anything to do with availability of farmland. The truth is there is enough food in the world to feed everyone. People die of hunger because they are poor, not because there isn't enough food. This is the upshot of a hundred and fifty years of the market system of capitalism. Western governments and banks, headed by the World Bank and the International Monetary Fund, impose a savage burden on the poor of the world while propping up repressive local regimes. In 1989 Third World countries spent £63,000 million more in debt repayments than they got in aid."

Fred, of course, had never said anything like that to her in his entire life. Fred's socio-political understanding was about as cramped and narrow as a *Times* editorial. But Alec had never said things like that to her either. All Alec had done was tell jokes and make her laugh and talk wistfully-urgently about love and the ghastly and difficult position they found themselves in. Al was different.

"It is a disgusting distortion of the truth," Al told her, banging his fist on the tabletop, "to suggest ordinary people in the West are to blame for famine in Africa, or that by consuming less ourselves we might in some way help. That is an

83

argument designed to make us feel we are individually guilty and the system is not! The truth is that feeding everyone in Africa in 1991 would cost half what the Coalition forces spent in a single day during the Gulf War! The truth is that Europe stores right now as surplus nine times the amount of food Africa needs! Three times as much money goes in maintaining the food mountains as goes on food aid! The truth was revealed by a U.S. treasury official who reacted to the idea of cancelling Africa's debt by saying, 'We have to keep their feet in the fire.' In such circumstances charity is never going to be enough! We need rid of the system that starves people!"

At first Al had shocked her with his ideas. Abolition of the royal family! In place of Parliament a revolutionary socialist republic based on Soviets! He used strange expressions like *surplus value* and *hegemony* until she felt her head would burst!

Later, when she had read *Manifesto of the Communist Party* and *Socialism: Utopian and Scientific*, her understanding began to develop. And that wasn't all. Thanks to Al she had experienced her first orgasm for forty-six years. Sex had never been very important to Fred (not that sort, anyway). Until she'd met Al her last orgasm (well, if the truth were told her *only* orgasm) had been in 1934. She remembered it well. It was the day Hitler had massacred the Brownshirts. Fred, who admired the Fuehrer enormously ("There's a chap who knows how to deal with the unions and the Jews!"), had seemed strangely excited by the news. He'd drunk five sherries in a row and put "Ride of the Valkyries" on the radiogram. She'd had five sherries too. They had gone to bed flushed and –. But that was an awful long time ago. In those days she had felt certain sex was not at all what it was cracked up to be. On the contrary, she had learned that it was a rather painful, messy business involving parts of the body that were best left in repose. Perhaps with Alec things would have been different – but all that was an unwritten and never-to-be-written story.

In those days her favourite song had been "Let the Great Big World Keep Turning". It reminded her of Alec. Well, the great big world had gone on turning, and millions had died in famines and imperialist wars and Alec had grown old and was probably dead by now, and here she was with R.E.M.'s 'Country Feedback" playing on her Walkman, ninety-one-years old, wrinkled but spritely. *Hell*, she thought. *My husband committed suicide, my son died in the Himalayas and my daughter is a class traitor. Thank goodness I have Marx, Luxemburg, Lenin and Trotsky to sustain and enlighten me in a barbarous and decaying world.*

She reached the last of the stripes and stepped on to the pavement. Strong gusts tugged at her frail figure. She leaned against them, pushed on towards Milford Post Office, where Al was waiting with the papers, a gleam in her eyes as her slip fluttered wildly, her stockings crackling, little shivers passing down her spine at the thought of the night ahead, a couple of beers and a curry, some serious hours with a book, then up before dawn to be on the picket line outside the sweatshop factory which was trying to stop the Asian workforce from joining a union, the one true marriage not a matter of a bourgeois lifestyle in a mock-Tudor detached house in a pseudo-Welwyn Garden City, but the marriage of revolutionary socialist theory and revolutionary socialist practice, good thoughts to have on a cold windy day in a dump like Milford, the rain starting, the wind getting stronger, like English conservatism, trying to push you backward, trying to cut you down to size, trying to weaken you, while pages from old newspapers cartwheeled along the street and wrapped them-selves around your throat, the decay of capitalism all around her in the boarded-up shops, the derelict warehouses, the old school with its broken windows and weeds splitting the grim Victorian asphalt playground, the police car on the corner ahead, the cold-eyed officer inside, writing her off at first as a dear little old lady then perhaps recognising her as the one that caused all the trouble, sitting down in the road that time the Mayor entertained a visiting dignitary from South Africa, getting arrested when the Territorial Army tried to recruit outside the Corn Exchange, plus six offences of fly-posting to

85

be taken into consideration.

Not to mention the time she'd slipped an egg down a policeman's trousers, a policeman who she was reasonably sure had never heard of the 26 Commissars of Baku, an action which had occurred for no other reason than that she'd been passing with half-a-dozen Size One eggs from Sunnyridge Farm when the officer had started kicking the black youth, an episode which arguably revealed a lack of discipline on her part, although as she explained to the magistrate, a goggle-eyed fool with three chins who'd looked oddly like Fred (without the moustache), she had always been someone who acted on impulse (thinking for the billionth time of Alec and that awful rainy night when she'd boarded the five-forty, then sprung off again at the very last moment and ran back to the flat, where Alec was waiting, where the bed was waiting, where a different life was waiting, a life which would, she rather suspected, have never led her to Marx, Lenin or Trotsky, but some ghastly bungalow on the Isle of Wight, and two or three babies, flabby miniaturised replicas of Alec, who was always late home from the hospital for one reason or another, growing old and dull and maternal, a life spent much like the one she'd been living in Milford, with church fêtes and teas and masses of embroidery), which needless to say had made not the slightest impression upon the magistrate, who fined her £200 and sent her to prison for three months, telling the court in a sombre voice that society simply could not permit people to go around slipping eggs down policemen's trousers.

She had devoted her time in prison to a close reading of Engels's *Origin of the Family, Private Property and the State*, a wonderful book, one of the many on her shelves, well thumbed, copiously underlined and annotated, and had emerged from prison a little underweight, and paler, but refreshed and invigorated, eager to help build the Party, enlarge the sales of the paper and prepare for the struggles that lay ahead in a crumbling world, where millions starved, and things decayed, where Milford Junction was a waste lot of rubble and weeds (the car park hadn't been built after all), a waste lot where derelicts burned rubbish and old railway sleepers and gathered around the flames and drank British sherry and cans of beer, bearded broken men who might have been something else, looking like sailors stranded on a desert island, like all the unemployed, stranded on barren land in the great grey ocean of capitalism, people whose lives had not blossomed as hers had blossomed, hers by a concatenation of implausible circumstances, the surrealism of life she liked to call it, thinking of the headlines on the whirling newspapers, and Fred turning to **a** spray of bloody mince and powdered rib under the iron wheels of the Boat Train, and the Junction's strange echoing reeking dreamlike green-and-white tiled urinals where Bobby had been caught in a cubicle with Mr Godby and which she couldn't resist peeping into that very last day, and the bar where she'd first met Al, who'd introduced her to many things, her clitoris for example, the pleasures of stout, the electrifying clarities of Marx and Lenin (not to mention Engels, Luxemburg and Trotsky), the theories of permanent revolution and of combined and uneven development, and much, much more...

And there ahead, outside the windy rainswept post office, she could see Al, holding up a clutch of papers, unmistakeable with his Lenin cap and blue raincoat, shouting something inaudible. She quickened her pace, thinking: *It is never too late to fall in love, never too late to clear your head of all the dust and dross deposited there over the long years, never too late to break through the crust of rubbish which grows over your life and discover revolutionary socialism. Nothing lasts really – not even (hard as it may be to believe at present) capitalism.*

She thought then of all the old footage at the start of the 1967 documentary *Ten Days That Shook the World,* a film which owed little to John Reed (not least in its bland quasi-Stalinist conclusions!) but which did at least have the virtue of being narrated by Orson Welles, old footage which showed the pomp and glory of the Czar's court, a world full of parades and galloping horsemen and flags and cheering crowds, a world at times oddly like the royalist rubbish they put nowadays on the

TV news, a world which seemed eternal, impregnable, immutable, but which had imploded with a sudden sharp puff of putrefaction, and had gone, astonishingly and abruptly and unbelievably.

And with a smile on her old wrinkled face, her eyes blazing, she drew closer to Al, who hadn't spotted her yet, the wind dragging at his raincoat tails and trying to wrench the papers from his hands, distorting his words, so that as she passed by the boarded-up hospital and came to the estate agents with the steel shutters next door he seemed to be shouting (but she knew it wasn't that: she knew exactly what it was really) *Surrealist Worker! Surrealist Worker!*

She hurried up to him.

"Give me some of those, comrade" she said gruffly, mockingly repeating a line from that absurd film, *Dr Zhivago,* which when it first came out in 1965 she had (*You're too sane and uncomplicated*) adored, but which as her consciousness had developed she had come to see travestied history through the simple device of telescoping Stalinism with 1918 Bolshevism, to convey the message that revolutionary socialists were cold-hearted, sneering, sinister, inhuman authoritarians determined to obliterate every spark of individualism and decency in people, and equally eager to requisition the homes of hard-working, sexy, poetry-writing hospital doctors and sweet, loveable, engaging old buffers like Sir Ralph Richardson – a message which, as anyone acquainted with Laura Jesson or her comrades would know, was utter

RUBBISH.

Nixon's Dog

And all because of Nixon's dog.

Nixon's dog was a bloodhound. He called it Barbour. It was a big, grey, sleek bloodhound with sad eyes and a long, dangling, slippery tongue. In fact, its tongue looked like an off-cut of raw steak.

Nixon lived next door. He was twenty-one years old. I was nineteen. Nixon was five-eight and seemed OK. I was five-two, short-tempered, interested in pulped wood products and firearms. I was originally six-four, genial, a keen reader of Leibniz, but the air crash changed all that. It was a Dakota. Guess you saw the wreckage on TV. I survived but my body was compressed by the impact. My brain has edges it didn't have before. Now I'm shorter and into Plato. My Aunty Babs was killed. She was decapitated. She was reading her *Reader's Digest* when – Hot damn!

There she is, improving her word power, when suddenly she can't seem to turn the page. Next she begins to wonder where her torso is. Confused, she thinks maybe she's wandered by mistake into Guatemala and been mistaken for a radical journalist. The words bubble from her mouth. "Don't do it boys! I'm an American citizen! I'm on your side! I got shares in rubber, armaments, cattle ranching *and* bananas!" she appeals to the phantom death squad in her fevered mind. Then night falls.

Her head was bouncing along runway nine, sprinkling blood from the ragged, torn neck. A Pan-Am steward saw it heading towards him. *He* thought it was a pumpkin. Hell, how was he supposed to know? He gave Aunty Babs's severed head a playful kick, sending it skimming over to the North West Airlines shed. A maintenance man in denim overalls grinned and slammed it across to the perimeter fence, where Nixon was walking his dog. Barbour reached a paw through the wire and chewed excitedly at the feast of gristle and jelly. Nixon didn't

89

seem to notice. He was staring at the sky. He was wondering if the Reds had downed the Dakota. He wouldn't have put it past them. On the other hand, it might have been those pesky Martians using one of their death ray devices he had read about.

It was a worrying thought that while Americans had automatic toasters, Martians were capable of inter-galactic travel in spaceships made out of gigantic saucepan lids. They even had little holes around the rim, but whether they were windows or to let out the steam wasn't known.

"Come on, boy. Home."

Barbour licked the succulent scraps of flesh from his chin and they set off back to E. 26th Street. The Martians were probably watching. They watched from millions of miles away, seeing everything in close-up. Those rustlings you sometimes heard. Odd noises. That was the Martians. They were always listening.

They weren't the only ones.

I remember one day Nixon pointed at the Dullards' black cat. It was lurking by a shrub in Nixon's backyard. It looked like it was trying to catch birds.

"That cat," Nixon whispered, "is working for the C.I.A."

"Aw, c'mon now, Nix. Like Plato says, cats don't have brains. They don't speak American. There's no way a cat can work for the C.I.A."

"Wanna bet?"

Nixon walks away with what can only be called a smirk.

Next day I'm sitting on the front porch thinking about Plato's contrasting of mathematical deduction which takes for granted its assumptions with philosophic dialectic which questions these assumptions inquiring what they themselves may presuppose thus moving backward reductively to a first principle, when an eighteen-wheel truck comes a-thundering down the street and – oh my gosh! That poor cat didn't stand a chance. It was Nixon's dog made the cat run out across the street like that. Barbour had been well trained. He stopped by the kerb, growling. He looked left then right then left again.

The truck didn't stop.

The funny thing was I could have sworn it was Nixon at the wheel of the truck. I must have been wrong, though, because right at that moment Nixon came running out of his house.

"The Dullards' cat," I said in a sombre voice. "Splattered." Barbour trotted over, slurped a little cat blood, then scampered off.

Nixon ran across to the bloody remains. He groped eagerly in among the torn fur and intestines and pulled something out. "Take a look at this!" He held up a piece of bloodstained wire. He licked his lips and groped some more. "See?" He wiped off the worst of the cat flesh and showed me some more curious items.

"I knew that cat was listening to me! See what the C.I.A. did? They cut the cat open, inserted this here transmitter in its abdominal cavity and ran an antenna up its tail."

The listening equipment glistened like twinkling stars in a sky of beetroot soup. Nixon carefully placed it back inside the animal's remains.

"Guess it's time to shoot out of here before ol' Ma Dullard finds out what's happened to her furry friend." And with a strangely metallic chuckle, Nixon was gone.

I was not surprised when soon after I heard the roar of an eighteen-wheel truck starting up and receding into the distance.

Nixon was quite a guy. In those days he was very interested in movies, science fiction and Latin. His face shining, he urged me to go see *The Manchurian Candidate*. He greatly admired *Invasion of the Body Snatchers* (the original black and white version, not the re-make). You might see Nixon as a regular fellow or you might see him as a repellent creep, but let me say this: Nixon wasn't stoopid. Whenever someone famous got shot in enigmatic circumstances Nixon used to take out an old placard he'd had painted by a skilled armless Korean immigrant. The placard read IS FECIT CUI PRODEST. The Korean, whose name is unknown, painted it by manoeuvring a paintbrush with his toes. Nixon stuck the placard on his picket fence, where it attracted a certain amount of attention. People used to gather and argue about what it meant. Some folks said the Korean couldn't spell. Others that the placard was obscene. There was general agreement that it involved profanity and an unwarranted attack on democracy and government, and finally, after the sixth or seventh assassination, someone came along one night and blew it away with high explosive (by a quirk leaving the picket fence miraculously intact, though scorched).

Nixon was a great fan of the sci-fi novels of Philip K. Dick. One morning he smiled at me across the white, gleaming, repainted picket fence. He was wearing a red sweater with a herring-bone pattern criss-crossed by bright blue lines of obfuscation. Nixon said, "Hi, Shorty! Hey, man, I got here a book you gotta read! *Time Out of Joint* by Philip K Dick. It's far out! You gotta read it!"

I have never liked science-fiction. The writing style is awful, just awful. I even once tried reading something by Dick, but I gave up after twenty pages. Not my scene. Besides, I didn't see why I should feel obliged to share Nixon's enthusiasms when Nixon didn't share mine. I had offered to lend Nixon *The Symposium* and *The Last Days of Socrates* and all he did was make excuses. He never showed any interest when I told him how in chemical pulping logs are chipped into pieces and then digested in either soda, calcium or magnesium sulphate or sodium sulphite. I even offered to let Nixon have a go at shooting my Pa's Magnum, but he wasn't interested.

I thought: there is something deeply un-American about a twenty-one-year-old male who isn't interested in shooting a Magnum. I knew one day I wouldn't be able to help myself and I'd be tempted to plug Nixon. Or maybe his dog. Of course, at this time, like most folk, I knew nothing of Nixon's farm, where he kept his anti-tank missiles and the herd of sedated elephants.

It bugged me, the way he always called me "Shorty". No one else did. Besides, Nixon was no picture. Somewhere Plato says that people who keep dogs grow to look like them and Plato never said a truer word. No sir. Nixon's cheeks sagged like old, withered dugs – the sort you see at the end of the news when the announcer clears her throat and looks temporarily extra-solemn and introduces a clip of some old black-skinned wretch starving to death on a hot, far plateau of sand and dead vegetation.

As for his eyes, his eyes. Nixon's eyes were great pools of troubled melancholy. I used to think maybe he was a great soul who had spent too much time alone in his bedroom listening to Frank Sinatra records or that he was a loner who had transcended earthly concerns (his spots, his bowel disorder, his head-lice) in order to devote more time to a thorough reading of *The Anatomy of Melancholy, What it is, with all the lands, causes, symptoms, prognostics & several cures of it. In three Partitions, with their several Sections, numbers & subsections. Philosophically, Medicinally, Historically opened & cut up by Democritus Junior, with a Satyrical Preface conducing to the following Discourse* as originally printed and sold by Hen. Crips and Lodo:Lloyd at their shop in Popes-head Alley, London, in 1621.

I was wrong.

Nixon was a patriot and what bothered him was his dog's behaviour. Nixon's parents had the biggest flagpole and the biggest Stars and Stripes in the neighbourhood. But Barbour just couldn't help himself. No matter what Nixon said ("Bad dog!" "Bad Barbour!" "Stop that!" "Don't ever do that again!") Barbour persistently urinated against the pole and left his droppings all over the lawn. And it wasn't just his own lawn, either. Barbour sometimes used to use our lawn, sometimes other people's. I swore that if I ever caught Barbour in the act I would shoot him where it hurt. But Barbour, clever dog, always performed between two and three a.m. when good folk are asleep.

In the morning people would be tucking into their sunshine breakfasts when suddenly they'd push the bowl away and run off to the bathroom. They'd just seen what was on their lawn.

The phrase "doing a Nixon" became part of the local language.

People began to shun Nixon, which bothered him. Despite his grotesque appearance and his propensity to sweat, Nixon craved popularity and affection. He was always offering to lend people SF paperbacks and Sinatra singles. But it wasn't books or music they wanted, it was a clean, odour-free lawn.

Nixon took to getting up at first light and creeping round the neighbourhood with a shovel and a bag. He started wearing a SQUELCH THE RUMORS badge. People shrugged. When that didn't work he gave the picket fence another lick of paint. Behind it he erected an enormous sign: THE COMPANY SAYS: SQUELCH THE RUMORS! But people still didn't understand.

Once or twice he was arrested by Deputy Sheriff Winner on suspicion of burglary but the D.S. quickly let him go when he heard Nixon's explanation and saw what was in his bag.

That didn't solve the problem of the flagpole. Despite regular applications of white gloss the flagpole was beginning to rot. Chunks would flake off at night. It was beginning to tilt.

"Barbour, if you do that one more time..."

Nixon's melancholy expression hardened into a rigid scowl of rage. He snuck off when Agnes Roosevelt wasn't around and checked out libraries and bookshops. Elections, Evictions, Erections... But there didn't seem to be any problem-solving guidebooks that dealt with emiction. Nixon had to fall back on his own resources.

He began to beat Barbour. At first he used a rolled-up copy *of Time*. That didn't seem to work so he tried a carpet slipper. Barbour wailed each time, then an hour later he'd trot off back to the flagpole and cock his leg.

"BAD DOG!"

Whack!

Waaaaah-grrrrrrrh-ooooh!

One day Nixon comes out of the house holding a baseball bat. He's wearing his DO NOT EMBARRASS THE BUREAU T-shirt. I'm warning you, Barbour..." he shouts.

Barbour wanders off. He spends a while sniffing the roses. Then he can't help hisself. He trots over to the flagpole and raises his right rear leg. He gazes mournfully across the lawn at

Nixon. Nixon's face is red with anger.

Nixon starts to run across the grass. He's swinging the baseball bat. He's so *angry.*

If there's one thing I can't stand apart from Aristotelians it's cruelty to animals. I ran inside for my deer hunting rifle and ran out again.

My lawyer told the jury to be sure they understood the distinction between IMPULSE and FOLLY.

"Members of the jury. The defendant is a young man in the full blossom of manhood. He has already suffered more in his short life than most of us will ever suffer. The destruction of a Dakota aircraft, a beloved aunt and a copy of the *Reader's Digest* – and all before his very eyes! But put away those handkerchiefs, members of the jury. I do not ask for SYMPATHY but for UNDERSTANDING. My client's actions were not motivated by cold-hearted FOLLY but by hot-blooded IMPULSE. The dictionary defines IMPULSE as 'an influence acting suddenly on the mind'. And what was that influence which made my client do the things he did? Was it the depraved influence of drugs? No, it was not. Was it the influence of excess intake of liquor? No, my friends, it was not. Was it the pernicious influence of some foul ideology alien to the American way of life? No, good people, it was not. The influence upon the defendant's mind was nothing else than PITY. Yes, PITY. PITY for that noblest of all the animals, a poor, defenceless dawg. PITY, which Plato describes as the most profound of all the human emotions. PITY, which shines out like a diamond amid mud. Consult your dictionaries, members of the jury. There you will find PITY lodged between PITUITOUS ('Consisting of mucus') and PITYRIASIS ('A chronic squamous inflammation of the skin'). The prosecution allege that the deceased, Nixon, was shot at least two-hundred-and-sixty-seven times, and afterwards cut up into small pieces. This may be so (though our ballistics expert Dr Surbase believes the correct number is, in fact, two-hundred-and-sixty-five). I ask you to put such matters at the back of your minds. I ask you to think of that poor dawg and of Plato's words. I ask you to forget the prosecution's fantastic claim that Nixon might, in the fullness of time, have become President of the United States of America. Just look at photographs of the shifty-eyed, droopy-faced deceased. What a preposterous notion! I ask you also to consider that my client's brief moment of charitable impulse resulted in irremovable stains upon not only his favourite lumberjack-style shirt and best denim jeans but also resulted in cracks across his parent's patio – cracks that have broken his poor house-proud Mother's heart. Lastly, members of the jury, I call upon the internationally acclaimed clairvoyant Mme Clare Vint, who will prove to you beyond all shadow of doubt that had Nixon lived his career would have been fatally impeded by pituitous blockage of both nostrils which, together with a chronic squamous inflammation of the skin, would have rendered him unsuitable for any work other than night lavatory attendant in a Negro district or lone Atlantic yachtsman. Ladies and gentlemen, all the way from Wordsworth, Arizona – Clare Vint!"

I raised my rifle and took aim.

"Nixon, if you touch that poor creature, I'm gonna blast your head off."

I don't think Nixon even heard me, he was so mad with that dog.

He lifted the baseball bat and brought it crashing down against Barbour's ribs.

The animal wailed in pain and crashed over on to the ground. Nixon raised the bat for a second swipe.

"Don't say you weren't warned, hog-face!"

I opened fire.

The jury found me guilty. The judge sentenced me to a hundred-and-twenty-five years in jail.

Nixon's dog reacted in terror to the first shot and ran off, barking hysterically. No one really knows what happened to it. Some said it was later seen walking along Highway 61, heading for Mexico. Others reckoned it had been abducted for experiments by the Martians. Deputy Sheriff Winner thought maybe he'd seen it in his garden, hanging around the septic tank. But nobody really knows. Whatever happened to it, it must, by now, be dead. According to Plato no bloodhound can live longer than twenty years.

I fired a second shot.

"Alarum! Alarum!" Nixon screamed. "Tro ro ro ro ro, tro ro ro ro ro, tro ro ro ro ro! Thomp, thomp, thomp, downe, downe, downe, to go, to go, to go!"

Three houses away Hank Wink was reading his *Newsweek*. How what the Reds were up to all round the world made his Dutch-American blood boil! They fomented strikes! They fomented disorder! They fomented insurrection!

Hank wondered how they did it. He took down his dictionary and looked up FOMENT.

FOMENT came between FOLLY and FOMES.

FOLLY meant "criminal weakness or depravity of mind" and FOMES was "a porous substance absorbent of contagious matter".

He was surprised to learn that FOMENT meant "to apply warm lotions to; to cherish; to excite".

Hank decided then and there never again to use shampoo. Next he took down the album of Wink family photographs, which showed his bearded grandfather gripping the edge of a basket, and his parents, grim, uncomfortable, surrounded by unknown faces, on their wedding day. He tore out several pages, urinated on them, then tossed everything on the fire. Finally he took a sedative and went back to *Newsweek*, feeling good, feeling he'd done his bit to keep back the red tide.

Hank's Mom and Pa came from Woonke (hence the reproduction Bosch triptych they used to hang over their bed, next to the portrait of Mozart hand-painted in Indonesia and the framed blueprint of Grandfather Wink's "family aerostat", of which three had been manufactured, and two sold, resulting in almost instantaneous death for seven members of two of the richest and most powerful Dutch families, including direct descendants of Rembrandt, the inventor of the world's first milk float to be powered by an engine which ran on the gases from rotting tulips). The Wink family fortune had been

97

devoured by litigation and awards for damages and Hank had departed for Byron, Texas, where he'd become big in land reclamation.

Hank, who was frightened by neither tiger nor porcupine but who had a mortal fear of eye-tests, optometrists and the sinister equipment they used, looked up from his periodical, thinking he heard knockings in his head. He glanced out of the window and saw Nixon on the ground.

It is not everyone who can wittily regurgitate lines from Bishop Bale's *King John*, a play which remained in manuscript until 1838, the year Arnold Ruge started the *Hallische Jahrbücher*, the leading periodical of the Young Hegelians, especially after being shot at twice, but Nixon's effort was wasted, owing to the wax build-up in Hank's ears.

Nixon seemed to be undergoing severe and painful spasms. His right leg jerked into the air and crashed down again. His left arm thrashed repeatedly the ground. His other arm greeted the Fuehrer.

"Must be that epileptic-fit impersonator I read about," Hank mused.

Hank did not stir, not even when (I am a terrible shot) a bullet sang through his porch.

The bullet was in a good mood. Before it passed on and buried itself away forever in Agnes Roosevelt's shagbark hickory it cried out in a lusty Hamburg accent,

Hoiho! Hoiho!

Hau ein! Hau ein!

which means

Hoiho! Hoiho!

Come on! Come in!

and which in the spacious minds of keen Wagnerians will instantly conjure up a cave, a forest and a large smith's forge, formed naturally from pieces of rock, with a rough, natural chimney and a large unnatural bellows, as well as a massive anvil and a miscellaneous collection of obscure tools designed to signify to a car-driving, coffee-grinding, VDU-using aud-ience the homely archaic workplace of a blacksmith, a bogus world of grey polystyrene and brown lath where a fat Tenor sits miming the hammering of a sword, which he then throws down, places his arms akimbo, and gazes at the ground in thought, provoking much booming song, briefly interrupted by some playful readjustment of the sword and a return to the hammering-mime, followed by more deep, booming song, at which point Siegfried enters, dressed in rough forest clothes, with a silver horn slung from a chain, a hearty, obese, boisterous lout who brings with him a large bear bridled with a bast rope, which in exuberant high spirits he sets at the blacksmith, who drops the sword in fright and runs behind the forge, while Siegfried urges the bear to chase him about, which no matter how many times they have seen *Der Ring des Nibelungen* before always has Wagnerians in stitches.

Whether or not the singing bullet was of German origin and an authentic Wagnerian or was simply a skilled impersonator who adored post-modernist pastiche and irony is not known. The bullet hit the hickory with a THUNK and remains there to this day, mute, snub-nosed, deeply embedded in the growth rings of the trunk which represent the years 1927-28, an interesting period in Nicaraguan history, when a squadron of U.S. airplanes conducted the first dive-bombing attack on a town in human history (Ocotal, 17 July 1927, 202 dead) and when Augusto Sandino gathered his followers together, warning them: "Henceforth our enemies will be, not the forces of the tyrant Diaz, but the Marines of the most powerful empire that history has known... We will be vilely murdered by the bombs that terrible airplanes rain down upon us; slashed with foreign bayonets; riddled by modern machine-guns."

The wood of the shagbark hickory is tough yet elastic and ideal for the manufacture of tool handles used in forestry and agriculture, a bast rope *is* rope made from the inner bark of the lime tree, and twelve seconds had elapsed since my first shot at Nixon.

One bullet had missed, one bullet had sliced through the Eustachian tube in Nixon's left ear, and one bullet had penetrated his thorax.

"Stop that," said Nixon indignantly. "You're hurting me."

I fired again. The bullet slammed into Nixon's throat, which was kinda strange, since according to witnesses of irreproachable repute I was standing behind Nixon at the time.

Time for another shot at Nixon. This time the rifle jammed. I ran inside and scooped up the family armoury. Then I came back and continued. I began with Pa's Colt .44, moved on to my own historic Colt .17, used up all the shells in Mom's shotgun, fired with my sister Jane's little .22 at Nixon's inguinal region, blazed away with the replica eighteenth-century Kentucky rifle that Uncle Abe had given us for Thanksgiving, and plugged Nixon some more with my brother Bill's Navy Colt. I made good use of deceased Uncle Ben's Heckler and Kock self-loading carbines. Then I stepped over and filled Nix up with a few well aimed shots from Mom's prized Derringer and Pa's punch-packing .357 Magnum. "Eat lead!" I yelled, which was kinda weird, since I don't usually talk like that.

"Gish," Nixon retorted. "Gish ug bloo!"

I paused, impressed. I'd never known his skill at languages extended to the Baltic regions.

"Hot damn!" I'd run out of ammo!

Then I remembered.

"Hot damn!" Hell, I'd clean forgotten about the 7.65 Mauser bolt-action equipped with a 4/18 scope and a thick leather brownish-black sling, the rear portion of the bolt visibly worn. Hey, did I just say a 7.65 Mauser? Forget it, guys. It was a slip of the tongue. I meant the Mannlicher-Carcano bolt-action rifle I'd gotten by mail order using the pseudonym "Dawlos Varhey Eel".

I dashed inside, grabbed the rifle, ran out again. First I set my stop watch, then I opened fire.

BANG!

BANG!

BANG!-BANG!

I have no great record as a rifleman, my aim is bad, the barrel was inaccurate, the trigger-pull leaden and sluggish, and Nixon was a-squirming and a-jittering like a worm on a hotplate, but by golly I did it!

I took a look at my stop-watch. Not bad! Nixon's heart and most of his head blown away in exactly 5.6 seconds. Not bad for one those creaky-squeaky crude-'n clumsy ol' fingernail-snappin' bolt-action jobs!

His last words.

Nixon's last words were:

(i) "Ohio" (or perhaps "Hoiho!"). Schucking argues for "I'm dying", which seems unlikely.

(ii) "cheeseburger." Schucking argues instead for profanity, which I utterly refuse to countenance.

(iii) "oil" (or possibly "isle" or "I'll"). Schucking, who rarely misses an opportunity of bringing in the Book of Job, suggests "Boil".

The neighbours had by now noticed that something was amiss, except for Hank Wink, who was still deep in *Newsweek*. Although I have no memory of this, I am told that after throwing down the Magnum I went indoors and came out with Mom's best pair of kitchen scissors. Then I began cutting Nixon up into half-inch strips. Next I laid the strips flat across the patio crazy-paving and began to bang them with a wooden steak-hammer. Sirens filled the air. I was still battering the strips of Nixon with powerful, highly charged Wagnerian motions when they took me gently by the arm, slipped on the handcuffs, and led me away.

The National Rifle Association sent me a replica M-12 sub-machine gun and a certificate saying I was a credit to the nation. *Pluto Quarterly* gave me a free life subscription. I received parcels containing lumberjack-style shirts and crisp new denim jeans. Young women mailed full colour photo-graphs and slyly asked for my measurements. The Liquidator Corporation sent me a crate of two-dozen bottles of Liquidator Stain Remover, the only effective and easy way to remove difficult stains and dirt from washable fabrics, carpets and many other areas. I was deluged by sacks of mail from sympathetic dog lovers. The mass media was in uproar.

Crowds gathered every day outside the jail. The President pardoned me in my second week of captivity. In a televised talk to the nation he explained that young men who wanted to do what was right and proper sometimes did impulsive things, and hell he understood that 'cos once, a long time ago, he'd seen an Indian stealing a hen and he'd blown that pesky thief away, even though he'd never told anyone at the time. A poll taken the next day showed that the President was the most popular President in the entire history of the United States.

They buried Nixon just before my release. Few realised that only approximately 90% of Nixon was being buried. I had done such a good job on Nixon that Deputy Sheriff Winner had been unable to resist slipping a few pounds of prime flesh into a bag. He popped the meat in the freezer and saved it for my release. When I came out he invited me round to dinner with a few close friends.

I guess you're wondering how the Deputy Sheriff cooked Nixon.

Like this.

He took out the bag of remains from the freezer and put them aside to thaw. He put Hank Williams's "My Bucket's Got A Hole In It" on the turntable to listen to as he worked. He set the record player to automatic replay so as not to get blood or grease on it. He filled a large pan with water and put it on the stove to heat up. He took six ounces of butter and dropped it into a large frying pan. He peeled two small onions and tears came to his eyes. He grated them using a silver grater. He put the onions in the pan and fried them gently for seven minutes. While the onion was frying, he opened a bottle of cheap Muscadet and drank two glasses swiftly and a third slowly. By now Nixon was beginning to thaw. I had of course comprehensively cut Nixon up into slices, so all that D.S. Winner had to do was to add the strips of flesh to the onion, which by now was beginning to brown. The Deputy Sheriff reflected that Nixon's flesh sure looked good. It was real red and juicy. He pushed the slices around the pan for eight minutes, turning them the whole time. The pan of water was beginning to boil and he dropped in a complete packet of fettuccine pasta made of the finest durum wheat, semolina, garlic, tomato, spinach and mixed herbs. He added some more butter to the frying pan. He threw in a pound of best Florida mushrooms and stirred them vigorously. Nixon by now was brown as a Peruvian Indian. He sprinkled Nixon with salt and pepper to spice him up a little. He poured six generous tablespoonfuls of sherry over the mushrooms. He stirred in half a pint of soured cream. He drained the fettuccine and laid out a generous portion on each plate. He ladled a helping of Nixon and mushrooms over the fettuccine and squeezed a cute spiral of cream on top.

"For what we are about to receive, we thank thee, Lord."

Heads bowed, thinking – Hmm, this smells good!

"Hey, this looks terrific!"

"It sure tastes terrific, too!"

"What's your secret?"

"Yeah. Waddaya call it, Sam?"

"My friends, I thank you. This dish is called – Stroganoff Milhouse."

"It's wonderful. It really and truly is!"

"It's great! It's better than great. It's *terrific*."

"Yeah. Not at all chewy, like you might have expected."

Of course, I was the only one the D.S. let in on his little secret. I guess he thought he could trust me. Afterwards we ate coffee-frosted walnut cake and I made a little speech. I quoted Plato, reminded everyone that among the Yoruba of South Nigeria the three months of February, March and April are generally given no specific name, and digressed a little to talk about Chaos Theory and the value of the walnut as a source of timber. This led me to ponder aloud as to whether the Chams of Indo-China still used a calendar of only ten months to the year. I reminded my listeners that the Toradja of the Dutch East Indies computed time in moon-months, but each year a period of two-to-three months was not brought into the computation at all and was omitted in time-reckoning. During this time, I explained, members of the tribe were free to do whatever they like – lie in bed until noon, strangle their wives, perform unnatural rites with pumpkins, and so on.

"It is known as *khushkrikki-tukotamm* or 'The time of desire', and ends with the Feast of the Boiled Dolphin. After this, members of the tribe return to the paddy fields, with slightly shamefaced expressions. Few live beyond the age of twenty-three and disease is widespread. Anthropologists who first discovered the tribe in 1927 found that they worshipped a sacred text known as *Kung-Glarr*, which turned out to be a Heinemann Educational Books edition of *Lear*, specially published in a simplified large-print edition suitable for missionary work. Each Sunday at eleven a.m. the entire tribe gathered in a forest clearing to consume fire-water and frenziedly chant the one-hundred-and-thirty-three references to animals in *Lear*."

"Is that a fact!" cried the D.S., slapping his thigh, and I was obliged admit that, though much of what I said was the naked truth, it was just possible I might have succumbed to a few trifling exaggerations here and there.

Somebody said that while it was true there were one-hundred-and-thirty-three allusions to a total of sixty-four different animals in *King Lear*, it should not be forgotten that the dominant image of the play was that of the human body beaten, pierced, tugged, wrenched, stung, scourged, flayed, dislocated, gashed, scalded, tortured, and finally broken on the rack.

The Deputy Sheriff said the way he looked at it, Shakespeare was using the play to dramatize the conflict between medieval society and nascent capitalism.

"Reckon so," said the red-faced man with the bottle of Cognac whose name I didn't catch (there was a massive gash in my butterfly net).

I brought my little speech to an end with a wild goose story. I pointed out that in none of the fifty-seven versions of the Lear story previous to Shakespeare's does the king go mad. This shows that W.S. probably knew the story of Brian Annesley, a gentleman pensioner of good Queen Bess, who in October 1603 was declared "altogether unfit to govern himself or his estate". Two of his stony-hearted daughters, Lady Wildgoose and Lady Sandys, tried to get him certified as insane, so that they could grab his estate, but the youngest daughter, Cordell, protested that her father's service to the late queen "deserved a better agnomination, than at his last gasp to be recorded and registered a Lunatick" (and here I offered to unfold a dictionary, the better to explain "agnomination" – but the assembled company begged me not to, and to proceed, which, reluctantly, and a little sullenly, I did). Cordell's dearest wish was granted, and her father was put under the care of Sir James Croft. When Annesley died, the Wildgooses contested the will, but it was upheld by the court of Chancery. A few years later, early in 1608, Cordell Annesley married Sir William Harvey, the widower of the Dowager Countess of Southampton, the step-father of Shakespeare's patron. It seems probable, therefore, that Shakespeare, who wasn't much good at inventing plot and whose plays are vast compendia of plagiarism (as Muir says, Shakespeare used other people's stories and then "pressed into service incidents, ideas, phrases, and even words from books and plays"), knew all this, and that it inspired his notion of Lear's madness and Cordelia's loyalty.

"Let me conclude by saying that Shakespeare was the first postmodernist, that at the heart of *King Lear* lies a Wildgoose chase, and that it is my firm intention to buy my sister one of those cute little Yorkshire Terriers from England."

Everyone cheered and they hoisted me up and carried me round the room, singing "For He's A Jolly Good Fellow". Then they put me down and we drank our way through three bottles of brandy. Everyone agreed it was one of the tastiest meals they'd ever eaten in their lives.

The next day it was a different story. Nixon must have had salmonella because we were all violently sick. Deputy Sheriff Winner had to take the day off work. He crouched over the lavatory bowl, watching as first the walnut cake and then strips of Nixon and fragments of onion and whole mushrooms coughed and burst from his burning throat and splattered against the curving china slope. It looked astonishingly like fomes, although of course he knew it wasn't.

Next came the two slices of buttered toast and lime marmalade he'd devoured earlier that day, a bowl of cornflakes, the ham omelette he'd eaten the day before, the strawberry milkshake and the burger with fries he'd had at Burger Bob's on West 42nd Street, the chicken nuggets coated in golden breadcrumbs and the walnut whip Lucy had given him, the pack of cashews he'd nibbled on Tuesday, the oxtail soup, three jacket potatoes, two chocolate-coated candy bars and, last of all, a three-inch-long caterpillar, evidently still alive, together with the cauliflower floret in which he had inadvertently swallowed it.

If only the Lord had granted that caterpillar vocal chords and a vocabulary of two hundred words, what a tale it might have told of its strange, dark journey down the Deputy Sheriff's gullet, a warm yet oppressive region where giants who liked Poe pressed rubber-gloved hands against its elastic, pulpy flesh – a droll metaphor for sequential peristaltic contractions of the oesophageal wall, needless to say – a journey which in its stark horror seemed to last a lifetime, but which in fact took a little over five seconds, and might have been even faster had it not been for occasional delays caused by the closing and opening of various muscular sphincters, further details of which are inevitably curtailed by our caterpillar's lamentably impoverished word-hoard.

D.S. Winner took hold of that sullen, apprehensive caterpillar and sealed it inside a matchbox, not forgetting to make some air holes with a pin or to include a good supply of fresh cabbage leaves. This he posted airmail, together with a full typed statement signed by two witnesses (both honours graduates) and stamped by a notary, to *The Fortean Times*, England.

His house never recovered from the stench. He burned it down, collected on the insurance and moved to Chicago. There, terrified of emetrophia, he wrote an emetology which became a surprise best-seller. At last he was able to give up being a law enforcement officer, something he had wanted to do ever since reading Marx's *Critique of Political Economy*. Later he came to understand that the eruption of a live caterpillar from his innards was not, as he had assumed, an utterly baffling and inexplicable event which in its own small way bolstered theories of sinister and bizarre other worlds and mysterious forces, facts and reality-dimensions shunned by narrow-minded orthodox science (theories popular with those who devoted spare time on Sundays to cracking open small boulders with sledgehammers in the hope of finding a living toad, full of spring and verve despite being entombed without food or water since the late Pleistocene era), but on the contrary made perfect sense in the light of the classic studies on gastric secretion carried out in the nineteenth century by Beaumont, working with Alexis St Martin, whose abdominal and gastric wall had been partly shot away in an accident with firearms, and who sportingly acted as a living test tube in which numerous fascinating experiments were carried out over a period of many years. Thanks to the pioneering work of Beaumont and his co-operative human guinea pig, it was now established that the secretion of gastric acids and the orderly onward movement of chyme might be inhibited by severe emotions such as fear and anxiety, or by infection with bacteria or viruses, or by chronic disease causing "achlorhydria", i.e. the absence of gastric hydrochloric acid.

D.S. Winner remembered the matchbox and the little blue airmail stickers, and blushed. Hell, how could he have known that a caterpillar could cheat death by a timely gastrointestinal viral infection causing both the absence of normal digestion and the eventual vomiting?

But then, of course, in those days he had barely begun to understand U.S. imperialism, let alone Marx. Now he had a much better grasp on the nature of things. For example, he had learned about the manufacture of consent. He had learned about the massacre in Colombia perpetrated by troops under General Vargas on 5 December 1928, in direct connivance with the United Fruit Company. He had learned of the stupefying

tunnel vision and ignorance of so many of his fellow countrymen when it came to a correct perception of their own society
and history, let alone that of the rest of the planet. What's
more, thanks to Beaumont, he now knew that many Americans
were walking around ignorant of the interesting creatures
lurking inside their smug paunches and/or distinguished,
greying, executive scalps – not simply the occasional vigorous,
wriggling, green caterpillar, but also clusters of lively maggots
and rich, colourful varieties of larvae. He had never realised
that Marxism-Leninism or gastric secretion could be so
interesting.

The rest is history.

The years pass, people change. Attitudes change. Sales of
shampoo soar. Every household in the U.S.A. contains at least
two bottles of regular-use shampoo. The best-selling video of
all time is *Shampoo*, starring Julie Christie and Warren Beatty.
Under President Shrubb the U.S.A. withdraws its armies from
Vietnam and all other outposts of the empire. The C.I.A. is shut
down and its leaders go on trial for crimes against humanity.
The defence budget is cut by ninety per cent. President Shrubb
announces his country's unilateral nuclear disarmament.
Foreign aid is ended to military dictatorships around the globe.
Shampoo is dislodged from the number one spot by *Reds*,
starring Diane Keaton and Warren Beatty. In every city
cheering crowds erect monuments of Lenin, which they subsequently take down, tenderly, with care, the sheepish
expressions on their faces saying that only now have they
encountered the concept of reification. The difficult question of
how the State is to wither away is eagerly debated on live
breakfast shows and news programmes. Capitalist democracy
is terminated and replaced by Soviets of workers deputies
elected at mass meetings. The number one song is *The
Internationale*, sung by the Detroit Red Army Choir. The top
ten best-selling paperbacks are *Capital, Volume One*, Rosa
Luxemburg's *The Accumulation of Capital*, Victor Serge's *Year
One of the Russian Revolution*, Lenin's *The State and
Revolution*, Trotsky's *The Lessons of October*, *The Loch Ness*

Mystery Solved, Tunguska: Cauldron of Hell, le Fanu's *The Vampire Lovers*, Bulgakov's *The Master and Margarita* and Chaikin's *Execution of the 26 Commissars of Baku*.

J. Edgar Hoover is fired. Under the Fat Slobs legislation he is obliged to undergo a ten-month dict of lettuce and grated carrot. Then, to atone for his evil life, he becomes stirrer of slurry (grade D) at the Roth Sewage Farm, New Jersey.

"Beware the Ides of March", Tony Blanchard warns President Shrubb. He is the new head of state security. "You have upset many corrupt and powerful people." Blanchard is a demolition and retrieval expert. If anyone should know, it's him.

"And just who's going to blow me away?" laughs Shrubb. "The Mafia? Cubans? The C.I.A.?"

Shrubb does not wear his armoured body vest, as advised. He does not travel in a closed limousine, as advised. American forces do not land in Santa Domingo on 28 April 1965 for the purpose of maintaining the enslavement of the people of Dominica by U.S. capitalism. On 9 July 1964, former C.I.A. director Alien Dulles doesn't say, "Nobody reads. Don't believe people read in this country. There will be a few professors that will read the record... the public will read very little." Direct U.S. military assistance in 1963 to the tyranny in Nicaragua does not amount to $1.6 million. On 8 May 1963, government troops in South Vietnam do not move in on a crowd celebrating the Buddha's birthday, machine-gunning them and killing nine persons, including seven women and children. The Phoenix Program involving the selective assassination of forty thousand Vietnamese civilians does not take place. And on the morning of 22 November 1963, Richard Milhouse Nixon does not fly out of Dallas, Texas, where he has just spent a short time obscurely occupied with his wide-ranging business interests.

Da-Da Vogt

Air thick as mud. Crushing, irritating, suffocating. Skin burning, room baking. Hot, hot, hot. Irritability, splitting headaches, itchings, insomnia. Thick as mud I tell you. Plus dust. Dust in my throat. Dust everywhere. Torrents. Dust avalanching in the motes. Skin burning, itching, throat furry, head bursting. Inflamed, yes. Inflammation. Lying in bed drenched in sweat, mind blazing, can't stop thinking. Daren't get up to put the kettle on, one of the children always wakes. All Vogt's fucking fault. *Egli è bugiardo e padre di menzogna.* Can't put him out of my mind. Go away, Vogt! Won't go. Vogt the itch-mite: scratch, scratch, scratch. *Sarcoptes scabiei!* Gets under your skin. Lurks, skulks, creeps, crawls. Stands the other side of the hedge, grinning through the hole. Haunts the other side of the street, pretending to eat a bun. Sits in the cafe, with the others, whispering. I can see you, Vogt! Don't think I haven't noticed. You're not going to get away with it, you lump of turd. I'll be revenged!

The Vogtiad! And what he says is – shit. Talk about the Contortions of History and the Grandmother of all Practice! Talk about the *rounded character* of the hereditary steward of Nichilberg! The Regent Karl Vogt! Inventor of Imperial Regency Passports with only one small shortcoming! Subsidised, indoctrinated, rascalised Vogt! Herr where-I-get-my-means-from-is-nobody's-business Vogt – *that is to say, from the central cash box in Paris.* Fatso! Slave and lackey of Heliogabalus Plon-Plon! Plon-Plon's Falstaff! Blood-bloated louse! General Vogt! Commander of the Mouse Tower at Bingen! Stomach wall distended like a drum! Ex-Reichs-Vogt! *Vogt from Giessen.* Old vaulted-belly! *Herr Vogt!* Da-da Vogt! Mr Punch! Small-time university beer blusterer and failed Imperial Barrot! Herr Jack-in-office, Herr Wire-puller. Herr Examining Magistrate Vogt! Herr Functionary. Wind is the only means that gentleman has of keeping his puny aerostat in the air.

Always whispering is Vogt. Drives you mad. To the edge. A core of whispers amid the noises of the day, the noises of the night. There in the grating of wheels along the carriageway, the snort of a horse. There in the hiss of gaslight, the cry of a boy selling apples. Libels, slurs, filth. Spewed by a police agent. Drives you mad. Wears you out. Exhaustion, edginess, scowls. A slight blurring of vision. The children shrieking, your wife sobbing. Tremblings, cups spilled, plates dropped. Furniture shifts a few inches in the night; suddenly you're cracking your pelvis on the dresser, your shins on the footstool. Sharp sudden noises, splitting headache, explosions of irritability. Shut up! Get out! Leave me alone! Can't a man get a moment's peace? Drives you mad. Forces you to frown, bridge of your nose a knot of angry wrinkles. Knife goes clattering to the floor, makes you want to scream. Vogt's fault. Get off my mind, Vogt. You just wait. I'll settle your hash, once and for all.

Sick and tired of all these books, these liars, fools like Vogt. Sick and tired. Wears you out. So many fools. Sick and tired of the mountain of facts and statistics, the notebooks on commodities, money, capital, wage labour, landed property, international trade, credit, population theory, the world market, colonialism, the production process, the riddle of exploitation at the heart of things. Enough to do without that shit Vogt and his slanders.

So little time to get things clear before the fog. What fog? Fog of dead days when nothing's done, fuddled fog of illness and old age, soft fog of slippage and fading of memory, cold-to-the-bone fog of blank cold mortality, fog of fuggy gossip, nudges and winks, lies and slanders and Vogt's libels and sneers and filth, all stuck to the muggy choking fog drifting thickly in from the river, curling through Soho, oozing into Camden Town, lapping the Heath. Fog fog fog. Cut through it. Dissolve it. Vogt stings like a wasp, hums in the mind like a wasp trapped behind glass. Very well: Vogt must be crushed. With a book.

A book! A book? A titanic book! Tit for tat. A bone-crusher, a pulverizer, a dirt-into-dust book. A book well worth eighteen months of anyone's life. *The facts are simply these.* Or: *Since Wolff's article in the 'Revue der Neuen Rheinischen Zeitung'' I had completely forgotten the "rounded character".* *I was once more reminded of the merry fellow in the spring of 1859 one April evening, when Freiligrath gave me a letter from Vogt to read...* Or: *The question remains: Is Karl Vogt paid to be an agent?* Or: *In order to reach a definitive view I subjected Hansard's "Parliamentary Debates" and the diplomatic Blue Books of 1807 to 1850 to a painstaking analysis.* Or: *While researching into the diplomatic manuscripts in the British Museum I discovered a series of English documents stretching back from the end of the Eighteenth Century to the period of Peter the Great, which reveal the constant secret collaboration between the cabinets of London and St Petersburg.* Or: *At the beginning of July 1859, shortly after my return from Manchester...* The facts! Put the little shit in his place once and for all. For all time. So that he'll never crawl out again. Squash the itch-mite flat, flatten him to a smudge.

Air thin as ice, cold, headaches. Old. So long ago. So many Bonapartes and Karls. So many old quarrels and dead thrones and broken empires. So much shit. Empires of dullness, somnolent lifelessness, blunted torpidity. Boring tip-toers and wool gatherers. Drudges. Quill-driving pug dogs! Penny-a-liners! Denunciations set in Garamond type! Stylists, civilisationists, Decembrists, Dentuists and dentists all! Chatterboxes. Self-important trinket-makers and rump-Parliamentarians. Clowns, claqueurs and bullies. Somersaulters, in tap-room congresses. Excessive verbal salivation. Tittle-tattle at Benz's tavern. Benz's tavern, where the Round Table of Parliament-arians had the long night of their exile enlightened and enlivened by the lies, tall stories, dirty jokes and bombast of Charles the Bold! Émigré squabbles. Loan Funds for the Fabrication of Revolution! A complicated affair! So many names. Tweedledum Blind and Tweedledee Schaible! The Bishop of Freiburg and the Countess C. and Dr Loening and Colonel Kiss! The notorious E. About! Not forgetting Abel and Abt and Arnim and Barthelemy and Bamberger and Berlinerblau and Benda and Bayard and Blanc and Biscamp and Bauer and Bangya and Decker and Bassermann and Bichot and Brass and Brentano and Boniface and Blum and Castella and Clossmann and Cherval and Crawshay and Cyples and de Cassagnac and Dietz and Drucy and Elsner and Faucher and Fazy and Fink and Flocon and Fleury and Gerlach and Gebert and Goegg and Goldheim and Galeer and Greif and Greiner and Gottfried and Guthschmidt and Guizot and Hollinger and Hirsch and Imbert and Jottrand and Jones and Jourdan and Jung and Kern and Kolatschek and Kossuth and Kolb and Klenk and Klapka and Kinkel and Lommel and Levy and Lelewel and Lippe and Lichnowksy and Liebknecht and Mayer and Maupas and Muts and Manteuffel and Ohly and Orges and Perrier and Rogier and Ranickel and Reuter and Reichardt and Reichenbach and Rings and Stahl and Simon and Struve and Schurz and Schapper and Schily and Scherzer and Stieber and Steffen and Stein and Stecher and Stieber and Schwarck and Schlehan and Schramm and Schlickman and Semrau and Schaller and Schimmelpfennig and Schulze and Temme and Techow and Trog and Thum and Tourte and Ulmer and Venedey and Vincke and Willich and Weerth and Wolff and Wiehe and Wysse and Zabel and –

What a waste! What effort! When you could be spending your time *more profitably* (as the bourgeoisie would say!) reading Ashley and Baynes and Cazenove and De Quincey and Eden and Fawcett and Gaskell and Hamm and Isocrates and Jones and Kopp and Laing and Mommsen and Necker and Olmsted and Postlethwayt and Quesnay and Roscher and Schouw and Storch and Tooke and Torrens and Ure and Vissering and Watson and Xenophon and Young. *In so far as he is capital personified, the capitalist's motivating force is not the acquisition and enjoyment of use-values but the acquisition and augmentation of exchange-values. The capitalist is fanatically intent on the valorization of value; consequently he ruthlessly forces the human race to produce for production's sake. What appears in the miser as the mania of an individual is in the capitalist the effect of a social mechanism in which he is merely a cog.* So much suffering, so much exploitation. So many documents, facts, so many books, so many revealing statistics...

Let me tell – let me tell you a story. Once upon a time there were three Karls – Karl Blind, Karl Marx and Karl Vogt. They were all Germans and they all grew beards. Karl Blind (1826-1907) was a petty-bourgeois democrat and journalist. Karl Marx (of whom you may have heard) (1818-1883) was a philosopher turned revolutionary socialist who as a young man wrote a few chapters of a comic novel in the style of Sterne, entitled *Scorpion and Felix*, but who soon abandoned ideas of becoming a novelist in order to plunge into the three main ideological currents of the nineteenth century – classical German philosophy, classical English political economy, and French socialism – fusing them into a system which laid bare the economic law of motion of modern society and provided the theory of modern scientific socialism.

That's what they'll say.

As for Karl Vogt (1817-1895), they'll say he was a miserable nobody, a nothing, a petty-bourgeois democrat, a secret agent in the pay of Louis Bonaparte. A nothing, a nobody, a dreg, remembered if remembered at all only because of Marx, a nothing who tormented him, tormented Marx, Vogt the nobody, the piece of filth, the pest, the itch-mite scratching at the scalp of greatness.

Air thin as ice, cold, cold in my chest, burning sensations, nausea. My left testicle aches. When I shit I splatter blood. Haemorrhoids, bloated, twisted lips around my anus. I strain to shit, I spend hours in there, straining, reading a book, thinking. Some of my best ideas have come to me in there. Stop banging at the door! Go away! Stop scratching, biting, chewing. Go away, Vogt! Miserable itch-mite.

Vogt called me leader of the Brimstone Gang! Preposterous! Perhaps Karl Vogt is averse to sulphur because the smell of gunpowder terrifies him? Or is it because, like other sick people, he hates the specific remedy for his disease? Did Vogt's zoological conscience remind him that sulphur is death to the itch-mite? Completely and utterly odious to those itch-mites who have already changed their skins! As recent researches have shown, only those itch-mites that have moulted are capable of reproduction and have thus achieved self-consciousness.

What a nice contrast: on the one hand *sulphur* and on the other *the self-conscious itch-mite*!

Air fogged and hot, cold as ice, prickling. I felt dizzy in the street yesterday. It's April. Old, aching. Dr Matheson says that my lungs are in excellent condition and the cough is due to bronchitis, etc. The same may affect the liver.

April 1871, and the news from Paris is tremendous! If you look at the last chapter of my *Eighteenth Brumaire*, you will find that I declare that the next attempt of the French Revolution will be no longer, as before, to transfer the bureaucratic-military machine from one hand to another, but to *smash it*, and this is the preliminary condition for every real people's revolution on the Continent. And this is what our heroic Party comrades in Paris are attempting. What elasticity, what historical initiative, what a capacity for sacrifice in these Parisians! After six months of hunger and ruin, caused by internal treachery more even than by the external enemy, they rise, beneath Prussian bayonets, as if there had never been a war between France and Germany and the enemy were not still at the gates of Paris! History has no like example of like greatness! The present rising in Paris – even if it be crushed by the wolves, swine and vile curs of the old society – is the most glorious deed of our Party since the June insurrection in Paris. Compare these Parisians, storming heaven, with the slaves to heaven of the German-Prussian Holy Roman Empire, with its posthumous masquerades reeking of the barracks, the Church, cabbage-junkerdom and above all, of the philistine.

A propos. In the *official publication* of the list of those receiving direct subsidies from L. Bonaparte's treasury there is a note that *Vogt* received 40,000 francs in August 1859! The case is proved! The case is closed! I fly through the window like a sparrow, I soar over the rooftops. I run like a child across

Parliament Hill Fields, laughing, free of it all, free of Vogt forever. Case proved, case closed. They'll say: that swine Vogt. They'll say: *filthy slanders*. They'll say: *Marx was right all along*.

Air thick as mud. Go away, Vogt. I am dying and Vogt is alive. Older than me and still alive. Filth. Nobody. *Sarcoptes scabiei!* Go away, Vogt. Judas. Spy. Contemptible toad. When the news came through about the 40,000 francs, I thought: *Now I am free of Vogt forever*. But I am not. Always whispering is Vogt. Drives you mad. To the edge. A core of whispers, whisperings. The night teeming with Vogt. Vogt sitting at my desk in the morning, sniggering. Vogt on that hill over there, beyond that clump of trees. Vogt pointing at me, whispering. Drives you mad, stops you thinking what you want to think. Soft fog of slippage and the Commune obliterated.

Algiers, Monte Carlo, Enghien, Geneva, the Isle of Wight. Bed bugs and itch-mites... And Vogt's there, wherever you go, his ghost, his wraith, skulking, lurking, scratching, peeping, spreading his lies, his whispers. But finally, you are finished with Vogt. Finally you get out of bed, into the study, sit down at the work-table and with one bound you are free, with laughter you bound out of the window, twenty-one again, run across the rooftops and, before the astonished gaze of the onlookers (but no, no one is looking, they can't see you, you are invisible!), you soar up across Camden Town, wheel round to Parliament Hill Fields, dive towards the Heath, where the kites are flying, small boys whooping, "Good-bye!" you shout, "Good-bye, Good-bye!", you did your best, your very best, you broke your heart and your life, you set it down, you exposed the workings of the foul machine (a capital achievement!), you sketched it all out, it's up to others now, and you rise over Highgate, and the stars are coming out and you rise towards them, free of Vogt forever.

Dead Iraqis

In a society like ours there are bound to be disagreements about this and that. It is only natural. But although we may disagree on many things, I think we can all agree on one thing. The nice thing about dead Iraqis is *they don't smell.*

Some years ago, as you may remember, dead Iraqis were turning up all over the place. At the time there were various theories about why this was happening but thankfully all that is behind us now and we can set aside our differences and get on with the business in hand.

Let me say something else about dead Iraqis. They are not nearly so much of a nuisance as dead Paraguayans. Dead Paraguayans are cumbersome, frequently blood-splattered and almost always attract flies. They smell disgusting. Dead Iraqis, on the other hand, are lightweight, portable and, on the whole, easy to manage. At most they give off a light powdery odour, not at all unpleasant, redolent of potting compost in a rose-bordered rural shed.

Of course, I am not pretending that there aren't sometimes difficulties. For example, you can (with much smoke, gasoline and difficulty) burn dead Paraguayans, whereas dead Iraqis are already so scorched and charred there simply isn't any more you can do in that quarter, no matter how great your resolve or your store of boxes of matches and jerrycans of flammable liquid.

It was a bright May morning when my wife Giacinta first came across Iraqi remains in the house. There must have been three or four dead Iraqis involved (it is always hard to be precise where dead Iraqis are concerned, because of the intermingling). They were scattered across the kitchen floor when she went down to make the breakfast. After the trouble we'd previously had with dead Sudanese she said it came as a pleasant surprise to find that all she needed to do was vacuum them away with her portable electronic Dust Devourer (it recharges itself at night and is a real money saver). The handful of coal black specks left smeared on the linoleum she wiped off in a jiffy with a few drops of lemon scented liquid multi-surface cleaner specially formulated to cut through greasy dirt, grime and human remains with the minimum of fuss.

Then there was the time my son Jason came home late one night and found half a dozen dead Iraqis in his room. Not at all perturbed, he called up his friends and invited them round. Soon Mike, Jake, Jute, Ike, Jock, Pete, Jack, Packer, Dibs and Luke were sitting around, drinking beers and poking at the Iraqi remains with my daughter Dune's knitting needles. Dune didn't know, of course. She was in Glasgow attending a conference on Dutch elm disease. After taking turns to taste the ashy remains on the tips of their tongues the boys decided dead Iraqi was best described as "gamey", "smoky" and "piquant". They popped half a cupful in the coffee grinder, then sprinkled the powder on eleven steaming hot bowls of tomato soup. "Hey, Jason, this is brill!" "Not half."

All through the night they played loud music by Iron Maiden and discussed setting up a rock group called The Argonauts. Until dawn they argued about who should learn to play guitar, who should sing, and who should drum, then they all went home to sleep.

Three days later Dune came home. She told us many remarkable things about fungus infections affecting elms. Then she went upstairs and began screaming.

There was a dead Iraqi on her bed!

I say a dead Iraqi, in fact it might have just been the burned remains of a piece of paper blown in through the window from somebody's bonfire. Some dead Iraqis are so insubstantial they are barely identifiable for what they really are. We didn't waste time pondering the matter. Out came our trusty "Dust Devourer" and the mess was quickly disposed of.

There was one occasion I don't think I shall ever forget. It happened one February. I woke up, pulled back the bedroom curtains and discovered a quite astonishing heap of dead Iraqis in our front garden. There were so many that some of them had spilled over the top of the hedge and onto the pavement.

I rang the Town Hall and asked for the Dead Iraqi Disposal Officer. At first the number seemed permanently engaged, and then when I did finally get through I was told by a rather surly woman that Mr Claggart, the Dead Iraqi Disposal Officer, was away on holiday. His assistant, Ms Winter, was off sick. In the end they put me through to Mrs Fish, who wasn't at all helpful. She told me she normally only dealt with dead Peruvians. She wanted to know how many dead Iraqis we had in our garden.

At that point I am sorry to say I became petulant. How was I supposed to know how many dead Iraqis were in my garden? You know how it is with dead Iraqis – they are almost always papery and fused together. It is like someone emptying two hundred packets of crisps in your garden and asking you how many individual crisps there are. There might have been a thousand dead Iraqis, there might have been ten thousand. I told Mrs Fish it was quite ridiculous expecting me to give her a number. Mrs Fish said it was no use me adopting that attitude. She said she had a form to fill in and it was bad enough her having to cross out "Peruvians" and substitute "Iraqis" without additional complications. She said if she didn't fill in one of the boxes then nothing would be done. The boxes started with "Under Ten Dead Peruvians" and went up to "Over Twenty Thousand Dead Peruvians".

I imagined Mrs Fish to be a large buxom woman with hair the colour of dirty straw, who spent a fortnight every summer in a caravan in Cornwall, although as I discovered later she was the spitting image of Marie in *The 120 Days of Sodom,* having almost no hair left, a nose which stood askew, dull rheumy eyes and a mouthful of teeth yellow as sulphur, as well as a buttock devoured by an abscess. She suffered from amblyopia and spent every summer working with clowns and Belgian acrobats in a circus in Dorking. Her husband, Mr Fish, who had formerly worked in the Chief Executive's Department, had left her when she refused to start wearing wigs and had gone to live in Tunisia, where he was slowly learning off by heart the *Collected Poems of W.B. Yeats.*

"Alright. Say five thousand!" I snapped, although as I hope I

119

have made clear I was not at all confident of the accuracy of this figure. I suppose it was because I am a bit of a stickler for facts and truth that I snapped, and needless to say, having snapped, I became completely paralysed and lay on the floor in two broken pieces, gasping for breath and unable to move, while the shrunken voice of my imagined blonde kept saying, "Hello, are you still there?" for some time, until she at last put the phone down and subjected me to the unending whine of disconnection until that joyous moment when my wife returned from the shops, saw at once what had happened, shrieked, dropped her dozen fresh eggs from Sunny View Farm and ran for the superglue and the string.

They stitched me back together in casualty and my wife drove me home in our Peugeot 605 SVE 24 with its peace-of-mind inducing ultrasonic alarm and optional extra security key pad. I relaxed in the electrically adjustable leather seat, ran my fingers over the Californian walnut double sealed door which had shut with such a deep, satisfying soundproofed thud. I felt the cares of life slip away even though we hadn't even left the hospital car park! I basked in the warmth from my heated seat, wallowed in the warm sunlight and the silent mastery of the electronic climate control system, gazed up at the electronic sunroof, admired what *Autocar and Motor* had authoritatively described as "the comprehensive and clear instrument panel" and took comfort from the knowledge that Peugeot's engineers had built in an automatic electronic ride control which would keep our journey smooth by constantly adjusting the settings of the shock absorbers between hard and soft, based on information received from sensors around the car (each of the shocks, incidentally, contains a tiny electric motor that carries out these adjustments in just a hundred-and-fifty thousandths of a second). It felt good to be in a car which, having spent seven hundred hours in a wind tunnel, had the best drag coefficient in its class. Just for good measure Peugeot had added three silencers to the exhaust and double sealing for any pipes or wires passing from the engine to the cabin.

They'd even mounted the engine on its own hydraulically

dampened suspension system!

I was grateful to Peugeot for helping me take my mind off our little front garden difficulty. As I'm sure you'll appreciate, I wasn't going out of my way to be awkward with the Town Hall. A couple of hundred dead Iraqis, say, is no problem for anyone. Because of their crisp, mixed-together papery texture even the elderly and infirm can shovel up dead Iraqis in that sort of quantity. Two hundred dead Iraqis will fit quite nicely into a single black rubbish sack (I know, I've done it). But frankly no one should be expected to deal on their own with five thousand dead Iraqis. For that you definitely need a skip or a light truck. I am sure everyone will agree with me when I say that five thousand dead Iraqis is a problem for the Council, not for the individual. This, surely, is what the Community Charge is all about.

Besides, as I have said, some of the dead Iraqis had spilled on to the pavement. A householder surely cannot be expected to be held responsible for the actions of the wind!

Just at that moment my wife, who had been overtaking a petrol tanker, found herself driving at speed towards a heavy goods vehicle coming right at us. She braked hard but it was too late, and there was a hideous wrenching tearing smashing noise as the juggernaut sent our Peugeot careering off the road and down an embankment.

I regret to say that Giacinta was rather badly decapitated in the accident. I didn't come out of it too well either. I had to spend six months in our local hospital, until it was closed in the latest round of sad but necessary cuts. When the hospital closed one of the consultants was kind enough to put me out into the car park. He even gave me one of his old plastic macs to shelter under.

By this time I had lost my job, but at least my son stood by me. Jason sent a registered letter from Hawaii, where he was working as a chartered accountant. The envelope contained a silver coin and enabled me to pay an enterprising urchin to transport me home from the hospital in his wheelbarrow. Dune, I am sorry to say, had long since severed all connections with her family and had become a revolutionary socialist. She always was a rather shapeless, restless girl. She left on a windy Wednesday, after spray painting REMEMBER THE 26 COMMISSARS OF BAKU across her bedroom wall, as well as on the wall of the local barracks. At present she is living in Croydon and (so I am told) has developed a special interest in Rosa Luxemburg's *Accumulation of Capital*. I last heard from her in October. "Imperialism," she wrote on the back of a postcard of the bones of a Tyrannosaurus, "stabilises capitalism over a long period but threatens to bury humanity under its ruins."

As the boy trundled me up the street in his wheelbarrow three of my stitches burst, and I began to drip blobs of bright red blood. But this was nothing to what I experienced when we finally reached the gate to number 13. I couldn't believe it. I was livid. I bellowed with rage, making the lad with the wheelbarrow jump so much he let go, tipping me out onto the ground.

The dead Iraqis were still in my front garden! The Council had done nothing, nothing at all! I gave the boy his silver tenpenny piece and ran indoors, bandages flapping, leaving behind me a trail of small shreds of flesh. Hungry starlings and sparrows swooped down excitedly; gulls squealed in the sky and wondered whether to join in the feast.

I telephoned the Town Hall and demanded an explanation.

In a tired voice the same surly woman explained what had happened. All the Dead Foreigner Disposal departments had been closed in the last round of cuts. Mr Claggart had obtained new employment as a home practitioner in Babinski's Reflex. Ms Winter, driven mad by autophony, had thrown herself off the Post Office Tower. She did not know what had happened to Mrs Fish.

Many years later I learned from another source that Mrs Fish had gone off to work as a lion tamer with the Lithuanian State Circus, until a mishap off the coast of Newfoundland led to her being swallowed by a whale.

As for the dead Iraqis... In the weeks that followed ceaseless rain reduced many of them to a dark, pulpy sludge, some of which I used to bed down my roses. The rest of the sludge my second wife Lorna placed in a bucket and stirred in butter and sugar. Then she baked the mixture in the oven for thirty minutes at gas Mark 4. The vicar said it tasted delicious and could she do some more for the church fête?

Those dead Iraqis who remained brittle and did not turn into sludge finally vanished from our front garden in various ways. The neighbourhood dogs found many of them reminiscent of bones (or perhaps there actually were traces of bone at the heart of those charred fragments) and helped themselves with a merry wag of their tails. The crispy papery sort were (from a householder's point of view) the best, as they simply blew away on the wind, or crumbled in a matter of days to a fine powder. Jason took a small packet with him back to Hawaii, "as a reminder of home". Of the rest, Lorna mixed an awful lot of them with water, in order not to disappoint the vicar. The five or six hundred or so that remained gradually vanished into the soil, or became hidden by our fine display of privet, violets and primroses. Soon, I am sure, we will all have more or less completely forgotten about that strange time when dead Iraqis seemed to be everywhere. Perhaps, for keen gardeners like myself, a certain darkness in the topsoil will remain, or perhaps a few black specks, stubbornly clinging to the underside of fresh green leaves. But probably not, probably all traces will wash away and vanish utterly. If we do remember them at all (and I cannot see it happening very often, what with inclement weather and then the ensuing fine sunny hot spells as well as the call of garden front and back not to mention the many small time-consuming domestic chores and also not forgetting the broad and varied choice of television that is available nowadays) it will be in small, inconsequential ways – the peppery taste of a bowl of tomato soup, say, or the sight of a dog waving its tail, or even the faint distant reassuring rumble of the refuse lorry as it enters our street, its stout rubber-gloved crew whistling cheerfully as they pick up the heaped black bulging sacks of rubbish and toss them, one after the other, again and again and again, into the dirty grinding jaws of the ceaselessly turning crusher at the back.

10.30am-4.45pm, 3 March 1991

Solzhenitsyn and Yogurt

From her lips he heard it, her cracked pinkish lips dappled with brown sores, those lumpy fissured clusters-of-small-dead-grapes lips which memory's magic turned to a rich flawless ruby-red of a type he did not again encounter until Lucy Johnson, better known by her pseudonym "Ava Gardner", devoured him through a nicotine haze from the irregular white sheet tacked to the wall of the village hut in Gdorsk, ten minutes from the lonely railway siding where the young man in the brown trench coat had three hours earlier loitered with his sack to catch the padded package thrown from fifth open coal truck of the belching wailing locomotive which hurtled past in a shower of sparks on its way to far-off Penza and which, when opened with seven trembling fingers (the eighth and the two thumbs long since turned to clay in the ruins of Stalingrad), turned out not to contain the hoped-for reels *of Five Fingers*, a gripping yarn about the British Ambassador in Ankara's valet, but *The Sun Also Rises*, a tale of idlers, parasites and social degenerates in which Errol Flynn was identified by those who knew the novelist as bearing an uncanny resemblance to Malcolm Lowry, a writer of whose existence none of those present were aware that icy September evening in 1959. And later, returning home through the dark woods, Solzhenitsyn thought again of those long-ago long evenings when his mother had repeated the thrilling story of the night they invented yogurt.

"Jorg" is the word for "wood" in that part of the vast, sprawling and now defunct Union of Soviet Socialist Republics, and "hutt" means "hut", and so it was that the new food was named by its inventors, Antip and Nastassya Belokonskaya, after the simple log cabin in which they had first had the idea of immersing in a pail of sour milk a decaying turnip "to see what would happen" – a story which Solzhenitsyn inevitably discovered to be a gross distortion of the facts, and which permitted a new interpretation to be put upon the bottle of water which his dear, red-faced, wheezing mother used to swig ("for my sore throat, dearest") all through those interminable winter evenings before the advent of colour television, perestroika and postmodernism.

He did not learn the full story until he was a lean man of about thirty, when he fell into conversation with a stranger on the stopping train to Perm. His tendency to lean was, it seems, inherited, and that tilt forwards and a little to the left rendered him helpless before the stranger's sudden thrust of allusion, ambiguity, anachronism, anagnorisis, anatomy, anecdote and anticlimax.

"Jorg-hutt!" roared the stranger, shaking his head. The stranger was of medium height, a little over eight feet tall, and skilled in the manufacture of ectoplasm and spectres. "Yevgeny Rogozhin," he said, squeezing Solzhenitsyn's hand as if anxious to extract a few remaining drops of lemon juice. He proceeded to tell Solzhenitsyn the true story of the night they invented yogurt.

It was a very long story set during the reign of the last Tsar and involved a Social Democrat, two jugs, a pan of boiled milk, some powder, and a window which in the morning was found to bear the frosty imprint of the crucified Christ, an astonishing phenomenon which by the time the nearest Kodak was rushed to the scene had, as you might have expected, melted, leaving only a teasing trickle of tears and a handful of gabbling peasants who swore by all that was sacred that every word of their blab was the straightforward, honest truth. It was only after the photographer had gone that anyone thought to look in the second jug. "Yah-hourt!" bellowed old Pavlishchev, the respected village elder and lackey of the corrupt ruling-class exploiters, by which he meant, "Astonishing rich protein food made by a miracle from milk and the blessings of Christ!"

"Flipping heck!" said Solzhenitsyn.

In the years that followed the contacts between Solzhenitsyn and yogurt became as numerous as those between the suction cups of some giant cephalopod and the sea-floor. For reasons which are as yet unclear Solzhenitsyn went to live in the crater formed by whatever it was which had crashed by the Tunguska river not all that long after the historic conference of Bolsheviks, Mensheviks, Bundists, Latvian and Polish Democrats held at the Reverend F. R. Swan's Brotherhood Church in Southgate Road, Whitechapel, at which Lenin spoke a hundred and twenty times, popping out one evening to a nearby music hall, where he greatly enjoyed a performance of clowns, commenting, "It expresses a satirical or sceptical attitude toward the conventional, attempts to turn conventions inside out, to distort them, and to show the illogicality of all our usual accepted practices. Complicated, but very interesting!"

During his fourteen years in the crater Solzhenitsyn found out that it was true, what they said about yogurt. It was slimming, versatile and easy to digest. Over the years he accumulated many jugs and thermos flasks, and became expert at beating a little hot milk until smooth, adding the rest of the milk slowly, injecting the necessary bacilli, adding half a teaspoon of microbes and then beating constantly until mixed. In time he grew bored with natural yogurt and developed many exciting new flavours, including sprout, smoked goat and swollen-bilberry.

One day he was walking along the river bank when a plump butcher stopped him. "Have you heard?"

"Heard what?"

"Stalin is dead!" The butcher could barely get the words out. His voice trembled. He mopped at his cheeks with a dirty red handkerchief. After the exclamation mark he blubbered.

"Who?" asked Solzhenitsyn, genuinely puzzled. Like a professional musician he had been too wrapped up in his artistry to worry about what was going on beyond the crater's verdant, emerald lip.

The butcher reported Solzhenitsyn to the authorities, and the great yogurt master was obliged to flee the region.

Near Ob he boarded a bus and sat next to someone who seemed familiar.

"Yevgeny Rogozhin!" he cried, remembering the tall stranger

who had set him on the correct road to a true and comprehensive understanding of the real nature of yogurt.

The man looked at him blankly, then smiled. "I see you have met my twin. Tell me, how is he these days? Still given to conceits, epic similes, hyperbole mixed with understatement, periphrasis, puns and synaesthesia?"

Solzhenitsyn explained.

The stranger nodded and shrugged. It was a bad habit he had developed from reading novels.

Later, at the inn, he beckoned Solzhenitsyn into a quiet corner and, over drinks (many drinks), told him the truth. The twin did not exist. Solzhenitsyn had been right first time. He was, in fact, the man who had once masqueraded as Rogozhin, but his real name was Ronnie Dobson, and he was from Penge. Bored with Penge, and having developed an admiration for Lenin, he had crossed to Finland, and then into the U.S.S.R.

The Stalinists had arrested him as a spy, but he had managed to escape with the aid of a silver badge, a bent pin, and an old uniform. He had been on the run ever since. But a man on his own is bound sooner or later to attract suspicion, hostility and denunciation to the authorities. Then and there he invited Solzhenitsyn to become his partner. Solzhenitsyn felt he had nothing to lose, and over the next three decades the two friends criss-crossed the U.S.S.R., always just one step ahead of the authorities.

At first Dobson was an old, dying actor, and Solzhenitsyn his faithful dresser; then they reversed roles and Solzhenitsyn was a geriatric yogurt technician and Dobson his young laboratory assistant. At Moscow University Solzhenitsyn posed as Visiting Reader in Dialectical Phrenology and gave a public lecture (with slides) showing that because Stalin had a skull which was large, well elevated and high above the ears, and because Stalin's head was well developed and thrown forward, so as to be nearly perpendicular to the base, it was clear that the General Secretary possessed a brain of greater power than anyone else in the whole of the U.S.S.R.; Dobson's clapped hands were the signal for a tumultuous ovation from the two-thousand faculty members who had crammed in to hear the talk.

In Minsk Dobson was a thief in chains and Solzhenitsyn his stern, bearded escort; in Leningrad Solzhenitsyn became an infirm Peruvian diplomat and Dobson his K.G.B. tail. Pursued up the Volga, Dobson was a missile expert and Solzhenitsyn his brother, a geologist.

Surrounded by armed troops in Dnepropetrovsk, the two men threw the Stalinists off the scent by lying on their sides, adopting a stiff pose and making crackling noises. In this way they successfully passed themselves off as the manuscript of *Materialism and Empirio-Criticism*.

If anything, the growing friendship between the two men was cemented by the joyous discovery of their mutual talent for immobility. This was vividly demonstrated by the occasion on which they caked themselves in glue, salt and icing sugar, and posed for an entire week as snowmen in a park in blizzard-swept Zhitomir. They could probably have kept up this subterfuge for another seven days had not a sudden thaw obliged them to wrench off their carrot noses and make a run for it, purporting to be survivors of the great Leningrad papier-mâché disaster of 1959 making a goodwill tour.

In Kiev they cleverly impersonated fourteen Young Pioneers and put on an outstanding performance of Sharpov's *26 Commissars of Baku*. In Poltava Solzhenitsyn wore a moustache made out of weasel hairs and gave a music lecture in a converted church, while Dobson stood outside in the street, attracting an audience with a virtuoso solo performance of Dvorak's 1865 Cello Concerto played, idiosyncratically, on a wooden tube doubled back on itself. As soon as twenty people were present Solzhenitsyn gave his firmly held opinion as to why consecutive fifths and octaves, though frequent in medieval music, became unpopular in the fifteenth century. Once, in Yelan, the two men narrowly escaped capture by a brisk display of slides showing freeze-fractured plasma membranes from two neighbouring cells in the endocrine pancreas.

Near Preluki they averted suspicion by staging a dazzling

two-man performance of *Romeo and Juliet*, following up their triumph with a very popular course of lectures on the one-hundred-and-ninety-seven instances of puns and quibbles contained in that play. Later that year, in Glazov, they impersonated crumbling stone statues of the Aloeids, those bastard sons of Iphimedeia, one of the daughters of Triops, who fell in love with Poseidon, and who used to squat on the beach, scooping up the waves and pouring them over her crotch, with the consequence (this was her story, anyway) that she became gross with twins. Fortunately the impersonation only lasted a week, which was just as well since, as everyone knows, Aloeids grow one cubit in breadth and one fathom in height every twelve months.

Perhaps their finest hour came in Red Square, where Solzhenitsyn, in the white trousers and smock of a psychiatric nurse, led Dobson, a sullen Trotskyite, under the noses of the Kremlin guard, causing them to sneeze and rub their eyes. I say perhaps. Perhaps not. For who could forget the time when a pack of yapping Alsatians closed in on them in the forest outside Svetlograd? There they evaded capture by a brilliant device – disguising themselves as miniscule objects.

The years went by until, under perestroika and glasnost, there was no need for such measures. The two men shook hands by the statue of Roussel in Krivoy Rog and went their separate ways.

In his later years, plump as a barrel, his face yellowed by jaundice and dyspepsia, heavily bearded, Vladimir Arseny Solzhenitsyn went to live in Belgorod, where on one occasion, in December 1990, an American tourist stopped him in the street and, mistaking him for his famous namesake, the writer, asked if he might take a snap.

Solzhenitsyn angrily shook his head, shouting that to mistake him for the recluse of Vermont was an outrage and an insult. He had never written (he screamed), nor ever would write (he bellowed), a novel of an archaic narrative form, complete with omniscient narrator, which portrayed Lenin as a frenzied fanatic with a crooked little grin and gimlet eyes which sometimes flashed angrily but which most of the time projected a piercing, quizzical look which always frightened people, and behind whom stood a sinister, shadowy fat Jew named Helphand, who, as you might have expected from a bloated monster with a name like that who moreover openly cavorted (lascivious filthy swine!) with plump blondes, lent Lenin a helping hand in order to destroy all that was pure and good about Holy Mother Russia, a lurid scenario set in a world where decent men convulsed their corrugated cardboard brows, thinking such polystyrene thoughts as "How difficult, how terribly difficult it is to master the lofty science of socialism! These grandiose formulas somehow refuse to fit in with your own poor limited experience."

"Lucy Johnson," Solzhenitsyn seemed about to conclude, "took on a new name. Vladimir Ulyanov took on far more! Ilin, Ivanov, Karpov, Meyer! Nikolay Petrovich! K. Tulin! N. Lenin! Jacob Richter, LL.D.! William Frey! Who could shrug off lightly the writings of a man who wrote under eighteen pseudonyms?"

The American tourist began to edge away apprehensively. This was not the response he had been expecting from the tall, dignified figure with a silver-streaked beard redolent of wisdom, the Bible, truth, and the movies of Cecil B. de Mille.

But Solzhenitsyn had not yet finished with the man. He seized him by the arm. He began to twist it.

"Down with the non-partisan writers!" he yelled. "Down with literary supermen! Literature must become part of the common cause of the proletariat. If I was to write – if I was to write fiction – you may be certain it would be something short... Something three or four pages at most... which would end... would end with eight words by Lenin." And with a groan of exhaustion he produced from his pocket (it was a trick Dobson had taught him) a four-litre pail of cockroach yogurt. This he at once emptied over the tourist's head, shouting that his detestation of Americans sometimes got the better of him.

The tourist staggered jerkily and sloppily away, like someone in an old silent comedy.

Solzhenitsyn returned to his bungalow in the woods, feeling good. Although in recent years he had gone right off yogurt, he still kept a few pails and cartons concealed about his person for emergencies. Whistling a jaunty extract from the 1812 Overture, he went into his study and began to gorge himself on a jumbo tub of thick bacon-and-mushroom yogurt with added walnuts, while adding a few more annotations to his much-underlined copy of *What Is To Be Done?*

A week later he died of author's cramp.

Dobson, whimsically made-up as Tolstoy with a long, silvery beard and a rather wild expression on his wrinkled face, gave a fiery oration at the graveside, full of quotations from Christopher Smart, Raymond Chandler, Victor Serge and *Halliwell's Film Guide.*

The ten-metre-high pink and green marble gravestone is exactly as Solzhenitsyn wanted it. It gives his name and dates of birth and death, above an engraving of a giant yogurt pot. Underneath, in very large letters, is Solzhenitsyn's favourite line from Lenin.

> # ENJOY YOURSELF, GET FAT, AND NEVER STOP LAUGHING.

The Epsom Flashes

"If, as you approach your front door, an Irishman with a wooden leg shoots at you once with a pistol and misses, what is the best course of action?"

"If someone invites you on a long and possibly dangerous voyage, to explore a distant river, at the end of which lie unimaginable reserves of gold and silver, do you go?"

As he sat at his desk eating a warm, buttered crumpet topped with berry-fruit conserve and a dribble of maple syrup, neither of these conundrums occurred to Bodsworth. His mind was fixed on the journey that lay ahead of him. Always that same, anguished question. What book to read on the long voyage towards the night? *Hamlet*? *Dark as the Grave Wherein My Friend is Laid*? *Martian Time-Slip*? *The Kill-Off*? None of these. *Tunguska, Cauldron of Hell*? *The Pan Jack London* ("London was a grand story teller... sheer grip and excitement", *The Times*)? Spurzheim's *Observations on the Deranged Manifestations of the Mind*? No.

Bodsworth was five-six. His nose, like Lenin's, was average. His brains had the texture of mushroom soup. He loathed donkeys, carpet slippers, sandals, churchgoers, caravans, shorts, abbreviations, jets, jests, Italy, the colour blue, ties, liver, petrol-driven lawnmowers, kippers, Cambridge, flags, the paintings of Van Gogh, *The Winter's Tale*, cauliflower, jazz, horse-racing and bourgeois parliamentary democracy.

When he was born he weighed 7lb., 1 oz., a month later he was up to 8lb., 3ozs.

He had decided. He emerged on to Unthank Road humming "Only the Lonely" and carrying a copy *of King Lear*. By this time he weighed a fraction under 11 stones. An ice-cream van passed, playing "Lara's Theme".

Bodsworth had emerged on to Unthank Road on many previous occasions. Sometimes he emerged in a state of thirst and anxiety, hurrying across the road to a small public house, the name of which subsequently slipped from his mind but not its sign, which continued to swing in the vast mental spaces of Bodsworth's cranium, noiselessly, an undistinguished wooden square showing the petals of a pink rose and a pale thorny stalk, the entire composition darkening a little each year, as if from a residue of traffic fumes.

Sometimes he emerged at the first light of dawn and hurried to a nearby baker's, where he purchased a large, warm, white loaf, which he took back to his room and ate with New Zealand butter, until it was all gone.

Once he emerged at eleven o'clock at night and ran towards the nearest red telephone box, shouting "O keep the infinite spark from being stifled by the measure of law!", after which, having sampled the box's fetid atmosphere of urine and nicotine, he retired once more to his small, dark room.

Sometimes he emerged after forty winks, smoking a menthol cigarette. On these occasions, coughing and spluttering, he invariably compared Virginia Woolf's description of "misty flat utterly stupid Bognor" with his own brief memory of a long-gone golden day when fishing nets hung out to dry flapped in the wind and the sea rushed at him, foaming at the mouth.

Once he had emerged on to Unthank Road and walked miles into the countryside, where, amid bird-chirp and the drowsy hum of bees, he'd stooped to pick up a mildewed stick at the roadside, whereupon a passing police car had screeched to a halt, and an aggressive uniformed brute had arrested him for theft of the property of Lady Unthank, a figure of whose existence Bodsworth had been wholly unaware, but who it turned out owned that particular chunk of Norfolk, including all wayside twigs and dead branches, a charge later dropped but an incident which must not be overlooked in any consideration of Bodsworth's slow trajectory away from the ideas promoted by the *Daily* and *Sunday Express* (the newspapers of his childhood and adolescence) towards Trotskyism, a *Weltanschauung* he had not at that time embraced, having only recently lurched through an empty, superficial, fashionable Maoism, then an infantile, gestural anarchism (his flash-lit face looming out of the outer darkness of the Town Hall steps in the local newspaper's front-page photograph of STUDENT MOB IN CITY-CENTRE RAMPAGE, a harmless affair involving a few fireworks, much crying of *Anarchista-Revolution!* and the stuffing of badly mimeographed sheets about radiant property-less communes where no one shirked the washing-up into the hands of hostile passers-by coming out of Tesco), arriving by this date at a solitary, undeveloped, somewhat academic Marxism, so that late into the night he poured over Marx's *Economic and Philosophical Manuscripts of 1844*, frequently underlining passages and inserting scarlet asterisks in the margins but remaining aloof from the working-class, with whose everyday struggles he had no contact whatsoever.

Sometimes he emerged in pyjamas with a jelly balanced on his head, or dressed as a giraffe, or as Robin Hood with a bazooka, and made his way to a surrealism party given in a far-off shed by Jacques, a vague acquaintance who was keen on Desnos and Schwitters.

Sometimes he emerged in the depths of winter, his teeth chattering. Over the years Bodsworth's teeth had grown increasingly voluble and opinionated. Sometimes they held long seminar discussions on the late novels of Henry James. Sometimes they mimicked Harold Wilson. Sometimes they derided members of the royal family, alluding to their libidinous private lives, their greed, barbarism and stupidity, and their risible interest in horses.

On the anniversary of the birth of Victor Lvovich Kibalchich it snowed, causing Bodsworth to smile and consume an entire bottle of cheap red wine, after which he emerged on to Unthank Road chanting, rather jerkily, the second stanza of Walt Whitman's "To a foil'd European revolutionaire".

Sometimes, when it was raining, Bodsworth would emerge in a torn blue raincoat and take the first turn on the left, pursuing a circuitous route through the dark streets and thinking about the mysterious flashes in a clear sky seen in Epsom, Surrey, on

8 August 1909. The night was fine and starry, and an alert contemporary observer had helpfully tabulated the mysterious flashes for each period of five minutes between 10 p.m. and 11.15 p.m.

Sixteen flashes, then fourteen, twenty, thirty-one, fifteen, twenty-six, twelve, twenty, thirty, eighteen, twenty-seven, twenty-two, fourteen, twelve, ten, twenty-one, eight, five, three, one, none, one, none.

The origin of the flashes remained a mystery.

Towards the end, only days before leaving Unthank Road forever, he emerged thinking about Lenin's nose.

By that time Bodsworth had long since ceased emerging in a dishevelled state, intoxicated, hurling in the direction of the sparkling stars loud, brief quotations from Chairman Mao. During his last months on Unthank Road he sobered up and began to take an interest in Trotsky. The last quotation he hurled at the stars above Unthank was on a warm evening in June.

"No achievement of the revolution is more important than the awakening of the human personality in every oppressed and humiliated individual!" he cried, a strange melancholy in his heart. "This process of awakening of the individual personality assumes chaotic form, in the early stages."

Bodsworth had a glum feeling that his personality had begun to wake but that its chaotic form was not due to a glorious proletarian revolution (for there had not been one) but rather to other things. The hot weather, a Simon and Garfunkel song, his squalid accommodation, the oppressive banalities of bourgeois parliamentary democracy, the news, girls, the symptoms of capitalist society's decay, that sort of thing. Grimly he put *Songs From a Room* on and sank into a profound gloom.

But all that came later. On this particular day it was 23rd April, Roy Orbison's birthday. Bodsworth emerged on to Unthank Road and headed towards the main railway station. In those days a large dream-like clock was strapped above the fog-wrapped entrance. Norwich station! Glimpsed in *The Go-*

Between, starring Michael Redgrave, one of the very few people to have received from the author an inscribed copy of the first edition of *Under the Volcano*. The station is in a badly decayed condition in Bodsworth's mind, the fog thick, the clock hazy, his memory of the station in the movie reminding him of what he supposes he used to remember.

Seven days earlier Julie Christie, star *of The Go-Between,* had celebrated her birthday, as had (dazzling coincidence!) Rod Steiger, her co-star in *Dr Zhivago.* Whenever he saw snow, leaves, polystyrene or hydro-electric power stations, Bodsworth could not help thinking of *Dr Zhivago.* But today, in spite of that tinkling ice-cream van, his mind was fixed firmly on sausages, hair oil and time.

He boarded the drab green train and sat down by one of the many dirty windows. He opened his edition *of Lear.* It had been published in London at 11 New Fetter Lane, EC4. Although he did not then know it, he would subsequently have two books published at that address, and would make two personal visits, once to discuss with an enthusiastic senior editor a proposed book, and the second time to collect the rejected synopsis and sample chapter after market research had shown that no one wanted a book of that sort. Small wonder that Bodsworth gave up that sort of book and turned instead to writing a book of recipes designed to appeal to environmentalists and those anxious about their diet after a nuclear holocaust. The recipes were all based around a single ingredient, the common garden slug. Eventually published at his own expense, the book was a failure of monumental proportions, and Bodsworth later used the remaining 5,986 unsold copies to make a shed in the garden for his children. But all that lay in an unimaginable future.

Bodsworth decided to skip the General Editor's Preface, Preface, Abbreviations (bah!) and Introduction. He gave only a cursory glance at the *Dramatis Personae.* First page: seven lines of text squashed between stage directions and small-print notes.

Kent. I thought –

Reg? Who's Reg? Who's Alb? What does Cor leave after eating an apple? Are Cor and Corn one and the same? Bodsworth realised angrily it was one of those editions which abbreviated the names of all those characters whose names consist of more than four letters. The Fool and Lear are laughing. And Kent. Not so Glou. Edm. Gon. Cor. Reg. Alb. Corn. Bur. Osw. Not so Bods.

The train gave a lurch and the station slowly reversed out of sight, porters with expressionless faces dragged backwards, accelerating stiffly, thin strips of empty platform and curly wrought-iron roofing hurtling after them, an irresistible vortex into which was sucked the backs of grimy buildings, a dirty brown river, fields and farms and far-off barns, a remote white cottage in a mist-bordered dream, windmills, ditches and an endless file of blurred, racing telegraph poles, still looped together from their recent jaunt down the Matterhorn and collectively late for their appointments.

2

In the opinion of many, it was the most brilliant company ever to set forth from Lisbon. Shakespeare was six. He had never heard *of Historia Regum Britanniae*, in which the ancient folk tale of King Lear first appears, still less had the notion of knocking-out a smarter play version. He spent his days like most six-year-olds, picking his nose, throwing things at his sister Joan, hiding behind doors or furniture and BOOH! jumping out.

"Stop picking your bottom like that!" cried Shakespeare's mother, in authentic Tudor prose.

Shakespeare squatted sullenly behind the water-barrel.

"Joan's got grease on her hands! Joan's been touching the pig! Greasy Joan, greasy Joan!" he whinged. He ran off into the garden to squash caterpillars.

An hour later. The kitchen. "It's my turn to stir the pot!" Shakespeare sobbed.

"Oh, go away!" cried Mrs Shagspur, exasperated. Joan, kneeling on the stool, smirked.

Blame Vasco da Gama for what happened next. He was the one who reported the gold and silver that was there for the taking. He was the one who had the bright idea that to get to it all you had to do was sail up the Zambezi river. A piece of cake. A few ships, the right number of soldiers, superior weaponry. Like all imperialist ventures it was dressed up as a noble endeavour propelled by the very highest motives – bringing Christianity to the black Godless savages in that far region.

Nowadays, of course, if someone was to invite you on a long and possibly dangerous voyage, to explore a distant river, at the end of which lie unimaginable reserves of gold and silver, you would probably reply, "To be quite honest that sort of thing isn't my cup of tea. But many thanks for thinking of me. And good luck!" or "Are you crazy? What kind of a fool do you think I am? Now I *know* you've never understood me. Never! You pathetic tool of Western imperialism!"

But if you were a sixteenth-century Portuguese you would probably have jumped at the chance of a great adventure culminating in massive financial rewards. Especially when the story of the silver and gold had been put about by Vasco da Gama. Vasco da Gama was nobody's fool. Vasco da Gama had circumnavigated the globe, and knew a thing or two. What's more, the expedition was to be led by Francisco Barretto. Francisco Barretto was the former Viceroy of India. He, also, was nobody's fool.

The expedition reached the mouth of the Zambezi in December 1571. Shakespeare was seven. He was still being horrible to his sister. She used to call him "Silly Willy". He continued to call her "Greasy Joan". Or so Bodsworth imagined, based on first-hand experience of children of that age.

Thirty-one-and-a-quarter years later, Samuel Harsnett's *Declaration of Egregious Popishe Impostures,* a treatise on diabolism and a bitter attack on the Jesuits, was entered in the Stationers' Register. Shakespeare (who by this time saw very little of his sister) read it, incorporating the names of some of the devils enumerated by Harsnett into his new play, *King Lear*.

Through the grime and smears on the window, Bodsworth saw that his train had arrived at Liverpool Street station.

3

Wilson? General Sir Henry Wilson?

Bodsworth had never heard of him.

With a worried look on his face he made his way to the underground, completely missing the small dirty blue plaque in memory of General Sir Henry Wilson which in those days was fixed to a wall in the ticket office.

April 23rd! In just over two months' time it would be June 30th! The day on which, earlier in the century, an unidentified object from outer space had flattened nearly eight hundred square miles of Siberian forest in a single devastating explosion! Forty miles away men had been thrown into the air! Women had lost their hair clips! A horror-stricken herdsman was left speechless for seven years!

In Bodsworth's experience most people had never even *heard* of the great Tunguska explosion, let alone suffered as he, Bodsworth, suffered, waking in the night's coldest and deadest quarter, in a cold sweat, half-thinking of a poem by Gerard Manley Hopkins and straining his ears to hear the approaching roar of a second devastating aerial intruder, expecting any moment the curtains to blaze with incandescent light and the walls to vanish in a blur of exploding radioactive gas.

It is always possible (he reflected) that the Epsom flashes had some sort of connection with the Tunguska explosion. But what?

Bodsworth sometimes emerged on to Unthank Road and made his way to social gatherings, where, after fuelling himself with two or three polystyrene cups of sweet cheap white wine, and suppressing the images of street-cars, balalaikas and Julie

Christie which churned in his over-heated mind, he'd loudly assert that in any rational and humane society the Tunguska explosion would loom large in the educational curriculum, and that people might say what they liked about Lenin (mass murderer/monster, etc.) but he, Bodsworth, rather admired the man.

In everything except his choice of narrative form, Bodsworth was a realist. He knew he did not live in a rational and humane society. He knew that those who reviled Lenin could expect publication and perhaps even a Chair of Modern History, while those who defended and applauded Lenin's incisive writings on imperialism, capitalism and the state, and the need for a democratic-centralist revolutionary party, could expect to spend much of their lives standing on cold, wet corners, trying to sell small-circulation revolutionary newspapers. Bodsworth knew that, among the throng of travellers passing to and fro at Liverpool Street station, more people would know that it was Roy Orbison's birthday than would have read *The State and Revolution*, far, far more people would know that Roy signed to Sun Records in 1956 than would be acquainted with Lenin's assertion that the doctrine of surplus-value is the cornerstone of Marx's economic theory, and at least 40% of those present would know that Roy's first group was called "The Wink Westerners", while less than 1% would have ever heard of Tunguska, let alone read Lenin's electrifying pamphlet on the collapse of the Second International or his blunt assertion that, to class-conscious workers, socialism is a serious conviction, not a convenient screen to conceal petty-bourgeois conciliatory and nationalist-oppositional strivings.

Bodsworth, though apprehensive about the approach of June, tried not to let things get him down. Even though the rest of his journey started from Waterloo Station, he went straight to Charing Cross. Like a Shakespearean actor, he walked slowly to and fro across the concourse, silent, medit-ative, an expression of profound thought upon his pale face. He was hoping, by random good luck, to tread at least one or two of the steps taken by Jim Connell that December 1889 day when he'd boarded the New Cross train at Charing Cross and, en route, in a sudden burst of inspiration, the great London dock strike blazing in his mind, scribbled "The Red Flag". Like most people Bodsworth knew only the slow, solemn "Tannenbaum" version, and it was only many years later that he heard the song sung more or less as Connell had intended, to the fast, jaunty Jacobite air "The White Cockade", on a 7-track, 45 r.p.m. Billy Bragg album (Utility Records, 1990), a singer Bodsworth was not particularly fond of, and who, he rather suspected, had never heard of Tunguska (for if he had, he would surely have written a song about it).

After his ghostly salute to Connell, Bodsworth walked briskly across Hungerford Bridge to Waterloo Station. His train left on time, and when he reached Havant he had almost finished *King Lear*.

Later, walking alongside the dark deserted fields of East Hampshire, he was alert for inexplicable flashes in the cloudless starry sky.

There were none.

4

It is November 10th, 1917. You come to page seven of your *Manchester Guardian*. The world is in its usual condition of chaos and confusion. How can anyone hope to make sense of it? As a bourgeois liberal who adores *The Mill on the Floss* and *Middlemarch*, you think: *If only people could be NICER to one another. Real change must begin in the human heart.* But then you cheer up. There is a bad news but there is also good news. GERMANS ON FINNISH ISLANDS. German troops have landed on an archipelago of eighty islands at the entrance of the Gulf of Bothnia. A useful map shows the whereabouts of the islands in relation to Helsingfors and Petrograd. And below that: WINTER PALACE SIEGE. Detachments of the Soviet occupied all routes giving access to the palace. Barricades were erected haphazard, made of logs taken from neighbouring wood depots, and planks from works under construction. About 2 a.m., the forces of the Soviet succeeded in entering the palace. While rifle and artillery fire was continuing in the vicinity of the former Imperial Palace, a performance was given as usual at the Orodny Dom, where a large audience assembled to hear M. Chaliapine, a popular singer.

ADVANCE IN PALESTINE. PURSUIT NORTH OF GAZA. FLEEING TURKS ATTACKED FROM THE AIR. East Anglian, Home Counties, West County, and Indian troops have pushed on through Gaza and occupied the whole of the enemy defensive line north-west and south-east of Gaza. A useful map shows the area in Palestine where General Allenby is advancing northwards and General Maude's position in Mesopotamia. In the far north can be seen Aleppo, still at present behind the enemy lines. The King has sent a message of hearty congratulation to General Allenby, expressing his admiration for the spirit of tenacity and endurance displayed by all ranks.

NO BRITISH PASSPORTS FOR THE "ANTI-WAR" CONFERENCE. A large number of Turkish dead have been buried at Tekrit. The crossing of the Tagliamento by the Austrians has caused a new flood of migration, fresh suffering, and new desolation. The incidents in the retreat from Udine were repeated in the retreat from Bordenono to Treviso. Babies were suffocated in the crush by their mothers, who suddenly became crazy. Trains attacked by aeroplanes took refuge in the tunnels, where thick clouds of smoke rolled over open cars so full that there was hardly room to stand. Many young children collapsed, and the frenzied efforts of their mothers were unable to restore them.

WAR COUNCIL FOR ALLIES. FOCH, SIR H. WILSON, AND CADORNAAS MILITARY COMMITTEE. The formation of an Allied Political Council for the front from the North Sea to the Adriatic, together with a permanent Military Committee, is authoritatively announced from Rome. General Foch, Sir Henry Wilson, and General Cadorna have been appointed to the Military Committee.

PETROGRAD GOVERNMENT. The so-called Red Guards of

Petrograd are armed to the teeth. M. Trotsky, President of the Petrograd Soviet, at the last meeting of the Maximalists said measures had been taken to prevent excesses, and the militia had been instructed to arrest pillagers. M. Lenin, on making his appearance at the Smolny Institute, received an enthusiastic ovation. He was accompanied by his lieutenant, M. Zinovieff. Both of them were unrecognisable. M. Lenin had shaved off his moustache, while M. Zinovieff had grown a beard.

What a day! What a world! You turn to page eight. You feel sleepy. You yawn, just as the door opens. It is your wife, bringing you a nice hot cup of tea.

"And how were your amputees today, dear?"

"Oh, not so bad."

5

Shortly after Shakespeare's ninth birthday, far away in Africa, Francisco Barretto died of malaria. It is not known what presents Shakespeare received on his birthday that year. Meanwhile the great expedition up the Zambezi was turning into a total disaster. The river wasn't navigable at all. There were endless rocks, rapids and massive waterfalls. Worse, the river was home to billions of mosquitoes and tsetse flies. Contemporary medical knowledge of disease was risible. Every day two or three men died of malaria. The oxen and horses collapsed from sleeping sickness. Those who were left continued on up the great river, until they encountered the Zimba tribe, who lived on the north bank. The tribe was unenthusiastic about a large column of armed white men intruding on their territory. They therefore killed them. The Zimba tribe were cannibals. Back in Portugal the whole affair was viewed as a disaster, but to the Zimba it meant many merry feasts and more than enough Portuguese chops for everyone.

The years passed. Shakespeare fathered two daughters, one

of whom married a quack doctor. Shakespeare died. His sister lived on for another thirty years. Many years later Lenin was born, and later still, Bodsworth. Bodsworth, like Shakespeare and Lenin, grew old.

Bodsworth looks quite different now to how he did in Parts 1-3. His hair is streaked with grey and he is going bald on top. He wears black horn-rimmed spectacles. He looks haggard, and has put on weight. Since reading the *Collected Works* of Lenin he has gained six inches in height and speaks more clearly.

It was three years ago, waiting at Liverpool Street Station for his wife, that Bodsworth drifted idly into the old ticket office and happened for the first time to notice the blue plaque. It had been placed close to one side of the large, plain memorial which listed the names of all Great Eastern Railway employees who had died in the Great War. The plaque stated that General Sir Henry Wilson had died shortly after opening the memorial in 1922.

Intrigued (heart attack? slipped off platform eight as the Lowestoft express thundered in?), Bodsworth went at the earliest opportunity to Hyde Park, in search of a time-capsule which might enlighten him further. He took with him a small trowel, a relic of his days spent on the moors above Haworth searching for buried letters by Charlotte Brontë.

He had thought carefully about the matter, and had devised a plan of action based on the Epsom flashes. He stood with his back to the Serpentine (at a point I am not permitted to identify, under the Time-Capsules Act, 1979) and walked forwards sixteen paces, then fourteen to the left, then forwards another twenty paces, thirty-one to the left, and so on. At last he came to a small, dry heap of light-brown excreta evidently deposited by a Yorkshire terrier three days earlier. Digging down to a depth of three feet, he found what he had been looking for – an old metal cigar box with a portrait of King Edward VII on the lid. It contained a newspaper cutting which explained everything.

The nation mourned. General Sir Henry Wilson, M.P., had returned to his home in Chelsea from Liverpool Street station, where he had just opened the memorial to the Fallen. As he stepped out of the taxi and approached his front door an Irishman with a wooden leg opened fire at him with a pistol. The Irishman was a Shinner, Sir Henry was a stout upholder of the Unionist cause and the year was 1922.

Sir Henry was now faced by the conundrum which had always eluded Bodsworth.

For a moment he dithered. Then, taking his sword from its sheath, he approached his assassin.

The Irishman had an armed companion, a biped sound in body and mind.

A sword is no match for two revolvers. Sir Henry approached the men, enlarging the target with every step. The Irishmen had another shot. "Glug," Sir Henry said, rather surprised. In fact the whole thing was beginning to make him extremely angry. "Glug! Gaaarg! Globbit!" he continued. Then he collapsed, playfully squirting blood on the pavement, and died.

The biped ran, and his companion hopped with him. With the unfortunate planning sometimes exhibited by Irish republicans, they clattered off in the direction of the nearest police station. Both were apprehended and swiftly, judicially, hanged by the neck until dead. And the wooden leg? Wantonly snapped in two, no doubt, to teach the Shinner's what's what.

Bodsworth filled in the hole and walked away.

6

Lenin's nose? It was sensitive to the bad smells of a rotting civilisation. When the Great War was nine months old, Lenin wrote that it was "doubtless beginning to do some good by revealing to the advanced class of the civilised countries what a foul and festering abscess has developed within its parties, and what an unbearably putrid stench comes from that source".

He was referring to the enthusiasm with which parties and individuals who considered themselves socialists or even Marxists supported the outbreak of the war. At the end of his pamphlet, *The Collapse of the Second International*, Lenin returned to the abscess question. "The crisis created by the great war has torn away all coverings, swept away conventions, exposed an abscess that has long come to a head", he wrote.

An abscess is a collection of pus, yellowish at the centre. There are numerous intriguing varieties, including the Gumboil. Not to mention the Whitlow Abscess, the Psoas Abscess and the Retropharyngeal Abscess. Anyone with an enquiring mind – anyone with a spark of interest in abscesses – should definitely investigate the role of pus in DISEASES OF THE BRAIN, BONE, RECTUM AND ANUS, LUNG, LIVER, SPINE, EAR, GLANDS and JOINTS.

In January 1916, Lenin and his wife went to live in Zurich, taking up residence in a single, small room in a sixteenth-century house overlooking a sausage factory. Here the metaphorical stench of the Great War and the bourgeois opportunists became literal in the intolerable stink which oozed from the minced flesh and offal from the adjacent factory. Lenin and Krupskaya kept their windows closed, even on hot summer days.

"He was always buying bottles of hair oil to cure his baldness," his landlord remembered, "and he forgot to turn off the gas jets, but he was a good fellow."

7

Bodsworth's comprehensive knowledge of history and the state of things has always been an enormous inspiration to me. One day, when I am older and have more stamina, I will give up watching movies on television and reading novels and join him in helping build up sales of *Socialist Worker*. He is one of the very few Leninists I have ever met who knows exactly what to do if you fall asleep at a water-hole and wake up to find yourself surrounded by a pride of lionesses.

Bodsworth has become, like Shakespeare, a father.

He has five strapping daughters – Cordelia, Immy, Rosa, Jojo and Alice. He tells me he has given each of his children a packet of woodworm and five pieces of advice to carry them through life.

1. Don't go up far-off rivers with imperialists.

2. If a one-legged Irishman shoots at you with a pistol and misses, throw a handful of woodworm at his leg and run as fast as you can in the opposite direction.

3. Study Lenin's "The State and Revolution" and "On Marxism" and you won't go far wrong.

4. If you wake up in the African bush surrounded by a pride of lionesses, get up slowly. Don't run. Don't let them see you are scared, even if you are. Walk in a straight line through the middle of them. Keep on walking until you are a very long way away. You may then run as fast as you like. When you are out of sight you may, if you wish, whistle, hoot, shriek, sing, dance the Dashing White Sergeant, pretend to be a windmill, make a dramatic intervention, a sandcastle or a powerful speech, investigate creatures invisible to the naked eye under a powerful microscope, impersonate Mao Tse-Tung, or juggle.

5. Finally, if you ever visit Epsom by night, be sure to take a watch, a piece of paper and a pen with you.

Sunday Morning in July

1

It was a Sunday morning in July in the future Communist society...

Michael and Julia lay on the silver sand by Lemonade Sea, absorbing ultra-violet rays and reading comics.

The unlions wandered by and gave them a friendly lick. Unbirds flew overhead, not defecating at all, whistling old Lennon and McCartney numbers.

Michael rubbed his scalp, as if still in the bad old days. He turned to Julia with a smile. "My God," he said, "I keep forgetting."

But something was happening. The Lemonade Sea was bubbling and boiling. Clouds began to appear and –

No. Not like that.

2

It was a Sunday morning in July in the future Communist society...

Michael and Julia huddled together for warmth in the cold, unheated two-room apartment, the walls peeling, the smell of cabbage oozing up from the apartment beneath, the rats scuffling behind the wall. Outside it was raining, there was the constant drone of the surveillance helicopters, the vista of barbed wire fences, the rumble of armoured vehicles passing by, filled with blank brutal faces, wearing Kronstadt T-shirts and sinister plastic masks of the fanatic Lenin, which captured superbly the spirit of his cynical lust for power.

His teeth chattering, Michael reached for the loose brick by the humble blackened hearth where they heated up their watery gruel, and felt for their treasured copies of *Nineteen Eighty-Four* and *One Day in the Life of Ivan Denisovich*.

"Thank God they're still there," he whispered in a cracked, poignant voice, and Julia nodded grimly, and smiled bravely, and he knew how much he loved her, and how one day they would be out of all this, just as James Bond had always eluded his captors and brought about their downfall. They held each other tightly and talked softly of Kerensky and Kornilov.

But just then the door burst open, and they were taken off in separate trucks to be interrogated and –

No. Not like that.

3

It was a Sunday morning in July during the transitional phase of the dictatorship of the proletariat...

Michael and Julia wandered, elated yet still a little nervous, through the debris of capitalism. The debris lay all around, jagged and dangerous. At times they were up to their knees in filth, at times they felt a burden pressing down on their brains.

They spoke of Marx and Engels, of 1848 and 1871, of Lenin and 1905 and 1917. They spoke of counter-revolutionary threats and of what happened to the 26 Commissars of Baku.

"The Party has already begun implementing the ten measures necessary to transform the economy and society now that the proletariat has taken power," Michael said.

"That is only to be expected," said Julia. "But let us never forget that none of these measures abolishes capitalism straight away but that each constitutes a partial intervention by the state in the economic mechanism of capitalism, and only in the totality, and over time, are they deemed to undermine capitalism completely."

"Hence a vigorously graduated income tax is okay for now but not in the longer term?"

"Precisely. The first phase of communism cannot yet provide justice and equality. Differences and unjust differences in wealth still persist but the exploitation of one individual by another individual has now become impossible."

They walked on.

"Thorough research into history uncovers communal property as the point of departure of all cultured peoples. The system of production founded on private exchange is, to begin with, the historic dissolution of this naturally arisen communism."

"You said it."

"Actually it was said way back in 1857. By Marx."

"The *Grundrisse*?"

"Uh-huh."

"A wonderful book. I love the way Marx plays off Carey the protectionist against Bastiat the free-trader."

"Carey, who believed that the harmony of bourgeois relations of production ended with the most complete disharmony of these relations on the grandest terrain where they appear, the world market?"

"The same."

"What Carey didn't grasp was that these world market disharmonies were merely the ultimate adequate expressions of the disharmonies which became fixed as abstract relations within the economic categories. When economic relations confronted him in their universal reality his principled optimism turned into a denunciatory, irritated pessimism."

"Whereas Bastiat presented fantasy history, his abstractions sometimes in the form of arguments, another time in the form of supposed events, which, however, have never and nowhere happened."

"It is impossible to pursue such nonsense any further. Away with Bastiat!"

They chuckled; they walked on.

"Something Marx never thought about," Julia added. "The role of scepticism in the transitional phase. I think we should get rid of it. Scepticism was fine in the run-up to the revolution. Scepticism was a valuable tool in exposing some of the glaring contradictions, not to mention absurdities and obscenities, of capitalist society. But frankly, do we need it any more? During the period of reconstruction and transition it's my belief we can get by without scepticism."

"In a pre-revolutionary society, scepticism is a progressive force. But afterwards? Scepticism and irony sap the will. They encourage cynical detachment. They're regressive. Is that what you're saying?"

"Something along those lines. Intellectuals are especially prone to scepticism and irony. Sometimes it gets completely out of hand. Take Mandelstam's Poem 395, the one where the Red Army man calls out, 'Don't worry, we'll be back!' Poem 395 wants you to snicker at the soldier. The soldier's cry, intimates Mandelstam, is unconsciously sinister, threatening, terrible. But all this poem really shows is that Mandelstam was incapable of distinguishing between Stalinism and the finest phase of Bolshevism. Mandelstam is, frankly, one of those pain-in-the-butt, don't-say-I-didn't-warn-you-this-is-what-so-cialism-leads-to types. To my mind Mandelstam's poem doesn't really mean what Mandelstam wants it to mean. Mandelstam's heavy irony falls flat. Put the poem back into the context of the Russian civil war and the soldier's cry is heroic, refreshing, alive with revolutionary optimism. Let's face it, the White cause stank. We can do without the luxury of Mandelstam's whingeing irony."

"I find it hard to forgive Mandelstam for Poem 103, 'The Twilight of Freedom'. To write of Moscow in May 1918 as a place of 'deepening twilight'! Incredible. One of the most electrifying moments in human history and all Mandelstam can do is whinge! Just goes to show that Mandelstam hadn't a clue as to what was going on. Mandelstam was just another of those dreary self-important, self-obsessed intellectuals."

"A bad end, though."

"A dismal end."

"I like his poem on Stalin."

"His poem on Stalin is one of the best things he did."

"I take back what I said about getting rid of scepticism. That smacks of pest-control and Stalinism. Let's just let it wither away."

"I agree."

They continued on amid the debris, hacking a path through a thousand obstacles, to victorious socialism.

It wasn't easy.

"It isn't easy," said Julia.

"It isn't," agreed Michael.

"Take revolutionary fervour, for instance. Revolutionary fervour is a problem in itself."

"It ebbs. Frequently."

"It has a tendency to fade."

"It can melt away overnight. Sometimes it simply fizzles out before your eyes."

"It is something to be reckoned with."

"Never underestimate the demoralising impact of power blackouts."

"Of water shortages."

"Of not being able to hear your favourite track by Billy Kingsley."

"Of being unable to freshen up, have a beer and relax, listening to Scott Richardson and the Gems singing 'Flashpoint'."

"Not overlooking the impossibility of spending a quiet evening running the Zapruder film to and fro."

"Devastating."

"Strange how important slo-mo and freeze-frame can come to seem."

"Some people are easily demoralised. Some people can get by with a good book, many people cannot."

"At the Third Congress of the Third International those delegates who had taken part in the preceding Congress could not help making the worrying observation that there was not much left of the revolutionary fervour which had been the dominant feature of the Second Congress."

"Much revolutionary fervour depends on objective historical circumstances. When these circumstances are unfavourable an atmosphere of easy-going scepticism may arise. Before you know it you are mingling with people who call you comrade but who run no risk of being carried away by revolutionary fervour."

"Radishes."

Then they came to the place. They knew they would know it when they reached it, even though they had never been there before.

"This is it," said Michael.

"Hold hands," said Julia.

And now their pulses are hammering with revolutionary fervour, their vision is lucid, their minds are free of all obstacles and illusions. Fervour is dynamic, intense, zestful; fervour is full-blooded, potent, stimulating. To have fervour is to go at things full tilt. A cloud of frantic multi-coloured butterflies billow thickly inside their taut stomachs.

"Jump. Now."

Fervour is the opposite of inertia, inaction, torpor, stagnation, passivity. Fervour propels them, defies the heavy gravity of things-as-they-are, gives them wings as (hurrah!) they make it, make that dreamlike, dizzying, fantastic, nec-essary, luminous leap.

4

Laughing, we ran down Cliff Road to the lake. In the distance the sea was calm, the beach crowded.

We saw lots of people we knew.

Everyone was happy except for Jack.

"What's wrong with Jack?"

"He wants to be a film director. But when the meeting saw his video of Coover's 'A Pedestrian Accident' everyone laughed. As Mary pointed out, apart from all the self-indulgent pseudo-experimental stuff with flashbacks and slow-motion, Jack has completely failed to grasp the meaning of Coover's story. What Coover demonstrated was the oppressed condition of the pedestrian – including the pedestrian victim's own fatalism – in capitalist society. Jack, however, has completely missed this, and instead has turned the story into a tale of individual angst with the social element completely absent. Reminds me of the way literary critics used to regard *Heart of Darkness* as a metaphysical text, or for that matter Huston's mediocre *Under the Volcano*, with all the politics missing."

"Daddy, what's capitalist society?"

"Something that happened a long, long time ago. I'll tell you about it when I've finished talking to Tom."

"So what happened at the meeting?"

"There was a unanimous vote against letting Jack become a film director. But Jane proposed we should let him go to film school. But only after he'd done a six-month stint on the sewage farm."

"And?"

"Passed unanimously."

"Jack doesn't look too happy. In fact it looks to me like he's sulking."

"He'll get over it. I expect it's the thought of the sewage farm. Even now some people hold very negative ideas about sewage farms. They remember how sewage farms used to be. They forget the bosses are gone. Nowadays most of the work is mechanised. As a matter of fact, I spent two years on a sewage farm. I had a great time. I managed to do some paintings, a lot of reading *and* I learned about new developments in the use of human manure in strawberry production."

"I remember it was the same with me when I did a six-month stint of road sweeping. I found it invigorating. I met some very interesting people – astronomers, museum curators, poets. Anyway, must dash – I said I'd meet Jane by the lake."

"Bye."

"Daddy, *please* tell me about capitalist society."

"OK, OK. Very briefly, it was a time when the means of production didn't belong to everyone but were owned by a tiny minority. This minority not only owned the means of production but also owned all the newspapers and controlled radio, television, the courts, the army, the police – *everything*. The rest of the population had to work for these people. It's a big subject. You'll learn all about it at school."

"But how would things be different *here*. If we lived in a

capitalist society. Tell me."

"Here? Well for a start this pleasant pathway leading down to the beach would be covered in dog excrement, because under capitalism people were encouraged to think only about themselves and not about other people. Many people were unable to form normal relationships and were reduced to animals instead. Dogs were very popular with inadequates because they didn't answer back and they were obedient. Most people, of course, were disgusted by the sight of dog faeces smeared across every pavement in the land, especially when they trod in it by mistake or went through it in their wheelchair or when pushing a pram, but the capitalist government refused to do a thing. Even when it was established that dog excreta resulted in 70,000 cases of toxocariasis a year, with some 15,000 children infected, the capitalist government did nothing. As usual the vested interests of the dog industry – pet-food manufacturers especially – counted for far more than young children going down with asthma, epilepsy, liver disease and even blindness. Fortunately, after the revolution, the American imperialist blockade resulted in the deaths of the entire dog population from starvation. About the last thing the royal family had to eat before their trial and execution was grilled corgi.

As for the beach, those ice-cream vendors you can see would have been working for a pitifully small wage, and the ice cream would have been mediocre, aerated to create a false illusion of quantity and perhaps even contaminated by bacteria as a result of the capitalist proprietor's drive to maximise profits at the expense of safety or quality. Overhead there would probably have been a military aircraft, costing the equivalent of a small hospital, its pilot practising the art of killing and bombing people. Those vessels in the distance would have been flying what used to be called "flags of convenience" in order to evade safety controls and to avoid unionised labour and minimum wages. The sea would have been contaminated by sewage, oil and other varieties of filth, and beneath the surface might have lurked a vast submarine bearing weapons of mass destruction, its crew contaminated by radiation to such an extent that their children would be born with harelips or other physical deformities."

"But that's awful!"

"It was. But like I said, you'll learn all about it when you're older. Some of the literature of that era is good – and very revealing."

We hurried on.

Soon the lake came into sight with its sparkling fountains and water chutes and brightly coloured rowing boats. Around the shore people sat at tables, drinking coffee and beer and wine, eating seafood, reading Aristotle, Iain Banks, Frank Key or Engels. Some were reading newspapers, others were simply relaxing, listening to the different bands.

It was a Sunday morning in July. I looked at my child. I tried to remember my grandparents, Michael and Julia. It was hard to believe things had ever been like I'd just described. No matter how many books I read, or documentaries I watched, I still found it hard to imagine.

The water of the lake was of an unusual depth but beautifully clear. I plunged in, began a slow crawl to the far shore, where the light was brightest.

The Hay Wain

One of those days when everything is pretty as a picture. Noon. The sun is shining, the sky's a blank blue. Just a trace of clouds, motionless, to the south. For some reason (not sure what) everyone has stopped. Everything's at a standstill. An old diseased-looking oak nearby, trunk puckered by boils, branches; leaves motionless.

Frake, wedged deep in the crowd, sees a high, lone swift pinned against the blue. Immobile. Frake wonders again why they have stopped. Frake, Jack Frake. A thin, wiry man of about thirty. Intense blue eyes and the white trace of a scar beneath his chin. Born in Birmingham, made his mark as an actor in Liverpool, his Hamlet astonishing. Hit one day in the street by a cart, bad leg injury, career in decline. Reduced to an attendant in *Antony and Cleopatra,* a harsh sluggish messenger, a servant, a limping Knight in Lear's train. Scene shifter in *Romeo and Juliet,* wheezy lugger of logs in *The Tempest.* Then out. Drifted the city, wrote comic songs, the occasional *jeux d'esprit.* Got by. Drifted south, drifted east. In a blue-lapelled coat a little the worse for wear. Pale waistcoat with two or three grey stains, kerseys, mud-splashed topped boots. And now they're off again, time to put your best foot forward, Jack Frake, and limp on into History.

At the front two rows of six youths, each holding a branch of laurel, followed by the men of several districts in fives. The band, playing on whistles and flutes, a drummer boy, a whiskery grinning toothless old man scraping jauntily his ancient violin. And then the colours, some of silk, gold on a green background: PARLIAMENTS ANNUAL, gold letters on a blue background; LIBERTY AND FRATERNITY, on a tall pole (further indicating the inspiration and influence of the French Revolution); a liberty cap, made out of crimson velvet, braided with the word

LIBERTAS and with a sprig of laurel pinned to it. Followed by the remainder of the men of the districts, in fives, from such places as Birch and Bowlee and Back-o'-th'-Brow, Hopwood and Heabers and Blackley, Wood-street, Heywood, Little Park. All labouring men, dressed in a white Sunday's shirt, with a neck cloth, and behind them a column of women and children, who dance to the music of the band, sing popular songs, make merry, and alongside the procession thousands of sympathisers, stragglers, well-wishers, including Frake, Jack Frake, in his stained waistcoat and muddy boots.

At Newtown the Irish weavers pour out of their huts and cheer, some dancing, some weeping, gazing at the great green banner, emblem of home, and the band strikes up "Saint Patrick's Day in the Morning". And so they come to the outskirts of Manchester, passing through the gully of a road below St Michael's, along Blackley Street and Miller's Lane, down Swan Street and Oldham Street, cheered by the townspeople, and in the footsteps of other processions from other parts, the Lees and Saddleworth Union marching with a black flag, on it in white capitals EQUAL REPRESENTATION OR DEATH, beneath it LOVE with two hands joined, and a heart, and on to Piccadilly, down Mosley Street, along the left side of St Peter's Church and into Peter Street, to a wide unbuilt space ahead of them occupied by an immense crowd, which cheers and applauds the arrival of yet more demonstrators. And as Frake stands there, amid the crowd, more and more marchers turn up, feeder columns, successive parties arriving, the multitude swelling, swelling astonishingly. No one there's ever seen anything like it, and they stand there, waiting, hearts thumping, talking, laughing, waiting, someone playing on a flute, someone dancing a jig, a man in the crowd saying something (can't hear what) to cheers and applause from those around him, waiting for the speaker, waiting for justice, equality, an end to things as they are and the start of things as they might be. And time goes by with a bright jaunty tick and a crisp merry tock, thirty minutes go by, and there's music, distant music. Music, distant shouts, cheering. It is the arrival of the speaker. Mr Hunt is here! Orator Hunt and his party, approaching from Deansgate, preceded by a band, people waving flags. How many there – eighty thousand? A hundred thousand? Cheering, shouting, clapping, hurrahing. And now here comes the barouche, with a woman in the driving seat. Inside the carriage: Mr Hunt (standing, smiling), Mr Johnson, Mr Moorhouse, Mr Carlile, Mr John Knight, and Mr Saxton, a sub-editor on the *Manchester Observer*. And now a single eighty-thousand-throated shout of welcome, dying away as Hunt mounts the hustings. And now the music ceases as Hunt steps forward, removes his white hat, and addresses the crowd.

Has scarcely begun before Jack Frake hears noises off, and a strange murmur back over by the church. Frake on tiptoe catches a glimpse of cavalry in blue and white uniforms, approaching slowly, swords in hand. "The soldiers are here," someone says. "We must go and see what this means."

Says someone else: "Oh, they are only come to be ready if there should be any disturbance in the meeting." Words hardly out when the cavalry raise their sabres, slacken reins, strike their spurs into their steeds and charge the crowd. "Stand fast!" someone shouts, a cry taken up by others: "Stand fast!" "Stand fast!" "Stand fast!" The cavalry begin to sabre people in the crowd. Swords slash down at hands and arms and heads and faces and shoulders and breasts, slicing through skin and muscle and veins and flesh and skull and bones. Shrieks and screams and cries and groans of agony terror shock anger fear anxiety. "For shame!" "For shame!" and then "Break! Break! They are killing them in front and they cannot get away!" and there's a general cry of "Break!" "Break!" Hunt and his companions disappear off the hustings, and now the Manchester yeomanry join in the attack, frenziedly destroying flags and flag staves, banners, wreathes, then turning to stab and hack at anyone in range, girls, young women, old women, boys, lads, children, who scream for mercy as the swords flash down and split open bodies with a sharp spurting hissing spray of blood. A massacre: the Manchester yeomanry aided and abetted by the 15th Hussars, the Cheshire yeomanry, soldiers of the 88th foot with fixed bayonets at the lower corner of Dickinson Street, four pieces of horse artillery at Deansgate and two hundred special constables. The man holding the green banner staggers as the staff is cut in his hand, next his shoulder is split in two by a saber slash from a member of the Manchester yeomanry. A young woman, her face all bloody, her bonnet hanging by the string, staggers away covered in big purple-brown bruises. A horse sends its fore-feet into the head of the big drum and rolls sideways. Frake, frozen, rage in his heart, a quarter inch of air between his soles and the grass. Frake frozen, a lean fiction unharmed by the swish of a sabre passing through his wrist. Frake coming to life, twisting, ducking, running. Frake dodges as the puffy-faced laughing shining-eyed yeomanry ride by, and seizes a broken stave. Jabs it hard in the rump of a galloping mare, which rears, upending its rider. Paunchy red-faced man with silver hair and bulging eyes. Frake darts forward and kicks the man hard in the crotch, sees him curl up in agony, choking and gurgling. An action witnessed by two of the yeomanry, who come at him with their sabres.

And now Frake's running for his life, dodging behind the wreckage of the hustings, jumping over broken and bloody banners, swerving past screaming bleeding figures, running towards the nearest house, swerving away when he sees the special constables by the door, darting towards a dark narrow muddy alleyway and hurling himself down it, hearing the thud-thud-thud of the cantering horses behind, leaving behind a sunlit deserted space littered with a crushed-flat, muddied, bloodied cap of liberty, and numerous other trampled caps, broken bonnets and crumpled hats, bloodied shawls, scores of shoes, scraps of torn bloodstained clothing, a dead body here and there, a mound of corpses over in the direction of the church, another heap by the new houses with the closed curtains and blinds, and nearby a man of about forty flat on his back and still alive, hands pressed upon a great bubbling gash across his stomach, not far from a lifeless girl with staring glassy eyes, flies flickering here and there in the sultry motionless air as the yeomanry dismount, wiping their sabres in the grass, easing their horses' girths, adjusting their accoutrements, a sunlit space where the only sound to be heard is the low murmur of the dying, the occasional snorting and pawing of restless horses, and the excited buzzing of flies. Frake runs like a madman into King Street and on into Market Street, not slackening his pace until he reaches High Street. Here he brushes back his dishevelled hair, unpins the sprig of laurel from his lapel and walks on in a slow, casual manner, as far as the hill at Collyhurst. Here, hiding in some trees, he narrowly escapes capture by a group of the Manchester yeomanry, who are combing the suburbs to capture stragglers, and who are looking in particular for Jack Frake, whose description has been circulated, whose name is not yet known.

At a nearby cottage he buys old clothing and returns to the clump of trees to set his actor's talents to work. Half an hour later a tall, pale, feeble old man with a handkerchief tied over his mouth and dressed in an old fashioned long-waisted surtout with broad metal buttons hobbles with his stick slowly back to Manchester. There, everything seems to be in a state of confusion: the streets patrolled by troops, police and special constables, the shops closed and silent, the warehouses shut up and padlocked, the Exchange deserted, the artillery on alert, and thousands of pikemen reported to be converging on the city from Oldham and Middleton and elsewhere. And next day, among the other notices, a charge concocted by the yeomanry in revenge for their colleague's badly bruised scrotum, WANTED FOR HIGH TREASON, JACK FRAKE, sometime ACTOR of LIVERPOOL. It's time for Frake to be on the road and he heads east. A month later he's in Norwich, three days later at Ipswich. A tavern keeper at Trimley St Mary reports him as a suspicious personage, and the constabulary come for him at nightfall. Three of them, big sullen heavy men with paunches. THUMP-THUMP-THUMP on his door at nine. "Open the door!" No answer. "We'll not say it again!" No answer. They kick the door down and rush in, truncheons held high. Too late. Frake's gone. He's half a mile away, running, by dawn a far black blob shrinking into the far grey misty fields. The constables depart.

They'll be back tomorrow with the dogs. It's their country. They'll flush him out. As Frake well knows, the tension in his throat tightening, a hammer thudding pain behind his temple, things – poverty, hunger, fear, illness, the cold, age, the forces of the State – closing in on him, while dark birds pass overhead in silent flocks, and unseen creatures scurry and slither in the dark undergrowth, Frake kneeling to claw at the hard soil, unearthing a turnip, squatting in the dew-soaked grass and gnawing at the tough white flesh, feeling sick and sick at heart and hideously alone, out-cast, a poor solitary wretch, a stranger in a mist-covered land of fences, ditches, far farms and barking dogs, shivering and sobbing in the chill dawn, under a blank colourless sky, then getting slowly to his feet, groaning at the aches and spasms of fire in his bad leg, going on across ditch and narrow stream, by hedgerow and winding path, across fields and water meadows, until, close to collapse, he sees the house.

A white house, deep in mist. Tall redbrick chimneys and a red slate roof. Filling out with colour as a blood-orange sun rises from the far flat horizon like an eye, the lurid unreal eye of a man who has been beaten, a man coming to in an empty space, raising his head, looking at the world with the one eye that opens, the other bruised and tightly closed, seeing a dreamy tranquil valley of romantic mists and motionless objects, a tree, a cloud, a ditch, a fence. And now it's an aerostat, a dreamer's device, a wild experiment rising across the sluggish villages, wiping away the dullness, putting a golden sheen on dirty cottage walls and stagnant ponds, heading for the stars, losing itself in the sky, becoming what it always was, the familiar sun, shining down on Frake as he crawls on hands and knees through the undergrowth, making his way round to the back of the house, the mist all gone now, discovering to his surprise there's a river there, cattle up to their knees, and in the distance a ferryman punting someone across the water, and a strange dull thumping which matches the tired beat of his heart. Sees an open door and crawls inside. Cool and dark in there. Cool and dark as the – Quick! Someone's coming. A maid. Bustles past, clanking some tin jugs. Didn't see him, crouched behind that high-backed chair. He slips through the deserted parlour, snatching a bread roll and an apple from the big table cluttered with tongs, saucers, spoons, cheeses, pans, a bowl of fruit, knives, and hurries breathless up a narrow twisty stairwell. Upstairs there's a short corridor, on one side a neat bare whitewashed bedroom, on the other a dark box room full of dusty old furniture, abandoned packing cases, a small table covered with boxes of apples wrapped in paper, miscellaneous junk draped with cobwebs barely visible in the opaque grey light leaking in from the tiny grubby window. Frake shuts the door behind him, makes a space on the floor, and lies down. Devours the roll and apple, throws the core under a nearby chest of drawers, then pulls a length of old frayed carpet over himself and goes to sleep. He wakes five hours later to the sound of housemartins chattering outside the window and a dull bronze glow over everything from the noonday sun. Goes to the window. Sees, over on the far bank, a man in his early forties, sat on a folding chair, reading a book. No, not reading a book. Holding a sketch pad and pen. Making two or three strokes, then pausing to look across the river. Looking right at Jack Frake. He seems to be drawing the big white house Frake's hiding in. A comfortable looking well-off sort of man. Distracted, suddenly, by a figure approaching along the riverbank, calling out to him. An officer of the law, carrying a truncheon. Asking him something. The man with the sketch pad shakes his head. Asking him something else. The man says something, can't hear what. Points in the other direction. The officer walks away. The man with the sketch pad fidgets with his neckscarf, brushes some imaginary crumbs from his blue expensive jacket. Waves away a wasp, continues sketching. Apparently drawing the big white house Frake's hiding in. Frake wonders what to do next. Stay in the house, in hiding? Doesn't look like anyone ever uses the boxroom. Or make a break for it? Too dangerous, in broad daylight. Almost noon, blue sky, bright sun, a few clouds. Scrap of pale windblown moon. Best to wait for dusk, keep to the hedgerows and the dark. Then, out of the blue, he hears the dogs. Frake glances wildly back out of the window. The cattle are gone, the ferryman's gone. The man with his sketch pad has folded up his little stool and is walking away along the riverbank path. He's bent forward, holding up his trousers, the sketch pad half-slipping from beneath his arm as he tries to keep the turn-ups out of the mud. Undisturbed by the sound which rivets Frake's gaze to the yard, the ferocious barking, brutes on leashes, brutes with studded collars, straining, slavering excitedly, towing behind them as they burst from around the back of the house half a dozen grim, burly constables. As they move towards the doorway below the artist on the far bank disappears from view. Now all Frake can see is the ferryman, back where he was before, punting across a bowed labourer who holds a scythe. The river is grey and empty and empty and grey there's still that strange dull thumping in the distance, merged with the hollow reverberating chimes of a nearby church ringing noon, chime after chime and the strange dull thumping, the batterings of heart and pulse, the unbearable close howling of maddened animals, chimes, the grunts and curses of the heavy constables.

2

Noon, and one of those days when everything is pretty as a picture. Sun shining, sky a blank blue. Just a trace of clouds, motionless, to the north. For some reason everyone has stopped. The people in wheelchairs wait patiently, the dancers pause. Everything's at a standstill. Time to look around. Robinson, wedged deep in the crowd, sees a high, lone swift pinned against the blue. Immobile. To one side a glassy tower, some trees undisturbed by any breeze. On the other the river. And nothing's happening, nothing at all. Why? And in the emptiness, the waiting, Frake's born. In Robinson's imagination. Frake. Jack Frake, let's call him that. Dressed in the clothes of a hundred-and-seventy years ago. And what would that be? A Tolstoy smock? No sooner born than ebbed away. A thing of scraps and patches, a paper creature. Paper Jack. The banners sway and they move off and Jack Frake fades. Along the embankment, passing the Rodin. Now they're coming to the Palace of Westminster, soon they'll be turning left up Whitehall to the square. The chanting's beginning now, NO POLL TAX! NO POLL TAX!

An old story, a long story. *Lords of manor as wel men of Holy Church as other make complaint that the villeins on their estates affirm them to be quit and utterly discharged of all manner of serfage due as well of their body as of their tenures and will not suffer any distress or other injustice to be made upon them and gather themselves together in great routs and agree by such confederacy that everyone shal aid other to resist the lords with strong hand and much other harm they do in sundry manner to the great damage of their said lords and evil example to others to begin such riots so that if due remedy be not the rather provided upon the same rebels greater mischief which God and BBC and ITN News forbid may thereof spring through the realm.*

And now we arrive at Old Palace Yard, now we come to the first of the statues and monuments to England's proud and noble history. First, children, there's war criminal, anti-Semite, mass murderer and religious bigot, Richard-the-raddled-with-clap-Lion-Heart, raising his sword above the Japanese cars in the House of Lords car park. A little further on, Oliver Cromwell, genocidal butcher of Irish folk and bloody liquidator of the Levellers. Across the road, hunched on his pedestal in Parliament Square, the gross, blister-faced figure of Sir Winston Twister Dardanelles-Disaster dulled-by-brandy dago-hating Edythe-Baker-in-the-hay-rolling Churchill ("*Edythe was hated by the Churchill family. But she was a great comfort to Winston*"), fan of Franco and Stalin, applauder of Mussolini's "victorious struggle against the bestial appetites and passions of Leninism", hater of Trotsky and Gandhi, acrobatic leaper from anti-Semitism to fanatical Zionism, admirer of that "indomitable champion" Adolf Hitler (*Evening Standard,* September 17, 1937), his language at times curiously like Hitler's, describing Soviet Russia as *poisoned, infected, plague-*

165

bearing ... and referring to swarms of typhus-bearing vermin ... political doctrines which destroy the health and even the soul of nations (1929). A helicopter chattering overhead, and men on the high buildings, dark figures with zoom lenses, video cameras, telescopic sights, binoculars.

And of this opinion was a foolish priest in the county of Kent called John Ball who would say thus: What have we deserved that we should be kept thus enslaved? What reasons can they give to show that they are greater lords than we, save by making us toil and labour so that they can spend? They are clothed in velvet and soft leather furred with ermine while we wear coarse cloth; they have their wines, spices and good bread while we have the drawings of the chaff, and drink water. They have handsome houses and manors, and we the pain and travail, the rain and wind, in the fields. And it is from our labour that they get the means to maintain their estates. Thus John Ball said on Sundays when the people issued out of the churches in the villages, for which many of the common people loved him, and such as intended no good said how he told the truth. And so they would murmur to each other in the fields and in the roadways, as they came together, affirming the truth that John Ball spoke.

Drums and tins banging, chanting, NO POLL TAX! Up Whitehall to the Cenotaph, lump of concrete TO OUR GLORIOUS DEAD, beyond it the shrunken figure of Sir Walter Raleigh, the political prisoner, the man who first brought lung cancer to England (*Go tell the court and Thatcher...*). Not forgetting bloody Haig, Earl Haig, half-witted, inept, blood-drenched Haig, emerging on his horse from the top of an escalator, still dreaming of forcing a gap in the Hun's lines and sending the cavalry on to the gates of Berlin... The paranoid imperial gates and high wrought iron fence unlawfully placed across the entrance to Downing Street, in a style curiously reminiscent of the Romanov dynasty...

Jakke Trueman doth you to understand that falseness and guile have reigned too long and truth hath been set under a lock and falseness reigneth in every flock. No man may come to

166

truth but he sing si dedero. *Speak, spend and speed, quoth Jon of Bathon, and therefore sin fareth as wilde floode, true love is away, that was so, and clergy for wealth worche hem woe. God do bote, for now is time. So these unhappy men of London began to rebel and assembled together. And the commons of Kent came to Rochester and there met a great number of the commons of Essex and those who came from Maidstone took their way with the rest of the commons through the countryside. And there they made chief over them Wat Teghler of Maidstone, to maintain them and be their councillor.*

Everywhere the rows of mounted police, ominously still and waiting, waiting, waiting; the police crammed into the side-street military-green coaches, hunched over their *Suns* and *Stars*; the police lined up and watching with overtime eyes, dead eyes, hostile eyes. *PO-LICE. COP-LIE.* A push, a shove. Sudden shrieks; turbulence. What's going on? What's that? A small sit-down. At the entrance to Downing Street. A baton charge – Some sort of trouble and – Everyone running this way and that, chaos. Enter the short-shield cowboys. A wave of grim constables, truncheons arcing, battering, a responding rain of cans, the sticks off banners. A flag from the Cenotaph is burned, the crowds swaying, shifting, lines of police move across both ends of Whitehall, trapping the marchers, diverting the others. Mounted police pour out of a side street half-way down Whitehall and charge at the marchers. Smashing glass. A woman sobbing on the kerb, uncontrolled, sobbing helplessly, another woman reaches down, comforts her. *If we look back to the riots and tumults, which at various times have happened in England, we shall find, that they did not proceed from the want of a government, but that government was itself the generating cause* (Tom Paine). The mounted police ride at the crowd, driving people back, back to where the skips are in the M.O.D. yard. The Union Jack is hauled down from the M.O.D. building, torn to shreds, cheers. Masonry is removed from the skip, broken into pieces, the windows of the M.O.D. building start to tinkle and smash. Chaos, confusion, shrieks, cries, sirens, yells, NO POLL TAX!

Frake, Jack Frake. And behind that white house where he hides? The parasites. Namely: 2,880 persons comprising the Royal Family, the Lords Spiritual and Temporal, the Great Officers of State, and all above the rank of Baronet, with their families, closely followed by 234,305 Baronets, Knights, Country Gentlemen and others having large incomes, supported ideologically by the toadies, the arselickers, the opportunists and creeps, to wit: 61,000 Dignified Clergy, Persons holding considerable employments in the State, elevated situations in the Law, eminent Practitioners in Physic, considerable Merchants and a rabble of Manufacturers upon a large scale, and Bankers of the first order, with their families. After which the Thatcherites of the era, the proto-fascists, the only-too-happy-to-assist-in-the-running-of nuclear power stations, guided missile systems, concentration camps, you name it, namely: Respectable Clergymen, Practitioners in Law and Physic, Teachers of Youth of the superior order, respectable Freeholders, Ship Owners, Merchants and Manufacturers of the second class, Warehousemen and Respectable Shopkeepers, Respectable Builders, scum like that, with their families, some 1,168,250 personages, give or take the odd sudden unexpected death from swilling too much port and the roast beef of old England. All bearing down like a ton of bricks on 1,279,923 menial servants, 8,792,800 Artisans, Agricultural Labourers, Working Mechanics and others who subsist by their labour in various employments, with their families, and underneath them, down there under the scowl of the fat, red-cheeked magistrates, out there in the fields, resisting the currents of the age, the Paupers and their families, Vagrants, Gypsies, Rogues, Vagabonds and idle and disorderly persons, supported by criminal delinquency, some 1,828,170 shocking and disgraceful persons. Not overlooking, of course, the forces of the State, an entity best perceived through the cool lucidity of Lenin's mind, remembering V.I.'s pungent, timely and unsurpassed definition of the State as a power which arose from society but places itself above it and alienates itself more and more from it and whose power consists *of special bodies of armed men having prisons, etc.* (ah, the big etcetera!), *at their command* which at this moment in time, children, amounted to the officers and non-commissioned officers of the Army, Navy and Marines, some 931,000 men, ready to order their subordinates to shoot, stab and imprison anyone who dared to upset the apple cart or the hay wain. Or to put it another way, to beat, maim, imprison or kill anyone who dared get in the way of the 47,437 families who comprised the British royalty, nobility and gentry, and whose income, though themselves being utterly unproductive, amounted to £58,923,590 per annum, at a time when the pound was worth a hell of a sight more than it is today. A time, children (1816-1822), of severe economic distress and hardship (you know who to) following the end of the war with France, e.g. end of 1816 a mass meeting at Spa Fields in London turned into a riot, the following month an attempt made on the life of the Prince Regent.

Trafalgar Square in chaos, hand-to-hand fighting outside St Martin's in the Fields, blue boiler suits in V-shaped wedges throwing themselves at the crowd, blue boiler suits crouched behind circular polycarbonate short shields 514mm in diameter, blue boiler suits hitting out with their truncheons, grabbing individuals at random, retreating. *It is considered an advantage to have the word "POLICE" on each shield as this may have an inhibiting effect on rioters.* Sticks and rocks raining down on the white South African Embassy, thick black smoke pluming upward, some Portakabins on Grand Buildings ablaze, NO POLL TAX! Bolts, fire extinguishers, rubbish, rains down on the boiler suits.

Therefore the king returned towards London as fast as he could, and came to the Tower at the hour of Tierce. And before the hour of Vespers the commons of Kent came, to the number of 60,000 (a figure disputed by the Metropolitan Police, who say that barely 8,000 troublemakers were involved), to Southwark, where was the Marshalsea. And they broke and threw down all the houses in the Marshalsea and took out of prison all the prisoners who were imprisoned for debt or felony and they levelled to the ground a fine house belonging to John

169

Imworth, then Marshal of the Marshalsea of the King's Bench and warden of the prisoners of the said place and all the dwellings of the jurors and questmongers belonging to the Marshalsea during that night. At the same time the commons of Essex came to Lambeth near London, a manor of the Archbishop of Canterbury, and entered into the buildings and destroyed many of the goods of the said Archbishop and burnt all the books of register and rules of remembrances belonging to the Chancellor, which they found there. And the commons of Southwark rose with them. And at this time the commons took their way through the middle of London and did no harm or damage till they came to Fleet Street, where the men of Kent broke open the prisons of the Fleet, and turned out all the prisoners, and let them go whither they would.

The window of the Army Careers shop is smashed, fragments of Jack Frake reflect from splintered glassy fragments. Someone hurls a rock at the Midland Bank, some people are pushing a crash barrier through a window in the Embassy. A police line forms across St Martin's Lane, preventing people from leaving the Square. Covent Garden, the West End. A TransAm car turned upside down like a beetle, amid tipped-over dustbins. Windows of the Hippodrome smashed. A showroom of expensive cars trashed, a stamp shop window broken, stamps pouring out into the street, escaping like butterflies... A barricade of burning sports cars. Cecil Gees stripped bare, clothes strewn along the gutter, sunglasses, porcelain ducks... Stragglers arrested, manacled so tightly hands turn blue, hurled into vans, eee-aaaaw, eee-aaaaw, away, gone.

Of a sudden four white police vans come speeding down the Strand and someone is hit, a body flies through the air and lands in a heap on the side of the road. A woman, furious, bangs angrily on the driver's window, spits on it, drags her hands through her hair. Two vans reverse away at high speed, two vans are surrounded, metal barriers are being pushed under the wheels, a torrent of bricks slam down on the mesh-protected windows, snatch squads come running to the rescue, blue helmets, round shields, truncheons slamming down on anyone not in uniform... Mounted police gallop in front of the Embassy, a woman is knocked to the ground and falls under the horses, astonishingly she's not killed. Mounted police charge a crowd of onlookers standing at the entrance to the Mall. Chaos, confusion, windows breaking along The Haymarket, Regent Street, Portland Place, Cambridge Circus, Charing Cross Road, Covent Garden. St Martin's Lane, Long Acre, Tottenham Court Road, Oxford Street... A strange assembly of – Flash cars catch fire, sirens, fire tenders, hoses, police running here and there, Alice in Wonderland smoothing her long hair, screaming NO POLL TAX! NO POLL TAX! A burnt out Porsche.

And then they went to the Temple, to destroy the tenants of the said Temple, and they cast the houses to the ground and threw off all the tiles. They went into the Temple church and took all the books and rolls and remembrances, that lay in the cupboards in the Temple, which belonged to the lawyers, and they carried them into the highway and burnt them there. And even the most aged and infirm of the lawyers scrambled off, with the agility of rats or evil spirits. And then they went toward the Savoy, and set fire to divers houses of divers unpopular persons on the Western side: and at last they came to the Savoy, and broke open the gates, and entered into the place and came to the wardrobe. And they took all the torches they could find, and lighted them, and burnt all the sheets and coverlets and beds and headboards of great worth, for their whole value was estimated at 1000 marks. And all the napery and other things that they could discover they carried to the hall and set on fire with their torches. And they burnt the hall, and the chambers, and all the buildings within the gates of the said palace or manor.

And in the Square, outside the National Gallery, a chair appears. A four-legged wooden chair with a back formed out of a single semi-circle of wood. The chair, tipped back, is suspended in the air, about ten feet from the ground. A dozen horsemen are grouped nearby, heads turned, staring through their visors at the chair. The chair has flown here from Borley Rectory, flown here at immense speed to linger amid the confusion. The spirit of carnival surges down the wide streets, the Lords of Misrule are cackling and shrieking, the World's Turned Upside Down: the Metropolitan Police are perplexed, enraged, terrified. The chair is tilted, as if about to launch itself into battle. The chair bides its time, enjoying every moment. Soon the chair will fly away; soon it will all be over, soon this will be yesterday's news, a tiny footnote in history. The historians will get to work with their Tipp-Ex and the chair will vanish as if it had never existed. Take a long look at the chair: appreciate the symmetries. No painter is on hand to register the Gallery's Hiroshima dome, the blackness of the chair's frame against the grey colonnade, the circle of bright light on the seat of the chair, the dark inhuman blobs of the helmeted heads of the mounted police. No surrealist is present to celebrate the strange conjunction of domestic chair and dark horsemen, dream-like dome and set of traffic lights. End the freeze-frame: let it roll on, let the chair go hurtling towards the horsemen and crash against the flanks of a horse. The snatch squads jerk into animated motion and grope their way towards the onlookers, rubbish showers down on the bodies of armed men, Robinson swerves and sprints along the edges of the crowd, aware of the snatch squad doggedly in pursuit.

1819 Peterloo. In the words of George Carter, M.A., *Outlines of English History: Facts, Dates, Events, People*, late Headmaster of New College School, Oxford, "in the terrible charge of the soldiers several persons were crushed to death attempting to apprehend a popular agitator known as Orator Hunt". A lie, a distortion worthy of BBC and ITN News.

1819 Peterloo. An event preceded by Memorable Events.

1812 The first steam vessel, the *Comet,* plied on the Clyde.

1813 Westminster Bridge was first lighted with gas.

29 July 1818, James Norris, J.P., to Viscount Sidmouth: "I am very sorry to inform your Lordship that from all I can learn, Messrs Drummond, Bagguley, Ogden, Knight, and in short, all the men who disturbed the public peace last year, have been most active for several months past in disseminating amongst the lower orders at meetings convened for the purpose in the different lesser towns in the neighbourhood the most poisonous

and alarming sentiments with respect to government of the country, and have continually inculcated the idea of a general rising, and I am disposed to think that this idea gains ground and that in consequence the working classes have become not only more pertinaceous but more insolent in their demands and demeanour..."

Respectable Manchester was frightened when the Blanketeers met, and laughed them to scorn when they were dispersed. No wonder at the laughter! What could be more absurd? And yet, when we call to mind the THING then on the throne; the THING that gave £180 for an evening coat, and incurred enormous debts, while his people were perishing; the THING that drank and lied and whored – when we think that the THING was a monarch, on which side does the absurdity really lie?

Swann's Way. Joseph Swann, a radical hatter from Macclesfield, up before the bench for selling illegal, unstamped radical newspapers:

BENCH: What have you to say in your defence?

DEFENDANT: Well sir, I have been out of employment for some time; neither can I obtain work; my family are all starving. I sell the newspapers for another reason, the weightiest of all; I sell them for the good of my fellow countrymen; to let them see how they are misrepresented in Parliament. I wish to let the people know how they are humbugged.

BENCH; Hold your tongue a moment.

DEFENDANT: I shall not! for I wish every man to read those publications.

BENCH: You are very insolent, therefore you are committed to three months' imprisonment in Knutsford House of Correction, to hard labour.

DEFENDANT: I've nothing to thank you for; and whenever I come out I'll hawk them again. And mind you, the first that I hawk shall be to your house.

Swann hustled out, out of the court, out of history, out of human memory, almost, but not quite, not quite...

Chaos, screams, sirens, crashings, NO POLL TAX! NO POLL

TAX! Trafalgar Square. Police on horseback charging the crowd like Cossacks, odd flashes of Eisenstein flickering in Robinson's mind. Robinson retreats, finds himself in a throng, looks up at the noble statue of King George IV, royally dressed in a rich white crust of pigeon shit, in the corner of Trafalgar Square. Rocks, bottles, scaffolding poles fly down on the far side, a shower of placards, sticks, *the rabble and dregs of the people, and the devil's agents on earth – the agitators* (John Constable, R.A.).

MEMO: *Find out more about Constable and Sir Robert Peel.*

St Peter's Field was obliterated from existence (as even now, children, they are physically destroying the field of Naseby). St Peter's Field was obliterated from existence, yes. The bourgeoisie tore up the grass, bricked over the bloodstains, built the Manchester Free Trade Hall there. "Unctuous Free Traders" Marx called them; 1846 "the introduction of the free trade millennium". Free Trade! *Free trade has exhausted its resources: even Manchester doubts this its* quondam *economic gospel,* laconically observed Engels in the Preface to the first English edition of *Capital,* 5th November (!) 1886. Free trade, which as Marx caustically noted meant trade with adulterated goods (6 kinds of adulteration of sugar, 9 of olive oil, 10 of butter, 12 of salt, 19 of milk, 20 of bread, 28 of chocolate, 32 of coffee etc.). The bourgeoisie built the Free Trade Hall, years later a grudging plaque. THE SITE OF ST PETER'S FIELD WHERE HENRY HUNT, RADICAL ORATOR, ADDRESSED AN ASSEMBLY OF ABOUT 60,000 PEOPLE. THEIR SUBSEQUENT DISPERSAL BY THE MILITARY IS REMEMBERED AS "PETERLOO". Beautifully vague, hey? Nothing about the eleven murdered demonstrators, or the four hundred slashed and mutilated by sabres.

In the nineteenth century Ford Madox Brown was commissioned to paint a series of murals on the history of Manchester: he was forbidden to include Peterloo.

Crushed caps on the road, police caps, a red wreath, score upon score of discarded NO POLL TAX placards. The ashen, burnt-out Portakabins, smouldering... And over there, the

National Gallery. You'll be safe there, Robinson. Culture will protect you. All those paintings will cushion you from what's happening outside. Robinson runs up the steps, one-two-three-four-five-six-seven-eight-nine-ten-eleven-twelve steps, pushes past the tourists, pushes through the revolving door, the pursuing police reflected in the glass like in an old jittery silent movie, his breath coming slowly, gulping like he was drowning, into the hallway. Ahead: two flights of steps, which he takes three at a time, then a tiled floor, COMPASSION beneath his feet, DEFIANCE, a fat man in a tin hat looking like Winston Churchill (it *is* Winston Churchill!), and on, into the shop, pushing his way up the central aisle, pushing past people buying art books and cards and the German language guide to the Gallery, and behind him the snatch squad, six of them, heads down, moving like rugby players.

And later, at Smithfield, the king sent the Mayor of London, William Walworth, to ask the common people to send their leader to him, whereupon Wat Tyler came forward and took King Richard by the hand and shook him warmly by the arm and said: "Brother, be of good comfort and joyful, for you shall have, in the fortnight that is to come, praise from the commons even more than you have had yet, and we shall be good companions." And the king asked what the common people wanted, and Tyler explained that there should be equality among all people save only the king and that the goods of Holy Church should be divided among the people of the parish and that there should be only one bishop in England and only one prelate and all the lands and tenements now held by them should be confiscated and divided among the commons and that there should be no more villeins in England, and no serfdom or villeinage, but that all men should be free and of one condition. To this the king gave an easy answer and said that he should have all that he could fairly grant. And then Tyler was attacked by Walworth, who slashed him with a cutlass, and one of the king's household, who sneaked up behind him and ran a sword through his body three times, and the king rode out to the commons, commanding that they should all come to him at

Clerkenwell Fields.

Ahead: some sort of exhibition, two mute uniformed attendants with fish mouths, staring at him, and staring beyond him, about to say something, wondering whether to intervene, as Robinson rushes past them and darts off to the left, into a side gallery, in his mind the dim memory of a North Entrance and a possible way out. Ahead: Titian's *The Death of Actaean*, though, turning left past it, all Robinson is aware of is a woman in dark, ripped clothes with an exposed breast and some sort of disturbance in the background, a red pain moving through his lungs as the yellow splash of Van Gogh's Sunflowers blazes by and slips from view, and directly ahead of him the washed-out blue of Seurat's Bathers, reminding him of the long time ago when he visited the Gallery with Martina and they stood before it with crackling pounding hearts in the high noon of their love, at the height of summer, that incandescent summer of the drought, which ended when she went back to her own planet, and he walked all the way to The Flask, saying much as now "Heugh, Heugh, Heugh" like an old winded broken horse, and just as he got to the cinema in Golder's Green where later he went alone to see *The Omen* the first few pattering drops of rain, metallic, a little unreal, like he was walking through the last lines of *The Waste Land* or some such, a poem which seemed to hang over them as they trudged here and there from airport to station, from hotel to hotel, from bed to bed, from park to park, exploring the green spaces, travelling to and fro on the Circle Line, the Northern Line, drifting through the City, into the Whispering Gallery, into St Magnus Martyr, a needle-sharp remote silvery memory quit at the sudden sight of a da Vinci, and there in the corner, hemmed in by an El Greco and a Rembrandt, much bigger than he'd imagined after seeing it all those times on biscuit tins and trays and calendars and hanging on the lounge wall of remote dusty relatives along with the Reader's Digest Condensed Novels and the 22" TV and the hideous china country maids and cherry-cheeked grinning shepherds, *The Hay Wain* by John Constable, R.A.

And while King Richard was soft-soaping the crowd (whose

heads at this juncture in History were alas stuffed with oppressive iron rubbish about the divinity of kings), Walworth, the Mayor of London, sped back to the City and commanded those who were in charge of the twenty-four wards to make proclamation round their wards, that every man should arm himself as quickly as he could and come to the king in St John's Fields. And when the king had reached the open fields he made the commons array themselves on the west side. And presently the aldermen came to him in a body, bringing with them their wardens, and the wards arrayed in bands (remember what Lenin said about the State, children), a fine company of well armed folks in great strength. And they enveloped the commons like sheep within a pen, a technique used by the forces of the British ruling class on numerous occasions since, e.g. Peterloo, Red Lion Square, Southall, Orgreave, Wapping, or for that matter Whitehall on March 31st 1990. *But this time it isn't working, the crowd's not running, it's all gone haywire.*

HAY, *n.* grass cut and dried for fodder. HAYWIRE (colloq.) tangled, in disorder, distracted [f. use of hay-baling wire in makeshift repairs]. WAIN, *n.* wane, a wagon; a carriage for the transport of goods on wheels.

The Hay Wain by John Constable, R.A., enormous after all those flat lustreless reproductions. Begins at knee height, rises up a couple of metres high, three wide, within a heavy fussy cumbersome Victorian gilded frame. *Suffolk was in many respects the most highly organised of English farming areas and* – And in 1822 Constable wrote: "My brother is uncomfortable about the state of things in Suffolk. They are as bad as Ireland – *never a night without seeing fires near or at a distance.*" The farm labourers setting fire to the HAYRICKS and HAYSTACKS and – The room's a dead end, no galleries off it, nowhere else to run, you're trapped. Stand there, Robinson. Don't panic. The room's deserted, the attendant's seat is empty. Don't panic. Pretend to be just another tourist taking a keen interest in our cultural heritage, ignore the tramp-tramp-tramp of your heart, which might be the nearing ominous clatter and thump of heavy police boots. Robinson glances at the green rope supported by a row of brass poles on circular stands which keep the art lover a discreet distance from the rugged surface of each masterpiece, preventing accidental scratchings and scrapings of the unique surface. Robinson steps across to glance at the white card pinned to the wall – *"The Hay Wain,* therefore, represents a link between the idealism of Claude and Poussin, and the future empirical vision of the Impressionists" – then moves to the left to stand, time spinning dizzily, before the very heart of the great canvas. *Tramp-tramp-tramp* goes the army marching past outside, Goodbye Leicester Square, and now he notices what he has never noticed before on biscuit tins or calendars or plastic trays or on the wall of his aunt's flat in Bradford, those tiny figures bending in the field beyond –

And after Walworth had set the wardens of the City on their way to the king, he returned with a company of lances to Smithfield, to finish off with his thugs the wounded Wat Tyler. But Tyler was not there. And it was told him that he had been carried by some of the commons to the hospital for poor folks by St Bartholomew's, and was put to bed in the chamber of the master of the hospital. And Walworth went thither and found him, and in the best traditions of the Israeli Gestapo occupation forces had the wounded man carried out to the middle of Smithfield, in presence of his fellows, and there beheaded. And thus ended Wat Tyler's wretched life, a man you'll never find pictured on British commemorative stamps.

The Hay Wain by John Constable, R.A. Dog, fisherman. Red vase in the window of the house. Tranquillity. A painting like *Top Gun,* all gloss, myth, fantasy. The judicious placement of flagpole or cart, runway or field, sunset or cloud, labourers or carrier in the Indian Ocean, until the two blur, and now that speck's a MIG fighter, behind the house lurks a blonde in leather, all sunlight and honey, in which there's no place for agricultural depression, recession, squalor, poverty, the all-night wage slave, the women in the electronics factories of Korea, the tortured of Palestine, the black children with puffy bellies and skull faces and big teardrop eyes, the masses blotted out by the sugar of individual destiny...

Then Walworth had Wat Tyler's head set on a pole and borne before him to King Richard, who thanked Walworth greatly for what he had done. And when the king saw the head he was, like the man in *Bring Me the Head of Alfredo Garcia,* delighted, and he had it brought near him to abash the commons. And when the commons saw that their chieftain was dead in such a manner, they fell to the ground for mercy for their misdeeds, poignantly demonstrating the dangers of personality cults and the underlying need for an organised revolutionary party ready and willing to meet a murderous ruling class on its own terms. *Then the king ordered Walworth to put a helmet on his head because of what was to happen, and the Mayor asked for what reason he was to do so, and the king told him that he was much obliged to him, and that for this he was to receive the order of knighthood. And Walworth made a great show of modesty saying that he was but a merchant and already fully occupied by trade and profiteering and exploitation of the masses, but finally the king made him put on the helmet, and took a sword in both his hands and dubbed him knight with great good will. And the king gave Sir William Walworth £100 in land, for him and his heirs. And in due course a great road was named after him, which is there to this day (Walworth Road, London SE17), and because Walworth sums up everything which it stands for – the market economy, double-dealing, toadying to the royal family, betrayal of working-class interests, opposition to anti-poll-tax campaigns, slavish obedience to the law, and unstinting support for the violence of the ruling class – the Labour Party has based its headquarters there, children, at number one hundred and fifty.*

Clatter of heavy boots and they're there, in the room, the snatch squad, grunting like hogs, and one cries, "That's him, Sarge!" and they come at him, six of them, truncheons drawn, rage on their faces, the same faces that you saw at Cable Street, the same faces Orwell saw at Olympia, the same faces you saw at Red Lion Square and Southall and Lewisham, the same faces you saw attacking the crowd outside Grunwicks, the same faces you saw at Orgreave, constable country, faces that don't alter

179

when Robinson folds his arms and says quietly, "There's no need for – ", a sentence, a life sentence, a foolish sentence coming from someone who has heard of the 26 Commissars of Baku and who ought to know better, a sentence that goes unfinished as the first truncheon smashes him on the left shoulder, sending a wave of pain through his body, a sentence that never will be finished as blow after blow rains down on him, the faces unchanging, the faces that hate these red bastard troublemakers, the faces that don't half have a larf as on the morning of the demo they're told that the loony left are going to be out in force and the day promises to be a tasty one, right tasty, the twisted, sweating faces that bob behind a shower of blows, a shower of blows that send Robinson spinning, that drive him down, that knock him to his knees, a shower that doesn't stop, a shower battering his shoulders, thumping his ribs, winding him, bruising his thighs, bruising his back, toppling him over that green rope, and the Sergeant's thump to his temple, the thump that sends a spurt of splintered bone and blood showering over the officers' overalls and over their blue helmets and spurting in a bright unreal slash across *The Hay Wain* by John Constable, R.A., closely followed by the soft hollow slippery brown noise of Robinson's body slumping against the painting, Robinson's split head smearing down the canvas, obliterating the two men and the wagon in a crude ketchup splash.

And afterwards, of course, came the bloody repression of the masses. The king sent out his messengers into divers parts to capture the malefactors and put them to death. And many were taken and hanged at London, and many gallows were set up around the City of London, and in other cities and boroughs of the south country. And some the king granted pardon, on condition that they should never rise again, under pain of losing life or members, and that each should get his charter of pardon, and pay the king as fee for his Seal twenty shillings, to make the blood-drenched little creep even richer than he already was. And after the end of the rising, a deputation from the people of Essex appealed to the King for justice and freedom and the relief of the poor. But the King repudiated his Seal, saying: Oh miserable men, hateful both to land and sea, unworthy even to live, you ask to be put on an equality with your lords! Serfs you were and serfs you are; you shall remain in bondage, not such as you have hitherto been subject to, but incomparably viler. For so long as we live and rule by God's grace over this kingdom we shall use our sense, our strength and our property so to teach you, that your slavery may be an example to posterity, and that those who live now and hereafter, who may be like you, may always have before their eyes and as it were in a glass, your misery and reasons for cursing you, and the fear of doing things like those which you have done.

Blood dripping from the gilded frame, puddle of slippery blood on the shining polished floor, and now Robinson is dying, dying unexpectedly on a Saturday afternoon in London, and his head flops and dying he has a sudden vision of the system in which he's enmeshed, in which they're all enmeshed, struggling muddily, half-blinded by blood and television and the dense laminated pages of the history books and –

And John Ball among the fifteen hundred people from various counties executed for their part in the rising. John Ball arrested at Coventry, taken to St Albans, and there, in the great tradition of English civilisation, hanged, drawn and quartered.

Robinson gazing up at "The Hay Wain", seeing for the first time a ghost in the murky water, seeing the small dark cracks like a falling net across that oh-so-innocent Suffolk sky, seeing what looks like a patch of rhubarb in the bottom left corner, seeing the red vase wobble like the amoeba under the microscope twenty years ago at school, the red vase now a red blob swelling, a drifting red balloon, a scarlet salty tongue and a thick sludgy voice calling, calling. *Christ, Sarge, you've killed the bastard*, the Sergeant undoing the straps of his helmet, taking off his black leather gloves, wiping his hands on his overalls, mopping his face, says *Fucking shut up, Briggs. Keep fucking calm. He was resisting arrest, right? Right mates?* (Right, Sarge.) *He was struggling violently, right? We used minimum force, right?* (Right, Sarge.) *Don't piss yourself and we'll see this thing through together, right mates?* (Right, Sarge.) *Everyone'll be on our side, remember that. The Commissioner. The Federation. The papers. And if it fucking comes down to it, the Coroner. Now fucking go and call for an ambulance.* (Right, Sarge.)

And there were numerous others, whose names mean nothing nowadays, men like John Shirle, of the county of Nottingham, who was taken *because it was found that he was a vagabond in divers counties the whole time of the disturbance, insurrection and tumult, carrying lies and worthless talk from district to district, whereby the peace of the lord the King could be speedily broken and the people disquieted and disturbed; and among other dangerous words, to wit, he said in a tavern in Bridge Street, Cambridge, where many were assembled to listen to his news and worthless talk: That the stewards of the lord the King, the justices and many other ministers of the King were more worthy to be drawn and hanged, and to suffer other lawful pains and torments than John Ball, chaplain. For he said that he was condemned to death falsely, unjustly and for envy, by the said ministers with the King's assent, because he was a true and good man, prophesying things useful to the commons of the realm and telling of wrongs and oppressions done to the people by the King and the ministers aforesaid. Which sayings redound to the prejudice of the crown of the lord the King. Therefore by the discretion of the said assigns he was hanged.*

Christ, Sarge, the picture's messed! Don't fucking panic! It's not fucking important! But Sarge, it's famous! It must be worth a packet! My sodding sister-in-law has it on the wall over her telly! Red, spreading. Reminds Robinson of the start of Roeg's *Don't Look Now*, the slow dreadful ooze, the sinister music, the prickling sense of doom and then – The deep, rich colours ebb. The room expands. Immense and grey as a mausoleum, and cold, cold as a mausoleum, and Robinson, dying, sees stone and bones and structures, things stripped bare, a vision (he drunkenly felt) a little like (don't be bloody ridiculous) Marx's, that cold pauper's winter of 1857, the winter of the seven workbooks, *Grundrisse der Kritik der Politischen Ökonomie,* "the antithesis to political economy – namely socialism and communism – finds its theoretical pre-supposition in the works of classical economy itself". Sketch of a sketch for six massive studies of CAPITAL, LANDED PROPERTY, WAGE LABOUR, THE STATE, INTERNATIONAL TRADE, THE WORLD MARKET, the skin of things stripped away, burrowing into value, money, credit, capital in general, sorting through capitalism's gubbish, *dissolution of communal property without* [Here the manuscript breaks off], vampire capitalism feeding on blood and young bodies, a dead thing, a husk, something like the personnel manager in *Martian Time-Slip,* or shall we say a hideous machine, a machine that has taken over, like – like that vast slow block-like unstoppable probe in *Star Trek IV: The Voyage Home,* bringing destruction to the planet, but not to be stopped by a couple of whales, surging over Stalin, getting him (state capitalism!) to do its bloody bidding, until no further use, then Gorbachev-Yeltsin-whoever, unending, yet not, finally, unstoppable, the final choice socialism or barbarism, the Culture or utter emptiness, choked canals, broken machines, mass graves, camps, a landscape of desolation, a Martian landscape of death in which, as the day wanes, wraith-like, Robinson glimpsed the Home Secretary, whose name he could not remember, a yellow eyed, sallow-pink, plump, shifty, curiously flaccid man, looking as if even *he* didn't quite believe the tide of half truths and oily insincere regrets oozing from his slug lips, and contriving to blame the Labour Party for the disgraceful scenes in Whitehall, which made Hatmadder very cross indeed, so that his seventeen chins wobbled uncontrollably, and denials slipped from those sherry-flushed wool-padded cheeks, Blabberhat was he called? Whatever he was called (and the names were crumbling, now; the buildings were beginning to crack and collapse; *Earthquake* was replaying inside Robinson's head) he wanted listeners to know that the Labour Party utterly condemned the violence and backed the police two hundred percent, Tweedledee adding *I hope there have been a*

183

substantial number of arrests, I hope the people responsible for the violence will be convicted and awarded very severe sentences, a message reiterated by Nellcock himself on the next day's news, Tweedledum Nellcock, statesmanlike, grave, full of gubbish and gas, not to mention the Commissioner's spokesman and the oily-tongued man from the Police Federation. The police investigation of the police the usual monstrous farrago of corruption and lies, moustaches shaved off, beards grown. The inquest held in the dark cramped rotting dilapidated Coroner's Court before the Coroner, Dr Arnold Rupert Adolf Tory-Bigot, who would refuse to call a jury until forced to do so by a successful legal appeal, the jury then being selected from an appropriately white upper-middle-class *Times* and *Telegraph* area of London, the jurors not chosen at random but selected by the Coroner's Officer who is – Catch 22! – a policeman, and whose directions to the jury would be biased, rambling, repetitious, confusing and confused, and who would put it to the jury that Robinson had perhaps *deliberately* cracked his head against the painting, the fracture being caused not (as everyone had assumed) by a police truncheon at all but by *the frame of the painting,* Robinson's motive possibly being a wanton and who knows even *anarchistic* desire both to discredit the police *and* to besmirch the one real masterpiece of English art. Robinson foresees it all, his eyes rolling, his eyes wandering about, his tongue stuck up, extremely dazed, unable to speak now, vague, confused, the Suffolk mist closing in, rubbing his head, the pain getting more severe, laid on the stretcher and rushed out of that place, the ambulance siren wailing, the surgical registrar running down the corridor, Robinson's pulse dropping rapidly, Robinson thrashing about, Robinson's left pupil dilated and unreactive, unconscious now, slipping from the grip of the police, running with Frake out of that white house, plunging with Frake into the brown calm river, holding his breath for half an hour just to fool 'em, surfacing underneath the hay wagon, hearing the thick Suffolk accents of the men on the wagon, hearing they've caught Frake, hearing the dogs, the bellows of the thick-necked red-faced bushy-moustachio'd constables, sinking back under the surface, sinking into the mud, worming his way into the mud, holding his breath spectacularly, watching from the back of the crowd as Frake is hanged by the neck until dead, deep now in the cold cold mud, respiration slowing alarmingly, bubbles and froth, blurry and frosty and smeary and salty and dizzy, taken straight to the operating theatre with symptoms indicating rapidly developing brain pressure, a large extra-dural haematoma on the left side caused by a blow which has fractured the skull, his condition deteriorating during the operation, dying at midnight precisely, buried in a grave which no one now visits, his sister dead in a car crash in Africa, his parents dead of grief, his friends drifted off into other lives, and Robinson (he sees it all, dying he sees everything) remembered now only in passing after other riots, other deaths, in revolutionary newspapers.

Reader, the police were completely exonerated. Sergeant Bull has just been promoted to Detective Inspector. The Coroner's jury's verdict was Death by Misadventure. And as everyone agrees, the restorers did an absolutely first class job on the painting, with not a trace of bone fragment or blood left visible. Our art critics are unanimous in their verdict that, since its restoration, "The Hay Wain" has an altogether startling new freshness and clarity. This assessment, together with the unfortunate Robinson episode (now thankfully behind us) has made "The Hay Wain" even more of a crowd-puller than before. Indeed, as someone remarked only the other day in *The Times,* though a cruel and ghastly accident, the Robinson incident was, taking the longer view, and from the perspective of art and aesthetics (not to mention Constable's reputation), the best thing that could possibly have happened.

Crocklefether Squiggs

Thrippsy blubberbod, darryah havermist obb addershronk annoof murrhwagh? Oazer ibbullthrush fraggors oym ider crocklefether squiggs? Ib sadderlabby yadder! Loymmed sinkglad dappersty jazzer crockly squiggs! Hubber drimp hubber oily thuttum! Flosky! Viddle squibble tog-a-tog! Wisty-inking hubbub madderisty hubbub yules drippsy crocklefether squiggs, Ailscess (hidd wanderlooned).

P.S. I also really want to talk to you about the October Revolution, to put things back into their historical perspective, to tell you how, far from being able to get on with their work in peace, the Bolsheviks had to prepare for war, and for a terrible war, since the attack came from all sides, and of how the bourgeoisie forced the Bolsheviks into war, how the pardoned rebel generals broke their word, how all the moral and material resources of a country already drained and exhausted by the Great War had to be thrown into a three-year civil war. I want to tell you about British involvement in the Russian civil war and of the forgotten 26 Commissars of Baku who were brought out of prison on 19 September 1919 "to be sent to India via Persia" and "to be kept as hostages" according to the story prepared for public opinion, the truth being that these men were taken out across the Caspian Sea by British troops and beheaded in an out-of-the-way spot. Did I say beheaded? In a lonesome left-wing bookshop I have just snapped up a copy of Trotsky's *Social Democracy and the Wars of Intervention in Russia 1918-1921*, which states that the 26 Commissars of Baku "were shot without investigation or trial, on a lonely spot between the stations of Pereval and Akhcha Kun in Trans-Caucasia, on 20th September 1918, by Teague-Jones, the chief of the British military mission at Ashkhabad, with the knowledge and approbation of the other British Authorities in Trans-Caucasia, notably the commander of the British forces in Trans-Caucasia, Major-General Thompson". I want you to read this book, and other books. I want to show you how what ended in 1991 did not end then but sixty-five or sixty-six years earlier. I want to break down your solitude and wrench you from this page and shout, "Things don't have to be the way they are!" I want to take you by the hand and dance among the rubble. I want to jump with you along the stepping-stones of all the severed heads of Lenin from all those gross, monstrous, mutilated statues. Tomorrow (viddle-squibble tog-a-tog!) I shall spell it out to you on Lenin's toes, toes the size of footballs. I've had a word with Lenin. I asked if that was okay with him. Lenin said he doesn't mind. In fact, he welcomes it.

Thingumajig

Days on end, days on end in the dark rooms, days on end holding on to things, dark conversations in the dark rooms, the long pauses, the things unsaid, days on end spent trying to keep the ending from happening, the last wave by, crying – From first gasp to last. A matter with grave repercussions. From first to last and all the ones between. Silent musings. Reaching for my glasses like the man at the start *of Twelve O'Clock High*. Tattered windsock. Desolation, decay, gutted structures. The ghost voices. Reaching for my glasses with both hands, deftly flipping them over. Licking the right lens. Wiping it with a big clean white handkerchief. Licking the left lens; wiping it. Middle of February. Lick and wipe; lick and wipe. Hearing voices that aren't there anymore, the voices you'll never hear any more. The faint chorus of the dead ones among the desolation. Putting the glasses back on, hearing the prop, the splutter of machinery, an engine starting up, a roaring coming from the sky, the story beginning all over again, the wild grasses harrowed. Dazed, dreaming. So drugged and loose with sleep. Out of breath, yes. Glasses fogged, eyesight failing. Not one-hundred-per-cent today. If I ever was. Not A1, so to speak. Time now to say something, yes yes! say something. Burn and rave. A word in your ear. A word or two. While the auricles and ventricles are still throbbing. While there's still a gleam in those dark eyes. Can hardly breathe in here and the story –. The story beginning all over again, again. Undo this button. Can't you see I'm –

past the dark lochans

Past the dark lochans and pale abandoned crofts and the derelict cars, past dark leaning pines and pale scrambling sheep, along that long winding lonely moorland road to the little port with its dark quiet houses and empty streets and grey quayside, the ferry there, blazing with light, the dull low noise of the engine, darkness, midnight, the surge of machinery at full thrust, the rock and sway and restless lurching, creakings, a sleepless night, slippage.

thingumajig

Go on! Tell. Kill it, time. Tell. For winter. Tell of the hospital. The bed. The blood. The room. Something was up. Or tell of that winter, say. That penniless winter. A sad –. The pier. The sea. The deserted town. Something was up. A royal wedding. The waves. Ramsay Macdonald Road. A long winter of everything falling apart, a long winter reading a three-volume biography of Trotsky. Go on, say something. Tell the story. Or how about... How about the one about the sewing-machine, the umbrella and the dissecting table? A lifetime's bummels. Jiggerypokery, adventures, triangles. Ron and Eth and –. Sundays, graveyards, boredom. Days on end alone, and then –. Numbers melting, numbers muddled, years slurring and blurring. Slippage and skip. Confused. Stop that mooching about, Sharp! Get a move on. No time to delay, not in your condition. Starting to forget names, street names, addresses. Time, please. Sum it all up. Come straight to the point. While there's still –. Can't be long now. Before the auricles and ventricles shut down. Before the old pitter-patter halts. Best to what? on a winter's day of pell-mell rain upon the pane. Speak. Before the mist blots everything out. Before the engine seizes up and the pipes freeze. Hair and eyes turning grey. Stop that mooching about. Get a move on, Sharp. Don't beat about the bush. Tell it while there's still life in the old dog. While there's still someone there, someone prepared to listen.

hat tooner daze

So fine so sweet so easy so much said and unsaid. Always did speak a different language. Too much sun, too much rain, in the drowsy house. Hymns pouring over the bed on Sunday

mornings from the church next door. Too much honey and –.
"Hey, alkie!" Lying amid green sheets listening to the
soundtrack album of *Pat Garrett and Billy the Kid*. Hearing
the bell tower chiming its tinny electronic chimes. Seeing it all
again, with blinding sight.

thingumajig

Our story begins in the ancient town of Thingamabob. Once
upon a time there was a biped named Ron. Not to mention –.
So I won't. But I'll mention the gnat, the rat, the cat, the dogs,
the toad, the frog, the throat, the lips, and fuchsia. Fuchsia
adored forsythia. It went yellow once a year, usually in March.
But not for very long. And now: a jingle of words. Say
something, yes. Anything. To be perfectly frank with you, what
I want to say is –. Something was up. And most of all let me
say that –. But I could not. My tongue was tied. I did not speak
the language. There was a frog in my throat. Besides, I was so
drugged and loose with sleep and what's more subject then as I
still am today to strange convulsive starts and odd gest-
iculations, not to mention the uneasy dreams, the scar on my
throat. An old itch. I scratched my head. I sucked my thumb.
Where was I? In Thingamabob with Thingamajig. I remember
now. I helped pick up the blue beads from the floor and –.
What then? Out to make the coffee, I suppose. Out for a bottle
of Martini Bianco that last time. Christ, the stuff I used to
drink in those days. Sweet fizzy wine. British sherry. You name
it (I can't). That last afternoon. What last afternoon? In Thingamabob with Thingamajig. What are you talking about? I am
talking about rented rooms. I am talking about Dorcas. I am
talking about the cloisters. I am talking about the skylight. I
am talking about the rain. I am talking about the Eighteenth
Brumaire of Louis Bonaparte. To be quite candid I –. I –. Liar!
I am talking about the forgotten bed, the cold bed, the
higgledy-piggledy sheets. The dying of the light. When all's
said and done I am talking about the tracks and traces. I am
talking about the brush-offs and the boredom, the buzzards

and the whoredom. I am talking about the vomit deposited in the yard of the state motorcycle repair factory. I am talking about a cold blue-grey dawn and a railway terminal. I am talking about the past, the present, the ramifications. Something was up. First the tragedy, then the farce. I am talking rot and rubbish and nonsense and stopped wrist-watches and shrieking alarms and congested hearts and typewriters and long abandoned beds and word-processors and the poor quality of nine-pin dot matrix printers and how you begin to forget things. Names. Especially names.

hat tooner daze

Sweet drowsy rain sun skin honey hymns gold. Lazing around and around and around and the bell tower chiming and much we didn't know, not then, not in those days. Never heard of the valorization process, had we? Never heard of the anomalous precession of Mercury's perihelion. Never heard of the secret of primitive accumulation. Never heard of the 26 Commissars of Baku.

thingumajig

When all's said and done say that in Aleppo once –. No. I will not say that. Let me tell you about Keith. Keith told the truth, so they turned him back at the border for moral turpitude. Let me describe –. Ah, if only I had the enthusiasm. If only it seemed to matter now the way it used to seem to matter. Growing old. Growing grey. When everything you do you do too long, too late, you can't expect to find the people still there. The people all are gone, into graves or marriages. The party's over. This train terminates at Seven Sisters. *All change.*

past the dark lochans

Slippage of fantastic scenery peopled by familiar faces. Back at the cottage dancing with Kate and someone wanting to interfere (go away, person, go away!), someone asking about Baghdad, someone tipping me into the London underground and lines I've never heard of, stations with mysterious names, the spine crumbling on the A-Z, the pages fluttering, pulling in to Powis Square Station and getting out, going up the escalator, emerging near the yellow H, mute, everything on the tip of my furred tongue, the thick rubbery texture of dream-things, rubbery unhelpful officials, stewards, receptionists, clerks, bum-bailiffs, functionaries, the police, all torn to shreds by the lurid yellow beaks of enormous gulls

thingumajig

I say, I say, I say. Did I ever tell you how a small part of me turned to stone? After the operation I kept it in a jar, it's probably still on one of the shelves. Or did I throw it away when it started to smell? I forget. Now all that matters is... What? Death and revolution? Keep the ending from happening. From first gasp to last, and all the ones between. The days short. A higgledy-piggledy time. Ah, I remember it vividly! Every last detail. I think. In Thingamajig with Thingamabob. Nothing but toast and beer, nothing but the old grunt and gasp and groan. Cold blue sky, sea blue as arterial veins. Blue beads. Say something. Maintain interest. *Once, I remember, many years ago...* Or *Have I ever told you about the extraordinary events that occurred in... during the summer of 19...?* No, not summer. Winter. What's that? How's that? Warm the chill emptiness of the room. Say something, something interesting and original and amusing. Something of the but-what-happened-next sort. So drugged and loose with sleep. Pick up the blue beads from the floor, pick up where things left off. Pick up the threads of friendship, unpick the tangle of the years. Pick out a book from the shelf, a poem from the collection of early eighteenth-century poetry. Pick out the pearls from the mud of lost time. Here is a ball of string, there is a bag of letters. Pick up the mail from the mat. Trying to stop things from ending, all that long grey winter. That winter. The winter, the pier, the sea, the waves. The rain. So drugged and loose with sleep. Something was up. Hearing the dull throb of auricles and ventricles, the warm soft pulse, the slow soft breathing, the roar of the sea, the squeal of gulls, the rattle of tramcars. I am talking about that time. The motion of a muscle. The dark mornings, the dark afternoons. Ways deep, weather sharp. Sun furthest off. The lighthouse winking from the hill. How I came to that place I cannot rightly say. The usual concatenation of haphazard happenstance, coincidence and destiny part random, part determined by the many levers of late capitalist society. Nothing to do all day but read Marx and *Wuthering Heights*, that is how I remember it, falsely. The empty railway station out of Tolstoy. Norfolk. Ontario. The branch line across the flat wastes. The unbearable desolation and emptiness. The longing. The frozen river. The snow. Something was up and everything fitted my mood to a T.

hat tooner daze

Hymns greensheets mirrors honey sprinklers soft time turning on fire in the big bed warm soft tempting recesses cracks and gashes and aureoles and thuddings and claspings and wrenchings. Slooberry and huxkinting.

thingumajig

Off to London one morning before dawn, in a fog of fatigue. The interview. Somewhere off Piccadilly, was it? The American. Have you ever been to Canada or the United States before? No. The cathedral. What, where? So drugged and loose with sleep. The hotel. The bed. Abscessedmoondead? At my last gasp. Cried out or grunted or mostly lay there, eyes wide open, all that winter, that dark margarine winter. Living off toast. Toast with this and toast with that. Went back two years later with Thingumajig. Early summer, blue skies, blue Cortina, the white gulls wheeling. Retraced the dark past briefly, then drove on, north. Loch Lomond slipping by. On.

Down the stony track to the grassy open space by the loch side. Finding again and over, the lineaments. Keeping half an eye out – you can never be quite sure – for monsters. Monsters? The diary. The torn letter. The motion of a muscle. The hospital. The bed. The room.

past the dark lochans

Lurid yellow beaks of enormous gulls, screeching, hovering, swaying past the cabin window, waking me, get up, brush teeth, get dressed, swaying, breakfasting on tea and bacon rolls, out to the upper deck, huddling by the funnel.

thingumajig

The pram. The prefab. The dark town where I was born. Where I was born. Where I was born. Where my first months were spent. In my pram, grinning at the big world. Knowing as much about its workings as a daily tabloid-taker. US vs SU, that time. So drugged and loose with sleep. Muh-me! Da-da! Learning to talk, learning my first words, yes. The school. Loathing it. Sobbing with despair. Lugging the big Union Jack round the playground on Empire Day. Learning to join my letters. Looning the allaphbed. Learning to make a name for myself. Getting to greasy grips with cutlery, chair and table, not to mention tablecloth, salt and pepper pot, as well as a table alphabeticall conteyning and teaching the true writing and understanding of hard usuall English wordes borrowed from the Hebrew Greeke Latin or French etc., with the interpretation therof by plaine English words gathered for the benefit and helpe of Children, Ladies, Gentlewomen, or any other unskilful persons. Whereby they may the more easilie and better understand many hard English wordes, which they shall heare or read in Scriptures, Sermons, or elsewhere, and also be made able to use the same aptly themselves. And later, litcrit. *"Ron" operates firstly as a seemingly coherent medium on the fiction, and then proceeds to become inconsistent, incoherent and the merest empty signifier whose "meaning" constantly varies in a thoroughly contingent manner. In cases such as this, what was taken as an ontological category becomes an epistemological problem.*

hat tooner daze

Wondering: are you asleep? Are you alive? In Toronto on Christmas Eve I walked the strange streets. In a store selling trinkets, badges, soft porn and miscellania, I bought a handsome edition *of Karl Marx and Frederick Engels: Selected Correspondence* (Moscow, 1965).

thingumajig

Ten thousand books out there, waiting. Thomas the Tank Engine, John Reed, *Troubles*. Not to mention good table manners, chess, kowtowers, road signs, theories of revolutionary socialism, dyversitie and chaunge of language. For a man may utter his commynycacyon and matters in suche maners and termes that fewe men will understonde theym. And thus bytwene playn rude and curyous I stood and stande abasshed. Sentenced for life. The cat sat on the mat. The big ship sails on the ally-ally-oh. There was (have a care to delete Obsenityes & other Scandalous matters) a little boy and a little girl lived in an alley. Dick, who secretly loved M – and who married Fanny... Bah! What could my sterile and ill-cultivated genius beget but the story of a lean, shrivelled, whimsical child, full of varied fancies? The use of points, pauses and stops is not only to give a proper time for breathing but to avoid obscurity and confusion of the sense in the joining of words together in a sentence. To wit. The worker exists as a worker only when he exists *for himself* as capital, and he exists as capital only when *capital* exists *for him*. The existence of capital is *his* existence, his *life,* for it determines the content of his life in a manner indifferent to him. Political economy therefore does not recognize the unoccupied worker, the working man in so far as he is

195

outside the work relationship. The swindler, the cheat, the beggar, the unemployed, the starving, the destitute and the criminal working man are *figures* which exist not *for it*, but only for other eyes – for the eyes of doctors, judges, grave-diggers, beadles, etc.

past the dark lochans

Misty cliffs, headlands, mountains, trawlers, mainland. A bell-owing tethered bull. Light drizzle. Pulling in to buy a paper, reading the headline.

thingumajig

The ground-floor flat in Thingumajig. Number twenty-seven, was it? The sea at the end of the road. The gales blowing in from the Baltic, the waves crashing along the pier. All that winter listening to "Winter". All that winter trying to keep out the cold, the ending. The little cinema, three programmes a week. Saw *The Getaway* there with what-was-his-name. Who went to America. The pier, the sea, the gales, the cold. The dole office. And later the upstairs flat in Whitehall Road. Whitehall? I am talking of the tricks and warps and glow of memory. I am talking of Saturday afternoons in bed. I am talking *of Star Trek* and desire. I am talking about the City of Norwich gaol 1827-1881. I am talking of men sentenced to walk a treadmill keeping a constant retrograde motion to grind corn. I am talking about sunbeams caught between finger and thumb in a Dores field. I am talking about the tracks of light. The thick shafts of light probing Smoo Cave. The rainbow mist. The huge screeching gulls. The graveyard we explored. The graves by the rough sea, the buffeting wind. White gravestone flowers under half globes of glass. Falling asleep drunk watching *Brief Encounter*. Occupation? Watching the waves break, watching the lighthouse wink. Listening to *Goat's Head Soup* all day long. Sent my poems to Jonathan Cape, 30 Bedford Square, who returned them promptly. Editor's Note: in Thingumajig that was.

hat tooner daze

Hymns green sheets rain. Somebody said you'd gone to England. For years I couldn't even remember the name of the band on the blues album you played all through that hot, honeyed July. Came across the album in the end, in a record store. Recognised the cover at once. Hymns poured through windows, dead dogs began barking, broken books reassembled themselves.

thingumajig

Morning, and all's confused again. Remember it well. Collapsing on the street in Lagos. The tent exploding in Scotland. Being stretchered to the ambulance and driven off to Portsmouth. The abscess in my mouth in Vancouver. Cut, hurt, drugged. Waking from the anaesthetic in the Jubilee. *You're a sharp one*, said the nurse. Knew at once it hadn't worked, said so. And later, in the North Middlesex, going into theatre. Surgeons in green. Watching them plant the electrodes on my chest. Just in case. Having my throat cut open. It could be malign, could be benign. Only one way to find out. Lay there, eyes wide open until morning. Cried out or –. The bed. Cried out or grunted or –. The prefab. The railway station. The airport. The car. The hotel. The cathedral. The sea. The North Sea, yes. Years pass. The grey years. Off to the big grey building on Forest Road. Mrs scowling what-was-her-name behind the counter. Snoop? Snake? Sneak? Mrs I've-met-your-sort-before. By which she meant: slugabeds. Idlers. Loafers. Lazybones. Sponging off the unspeakable generosity of the capitalist state. Snoozing. Forty winks. Lazing around all day listening to Bach and reading Marx. Intellectuals – bah! Never done a day's work in their lives, not *real* work. Reading books when they ought to be doing something useful like fitting exhaust pipes to Ford Sierras or smashing down the doors of debtors or sitting grim-faced on Social Security Appeals Tribunals or making a name for their selves.

past the dark lochans

And fourteen years later, the statues coming down, the afternoon grey and smoky, the yellow-and-rose-coloured evening, at the end of a hot sticky day an ice-cream van moving along the grid of streets repeatedly tinnily playing *O Sole Mio*. Next thing the winter sweeps in, the road's too long, death everywhere, the days beginning to darken at the edges.

thingumajig

Remember it well. Going to see *I'll Never Forget Whatshis-name* at a long forgotten cinema, going to see *Vampire Circus*, going to, going, going –. The old familiar motion of an old familiar muscle. Thingamajig put my in her sad to say, began the old gasp and grunt and groaning, the what-happened-then, the what-happened-next, the what-happened-after, the what-happened-after-that. Forgot most of it and moved on. Met Thingamajig and went back to her place. Began the old gasp, the what-happened-after. The years passing by. That time on the dole, never forget it. Days on end. The shabby halls, the shabby offices, the Dostoyevskian clerks. Waiting around in tatty smoky waiting rooms where slumped the defeated, grey people, hopeless folk, the corrugated faces, coughing. "How did you get here Mr Sharp? By car?" "No, I walked." Nonplussed. Eyebrows raised: "Walked?" Suspicious: "That's a long way to walk." "I like walking." Suspicious: "You *like* walking?" "Yes." "And you don't have a car?" "No, I don't have a car." "You're quite certain about that?" Baggy-eyed, weasel-eyed, ratty moustache, navy blue blazer, sludge-brown tie, Brylcreemed hair, shiny black shoes.

hat tooner daze

As for the handsome edition. The photographs were sludgy and mediocre. Translated into English by the late I. Lasker. It was one way in to the one way out of here.

thingumajig

Tomorrow, yes. Tomorrow and –. Don't know where, don't know when. Can remember, just about, heading west, then east, at five thousand feet. Looking down at the grid of streets, the familiar buildings. Collecting my possessions in carrier bags while the Vivaldi played over and over. My possessions? A dozen albums (*Desire*; *Blood on the Tracks*; *New Skin for the Old Ceremony; Berlin*). A scratchy Bach Cantata. *Die Zauberflote*. A lifetime ago. The people all are gone. The party's over. Another lifetime takes over. Years. Slippage. Slip and slide and sun and ice. The frozen river behind me. Summer ends now. Walking to and fro in the car park. Won't be long now. Old songs in the blood every inch of the way. Checking the new-born babe on the Apgar scale, rinsing off the blood and slime, wrapping it up in a shawl, laying it on her breast, the little lips fastening on the brown nipple, beginning, beginning the great suck-suck-suck, the slurp and guzzle, the longing, the pangs, the continuing hunger for more, the open-mouthed cry, every inch of the way. Putting on clothes, zipping up zips. All said, done. Fastening the hooks of her white bra, buttoning up buttons, pulling on shoes, pulling the door to behind you, pushing to check it's locked, walking away from the room for the last time, never going back, never never never. Tickets, documents, platforms, trains, ports, ferries, terminals, airlines, I.D. The key twists in the ignition, firing a mixture of gases and air, the silver train pulls away from the station with a sudden jolt and heads into the dark, the ferry pulls away from the quayside, the airliner gathers speed along the runway. Weeds growing down the middle of the single-track road at Woolsery, weeds sprout on the disused platform at Thing-amajig, weeds cracking open the hardest surfaces. The grass on the embankment consumed by fire. Can't go back now. All gone. The party's over, it's time to –. Time to make yourself scarce. Do not go –, no. Show the bastards you saw through their –. The luminous revolutions! Leon Leon. Middle of February, were I to take a turn –. Bright day done, now.

Heading away from the shore. Going down through the clouds. The brine in my throat, the air on my tongue, every inch of the way. Bedsprings snap with a plangent whine. Cloudy-bright, then cloudy. Out of breath. What's the matter? It's a matter of −. Rattle in my throat, words dying on my tongue. Remember, remember. The hotel, the bed, the morning, the snow, the cold. Remember the 26 −. Re −. Mixture of gases and air, motion of a muscle, all consumed. Out across the Caspian Sea and − It is, however, not difficult to perceive that −, that −. And back of all, back of everything, the metallic motion of the old, foul machine, its blood-drenched jaws, its cold coppery touch turning human life into krugerrands and pounds sterling and yankee dollars, its engine of profit, its accumulations, wearing out bodies, producing capital and death, its almost inescapable grinding rhythm everywhere, as if the earth had died and in its place an iron heart pumped slump-boom, boom-slump, slump-boom, boom-slump, slump-boom, boom-slump until, until −. Until the dreamable unknown half-unimaginable end.

Afterwords

This book's improbable-sounding Winston Churchill epigraph is authentic, as is the quotation from Lenin at the end of "Solzhenitsyn and Yogurt". I am indebted to Frank Key, who suggested the title of this latter story.

The episode in "Nixon's Dog" describing how the C.I.A. converted a cat into a listening device is also genuine: I came across it in Mark Lane's fascinating and persuasive book about the Kennedy assassination, *Plausible Denial* (New York, 1991).

Accounts of extra-terrestrial visitations in "Martina" are taken from John Michell's *The Flying Saucer Vision* (London, 1967); the references to Marx and Engels in the same story are: Marx, letter to Engels dated 25th March 1868, and Engels, letter to C. Schmidt, dated 12th March 1895.

Al's analysis of famine in "Rubbish" is borrowed from a 1991 article by Ian Taylor entitled "Charity is Not Enough".

Kollontai's novella, mentioned in "Lenin's Trousers", refers to Alexandra Kollontai's *A Great Love* (trans. Cathy Porter, London, 1981).

"Da-Da Vogt" is, of course, indebted to R. A. Archer's translation of *Herr Vogt* (London, 1982).

The seed of "Sunday Morning in July" was sown on a Sunday morning in July 1991 in the Prince William Room of the Royal National Hotel, Bloomsbury.